Freddie's Dead

Richard Torres

The
X
Press

Published by:
The X Press
PO Box 25694
London, N17 6FP
Tel: 020 8801 2100
Fax: 020 8885 1322
E-mail: vibes@ xpress.co.uk

Printed by Bookmarque, UK

Distributed in the UK by Turnaround Distribution
Unit 3, Olympia Trading Estate, Coburg Road, London N22 6TZ

Distributed in the US by National Book Network
15200 NBN Way
Blue Ridge Summit, PA 17214

ISBN: 1-902934-35-0

Freddie's Dead

Richard Torres

Acknowledgements

So many to thank, so little room. Here I go anyway: The X-Press crew, my pal Jeffrey Scott, Anita Franklin, Helen and Stephanie Collier, Beth Krakower, Frank McCourt, Paula Garzon, Kristina Hathaway, Bambi Jones, Joseph Trigoboff, Lisa Cortes, Coati Mundi, Kellie Jones, Janine Coveney, Tom Terrell, Benj DeMott, Quentin Tarantino, George Lopez, Joan Plaza, Armond White, Justice Edwin Torres, Joe Cuba, Joe Conzo, Patrick Cole, Lydia Offord, Jamie Okubo, Donna Lamback, Gianluca Tramontana, Tommi Jackson, Andrea Alvear, Joy Bell, Yvonne Marie Harris, Michael Gonzales, Brenda Phipps, Charles Raisch, Walter Mosley, Sheena Lester, Dan Ouellette, David Hajdu, Barbara Rice Thompson, Robin Roberts, Monifa Brown, Diana & Errol Nazareth, Tracey Ann Jones, Rob Tobias, Jane Bunnett & Larry Cramer, Danilo Perez, Sandy Kenyon. (RIP Angelo Gonzalez, Clinise Johnson, Ana Araiz.) Also - deep breath now - Valerie, Michael & Terri, Elsie, Kim, Deidre, Susan, Denise, Karen, Alice, Bruce, Nina, Jana, Angie, Gaby, Tim & Amy, Laura, Angela, Liz, Debbie, Jenni, Bob and Rosemarie, Jo, Deborah, Jason & Sam, Helene, Charlene, Bryan, Judith, Pamela, Joanne & Jim, Charlotta, Dawn, Jim & Sheila, April, Rosanna & Maria, Chrystal, Zelda, Lauren & Rosemary, Louisa, Sujata & Todd, Grace, Robin, Sofia, Ellen, Peter & Janet, Blanca, Chandra, Albert, Greg, Jose, Barry, Tony and the rest of the Command Bus Posse. My entire family - past, present & future. Special thanks to my father, my mother, my sister, my brother D-ski and my much-missed and much-beloved grandmother Marie.

ONE

ALL RIGHT, I'LL admit it, I am a lazy person. It's just my nature. I always have been, shall we say, a little lax. As a kid, this was my idea of fun: I'd memorize the TV Guide, run home after school, fling my ancient textbooks onto the faux-leather living room couch and just before I'd park my lean, skinny, tiny, puny, wimpy ass next to them, pop on the television - obviously these were the pre-remote days - and do my studying and homework during the many, many, many commercial breaks.

Flashforward some thirty years later and my priorities still hadn't changed. Go out? Ah, fuck that shit. I'd rather mosey around my apartment, sneaking a few catnaps throughout the day, than to slave over a regular nine-to-five. I guess that's one of the reasons I chose my line of work. There's tons - TONS - of downtime and ninety-nine-point-nine percent of that I spend at home. Still, while I may grant you that to the uninformed observer I may seem like some sort of slothful shut-in, I insist to you I'm not. Deep down, I knew all of this.....inertia was preparing to something special. (At least, that's the lie I kept telling myself.)

Having said that, let me say, in my wildest of dreams, I never expected to have a life-altering experience take place on one cool November afternoon while lounging on my Castro Convertible. But I did and it changed my outlook forever.

Allow me to backtrack just a little. See, it's a horrific moment when a man realizes he's getting older. (Sort of like making the transition from athlete to ex-athlete.) For some, it occurs when they discover they can't wedge their slowly-spreading keister into their favorite pair of jeans. Other experience the crunching terror of Playboy Playmate-itis. That's when you discover the Centerfold you're drooling over is some two decades younger than you are thereby being someone you could have sired. (A milder case of P P-itis can occur when the Playmate is younger than your baby sister.)

When it happened to me - when I had my epiphany - I was having a sit down on my sofa bed catching some tube. To be more specific, I was watching the Jenny Jones show. Now, I'm not really a fan of chatfests. I'd much prefer checking out old flicks. But I reside in Nueva York proper, in la isla Manhattan, without cable. (It's not a political statement...I just can't afford it.) Consequently, I am marooned in the VHF wasteland, the local channels, where, from 9AM to 6PM, all that is broadcast are soap operas and talk shows. I can't stand the soaps - who wants to watch a story which lacks the guts to end? - so I'm left gazing at a dysfunctional cathode parade which ranges far beyond the scope of even the late, great Fellini's imagination.

That afternoon, I had witnessed interracial couples and their families who opposed them, White supremacists and their grandchildren, snarling wives whose simpleton husbands must pay them for sex, flamboyant drag queens who very much enjoyed being a girl and a Osmond family reunion.

For some inexplicable reason, it was the aforementioned Jenny Jones show which pushed me over the edge. The show's topic was arguably an important one: men-who-were-confronted-by-the-women-they-dumped-after-a-one-night-stand. Important, that is, if you believe the McMillanized fantasy that all men are dogs and all women are overworked underappreciated saints. The female panelists certainly believed the hype. Their attitude was full of anger and disbelief: how dare you leave me, you panting dog boy, after I gave up the goodies? The guys in question, the preening Rovers and the insipid Rin-Tin-Tins, weren't any better. They had this depraved satisfaction in affirming their conquests to millions of television viewers. And the mainly distaff studio audience was a-disapproving and a-hectoring as if they never sinned or indulged in the wayward pleasures of the flesh.

Through all the name-calling and the hump-slinging, our hostess Jenny smiled, scolded and led all of the involved parties through a cursory examination of the sordid activities that even I, a thirty-five year old man with a twenty-five year subscription of Playboy - precocious, wasn't I? - felt was better left private.

But like a good ringmaster, she seduced both the guests and the audience into revealing the pathetic look-at-me-Ma nature we Americans love to unveil at the sight of a key light and minicam. And, she allowed the viewers at home to feel something they probably rarely got the opportunity to experience all day: superiority.

Now, perhaps it was the talk show overload - after all, I had nothing better to do - but I was appalled. (Hooked but appalled, a conveniently pious combination.) I yearned for a simpler time, my formative youth, when game shows ruled the daytime airwaves.

A child of television - I didn't have much to do back then either- I was raised on a steady diet of The Price Is Right (with both Bill Cullen and Bob Barker), Split Second (with Tom Kennedy), Jeopardy (with Art Fleming), The Match Game (with Gene Rayburn), The Hollywood Squares (with Peter Marshall) as well as every Allen Ludden-hosted permutation of Password there ever was. Gosh, I ached of the honest sleaze of the Chuck Barris television empire. Barris, a sleepy-eyed mogul, was the evil-genius mastermind behind such boob tube classics as the Dating Game, the Newlywed Game, Treasure

Hunt and the Gong Show.

Now, sure the emcees on these programs (respectively, Jim Lange, Bob Eubanks, Geoff Edwards and the schlockmeister himself, Chuckie baby) were tremendously smarmy. Yes, the contestants were intentionally humiliated and em-Barris-ed but, hey, at least, they were doing it for sport. They wanted to win a prize, a living room set, an automobile, a weekend in the fabulous Puerto Vallarta, something. The on-air debasing was understandable: they were getting paid for it. The America of my youth knew the real deal; you can't get something for nothing. For a thirty-minute segment of their lives - commercials included - they would happily give up the booty running through a Money Maze or playing Musical Chairs if it meant coming home with a new dinette set. Face it, dignity is fine but you can't eat chicken off of it.

On talk shows, people pimp themselves for nothing. Nada. They just want to be on television. It was then my moment of truth transpired. I realized I was now old enough to be disgusted by the actions of others. My arms broke out in gooseflesh. My long feared nightmare had come true: I had become my parents. Lost in a self-pitying reverie, I sat frozen on my couch. This was not the way of my life, mi vida, was supposed to turn out. I was educated, a possessor of two bachelor degrees in both political science and journalism, not bad-looking and in pretty fair physical condition. I was also unemployed, deeply in debt, depressed, ten to fifteen pounds overweight, living in a tiny two room (if you count the toilet) flat over my uncle's bar in East Harlem, estranged from the rest of my family, abandoned by my longtime girlfriend for my former best friend and had just had the grand revelation of my life while watching the fuckin' Jenny Jones show. Man, I tell you when I heard my telephone ring, I grabbed that motherfucker as if it were a lifeline from a passing ship.

TWO

"HELLO." IT HAD been so long since I'd spoken to someone my voice felt super-strained. Man, I needed contact. Now. There was a pause for the cause on the phone and then the sound of a familiar feminine purr.

"Freddie, this is Mayra Molina. Remember me from One-forty-five…Chulito, I need your help."

Wowie. A mega-ton blast from the past. Mayra Molina and I went back a quarter of a century. We attended grade school at Public School 145 in Brooklyn's scenic - we're talkin' nothin' but projects and tenements - Bushwick section.

The school itself was a decrepit blood red brick building located in the epicenter of the old Schafer brewery factory complex. Surrounded by a beer bunker, with the intoxicating scent of malt and hops permeating the air, P.S. 145 felt more like an alcoholic training center than an actual educational institution. However, the majority of us students, despite our slight inebriation, managed to muddle through our lesson plans and received our diplomas. Mayra and I graduated as co-valedictorians.

Truth to tell, even though she was an older woman - she was born in May, me in June - I'd always had a crush on Mayra. She was pretty, intelligent and the very first to sprout some boobies

11

in our class. (This made her very popular.)

I remember one day we were with a few classmates in the neighborhood public library (a block long, faded gray building on Bushwick Avenue with a mountain of shit-yellow cracked stairs out front) studying for the next day's exam - trust me, only the thought of seeing Mayra could tear me away from my beloved game shows and cartoons - when five high school age thugs we'd never seen before came over to our table.

Us schoolkids looked up in horror as the five guys recounted, in the most graphic terms, what they wanted to do to Mayra. In fact, they told us they'd decided to wait outside for her so they'd have the chance to fulfill their sordid fantasies. Before they left, the tallest guy, the one who looked a lot like "The Rifleman" Chuck Connors, instructed us all, in a most indelicate manner, not to notify the librarian or any other authority figure. (I believe his exact words were 'or everybody's gonna get fucked.') Well, I tell you, that struck the final chord of terror for all concerned. Nobody said a word for ten minutes. Finally, one of my classmates, Willie (the Weasel) Vincent spoke.

"Somebody's gotta take Mayra home, " he said.

We all agreed. Especially Mayra. However, there was a problem. Home was some twenty blocks away. This I knew because...

"Freddie," said Willie, "don't you live down the block from Mayra?"

All eyes turned to me. I had been set up. "Technically," I croaked.

"Great, Freddie can take her, " declaimed the Weasel.

Never mind that I was a Cuban heel taller than being declared a midget, now I was supposed to overcome this height disadvantage, pass a gauntlet of wannabe rapists and ruffians and then dash about a mile to get this chick home safe and sound. I didn't think so.

My face must've registered my lack of enthusiasm because Mayra made sure to lean in real close to me. Her eyes were the darkest brown. I was hyp-mo-tized. Did I call this girl a chick? I meant a goddess.

"Promise me, Freddie, you'll protect me, " she said.

I nodded.

"Always?"

"Yeah," I gulped. "Always, Mayra."

We put our books into our cartoon-imprinted knapsacks. (Hers said Barbie, mine was Batman.) I made certain that the snaps were secure when we put them on. The last thing I needed was for our textbooks to go flying out onto Bushwick Avenue while Mayra's gentlemen callers were in hot pursuit.

Willie snuck a peek outside one of the side windows. He turned around to us shaking his head. "They still out there, Freddie, " said the Weasel. "They sitting on a blue Chevy about ten feet past the steps."

"To the left or the right?"

"Left."

Good, I thought. We've got to head out right anyway. Sitting down on a Chevy. That'll give us a running start. I told Willie if I didn't call him at home in a half an hour to dial the police. He looked nervous but he agreed. I placed my shaking right hand in Mayra's soft left. It felt goooood. I guided her to the building's exit. We stared at each other. We were two terrified kids. I tried to sound like John Wayne.

"Just hang on to me, don't trip and run like hell," I drawled. Mayra smiled.

"I will, I won't and I will," she said.

"Good."

We burst through the library doors as if propelled by jetpacks. Like a skier goes down an icy ramp, Mayra and I used the steps to build up some momentum.

We caught those jerks outside flatassed and flatfooted.

They chased us for a little while but not enough to worry us. Fear is a great motivator. We dusted them. After five blocks, they gave up.

Just to make sure, however, Mayra and I ran all the way home. She lived with her parents and baby brother Junior on the flight above the butcher shop at the corner of George Street and Wilson Avenue. (I was a half a block south on George Street proper between Wilson and Knickerbocker Avenue.)

When we got to her door, I realized we were still holding hands. Now, this thrilled and terrified me. Mayra's folks were like most Latino parents who've spawned an attractive daughter: homicidally super-strict. In fact, her mom was known to brandish a hatchet to shoo away her nena's suitors. (The joke in class was it was Mrs. Molina who taught the butchers in the shop below how to chop.)

Lizzie Borden or not, I was gonna angle for a kiss. After all, did not I just rescue the fair maiden from the monster men?

Mayra put her key into the hallway door to the right of the butcher's window. I peeked in. Just saw the backs of some couple by the counter. No sign yet of the Molinas.

"Thanks so much for protecting me," she said.

Man, I was sweating profusely. Some of it was the run but mostly it was the wonderful sight of her.

"Mayra," I said nervously, "can I have a…"

"Chulito!!"

I froze. That high, shrill voice. Oh no.

"Chulito!!!!"

It came from the butcher's. I looked left, then gasped. This was worse than Mayra's mom. This was my mom. And she called me by my dreaded family pet name. I had been outed.

"Chulito," growled a deep voice, "come help your mother with these bags now!"

Great. My father too. The couple by the counter. Stupid, stupid me. I was trapped. I looked at Mayra, pleading with my eyes for her not divulge my nickname.

"Chulito, huh? No problema," she said. "It's our secret."

With that, Mayra turned the key, opened and shut the door and killed the only chance I ever had to kiss those luscious lips. I was left with my parents, a passel of cold cuts and a raging woody. Talk about your Freudian nightmares.

After we graduated from One-forty-five, Mayra and I remained close. Together we attended and survived our rough, fight-filled neighborhood junior high: Enrico Fermi Intermediate Junior High School 111. (Like Fermi's life work, one-eleven was an A-bomb waiting to explode.)

In one-eleven, Mayra would always look around to make

sure we were alone before calling me Chulito. I liked that. It affirmed my trust. We were named, once again, co-valedictorians.

It was our choices of high school finally split us apart. She chose a Catholic school, Cabrini in upper Manhattan. I picked Stuyvesant, a 'specialized' school in lower Manhattan. Still, every once in a while, we'd run into each other on the double L train stop, Morgan Avenue, heading to or from class and have big fun. We'd swap lies, gossip about old classmates and promised to always, always stay in touch.

We didn't.

The summer before senior year, Mayra and her family moved out of the neighborhood to Queens. (Woodside, I believe. I never got the address.) Three months later, my family joined the George Street exodus. Being Brooklyn loyalists, my parents moved us to Canarsie - the Rockaway Parkway stop on the double L- where they still remain.

Bumping into some old classmates, I heard Mayra went away to Harvard where she met and married some rich, uppity white boy. I passed along my well wishes and that was that.

Until this call, a decade later.

THREE

"**HOW'D YOU GET** my number, Mayra?"

"I was in the city yesterday, waiting on the Eighth Avenue platform to take the double L from Eighth to Union Square, when I ran into your mom."

Yes, indeedy. Mrs. Perez does get around.

"I told her about my situation, " said Mayra, "and she gave me your number. She said you wouldn't be busy."

That's my mama. A rock solid temple of support.

"You're fortunate, Mayra," I said. "There does seem to be a hole in my calendar." About three years worth, I thought. "Now, what can Freddie do for you?"

"It's my kid brother."

"Junior?"

"He's missing."

"What? For how long?"

"It's been a couple of months."

"That's a long time, Mayra."

"I know. We went to la policia but there hasn't been any progress."

"Who's 'we'? Your parents?"

"Si," grunted Mayra," and my husband Oswald. He's been there for us Chulito."

Aha! The husband at last. Oswald? I hated myself for

16

thinking it but I was more curious about Mayra's hubby than Junior's whereabouts. I *had* to know more about Oswald.

"What does Oswald do?"

"Oh he's a doctor. A plastic surgeon, actually."

Interesting, I thought, she married a face re-tooler. She must look *fabulous.*

"Does Oswald work in the city?"

"No....sort of, Chulito. Oswald lives...we live in Los Angeles..."

Figured.

"...but we have an apartment in Manhattan, in Tribeca, for our trips back here."

How chi-chi. Man, I was so jealous.

"Do you and your spouse," I asked, "get back this way often?"

"About three months out of the year total," she said. "That's when Oswald works out of a satellite office of...have you ever heard of the Carrington Foundation?"

"No."

"It's a nonprofit organization designed to assist unwed mothers and their families. I'm on the board."

"Real popular nowadays."

"Tell me about it, Chulito. These are the days of 'blame the victim and forget the problem.' Anyway, we come back here a lot for fundraisers."

"The old hat-in-hand routine."

"Yeah," laughed Mayra, "but it works. You know, White people love to see people of color begging for financial assistance."

"You should know," I thought

"Reminds them they're in charge," I said.

"Anyway, since we are based in L.A., I thought it'd be a good idea to let Junior live there to, you know, watch the place."

I bet the lucky bastard lived there rent free.

"We flew into town six weeks ago," continued Mayra, "and headed to the apartment. The place was a wreck."

"Did it look like somebody rummaged through the place?"

Mayra paused a few seconds before answering. Her tone

was cold and clinical.

"No," she said. "It was more like a slob hurricane. Tons of empty and half filled pizza cartons. Cans of beer and soda left all over the floor. Dirty clothes flung around the apartment. His bed was filthy and unmade."

It sounded to me like Junior was on a major bender.

"Is that unusual Mayra? Was Junior messy?"

"Are you kidding, Freddie? With my parents? He was a Molina. Junior was the second coming of Felix Unger."

"A tip-top neat freak, huh?"

"Uh-huh. When I saw the place I knew something was seriously wrong."

"What did the police say?"

"Nothing," Mayra said disgustedly. "They saw no sign of trouble just some piss-poor housekeeping. The pizza left in the cartons was about two weeks old. They spoke to the pizzeria owner about deliveries. That's how they placed the date of Junior's disappearance. We waited a few days and then filed a missing persons report. Since then, nada. When I ran into your mom and she told me what you are doing now, well, I simply thanked God for my good fortune."

Well at least one of us can praise his name, I thought.

"So, Chulito, can you take the case? I'll pay you accordingly. What's your rate?"

Hmmmm. A missing person. The brother of an old childhood friend. I should cut her a break on my usual rate, thought I. Then I glanced around my apartment. There was a musty bathroom replete with peeling green tile, a leaky sink, a busted mirrored cabinet and an mold-encrusted tub with a bare lightbulb hanging four feet above it. Next to the bathroom was an old grease-splattered four-burner gas stove. Besides that was a five-foot high icebox with a corroded steel Colt 45 six shooter lamp on top of it. There was my faux-wooden kitchen table which rocked from side to side for two minutes whenever a cup was placed on it with the single folding chair I'd swiped from my college graduation in Washington Square Park. Next to the chair, to the left of my only window, was a plastic milk crate holding my self-help books. Against the wall, to the right of my window, was a collapsible flowered breakfast tray with the fifty compact discs my ex-girlfriend allowed me to take from our... no, no, no, ...her apartment on top. Under the tray was the cheap boombox my uncle Chubby lent me. Next to my mini-stereo system was my 13-inch black and white television propped up on two cement blocks. Under the TV, between the blocks, was a growing pile of unpaid bills, threatening missives from collection agencies and a lot of postcards with the words Final Notice printed in puke-green lettering. All that and a sofa bed with a rotary phone balanced on its left arm too. (I did have a couple of closets in the back, however.) Fuck friendship, I thought, Mayra's just gonna have to get soaked. I tripled my rate.

"I'm about a hundred and fifty bucks a day plus expenses," I said.

"Is that all, Chulito?"

Ah, shit, I thought. I could've really rooked her. I was going to have to really pad my expenses.

"Eh, yeah," I said, "that's my price."

"No, Chulito, I won't hear of it. You're not going to cut your price for me. I want to..I demand to pay your regular fee."

Score one for the almighty. "Mayra," I said, "I won't take any more than three hundred per. After all, you are a friend."

"Plus a bonus," she added.

"Okay, you talked me into it. Plus a bonus of *your* choosing."

"Done."

Get me to a notary public, I thought. Fast. If I were really lucky, this case could drag on a couple of weeks and then I'd be debt-free at last.

"Okay, Mayra," I said, "I'm gonna stop by your place tonight with some papers to make this official. Before that, I'll cruise by my local neighborhood police station this afternoon to nose around a bit and see what they might have heard. Answer a few more questions for me?"

"Sure."

"What's Junior's first name?"

"Junior."

"Junior Molina?"

"Yeah. My mother didn't want my father to burden his son with a name that had the built in pressure of following exactly in his dad's footsteps but my father liked the idea of a junior so much that they compromised and so they named him Junior Junior."

Imaginative, I thought. I asked Mayra for a current description of Junior.

"You mean, height, weight, etc?"

"Yep."

"Dark brown hair cut in a fade, fair skin with a hint of acne about the cheekbones, brown eyes, bushy eyebrows, clean-shaven, five foot eight, one hundred and fifty pounds, a mole on his forehead just over his left eye. That's about it. There should be a poster of him at the police station. The police promised me they'd forward them to all precincts."

"Fine," I said. "Now what's your address?"

"150 Franklin Street, right off the number one train. Just push the buzzer with our last name."

"What's that? Molina?"

"I didn't tell you?" asked Mayra.

"No."

"It's Velleto."

So that was the husband's full name. Oswald Velleto. Correction. Doctor Oswald Velleto. With a name like that, he best be good.

"I'll be there about eight," I said.

"Great, Freddie. I'll make supper. Arroz con pollo." Mayra paused and continued in a choked-up voice. "Thank you, Chulito. You've always been there for me."

"I try."

"Eight o'clock then."

I was about to hang up when Mayra decided to ask me a question. She wanted to know why I decided to go into this kind of work.

"What? To help you?" I asked.

"No, silly," she said. "To be a private detective."

I could have told her the truth. I was a chronic fuck-up too frightened to try a real job. Dealing with the public scared the shit out of me. This career was simply my latest reality stall tactic. For the past year, since I got my license, the only case I was working on was trying to find myself and that was one mystery which remained unsolved. I was at the point where I had the terrible feeling I had grown attached to my misery and would do anything to maintain it. I could have told Mayra that.

Instead ...I lied.

"Mayra, honey," I said, "I just enjoy helping people."

FOUR

AFTER MAYRA HUNG up, I hopped off the sofa and headed to the bathroom to shower and shave. Man, the spurting hot water from that rusty spout never felt so good. (Just as long as I didn't get any in my mouth.) As my ten-cent razor removed the three-week stubble off my chin, I began to rejoice in my sudden good fortune. Finally, I thought, I'd made it off that goddamn couch. Seemed since Clarice Jean had kicked me out, I'd set up shop there. All that was needed to make my surrender official was a tent and white flag. Anyway, I hadn't had a good reason to move off that Castro in eons. Baby steps, I thought as I washed my face, I'm taking baby steps.

I rummaged around in the bottom of my closet and pulled out my manual typewriter from high school and a ream of paper. After blowing the dust off the cover and taking it off, I slid a sheet in there and typed up a deal memo. The ink was slightly faded but legible. After I finished I checked it for typos - none, I'm proud to say - placed the paper on the couch, locked up the portable printing press, shoved it back in the closet, washed my hands and started to get dressed. I put on a black pocket T-shirt with matching boxer shorts. I folded up the memo and jammed it in that pocket. It was going to be a day of running around so I decided to dress informally. Because my ass had gotten too fat to wear the regular size, I put on a fairly new pair of indigo blue relaxed-fit Levi Silver tab jeans and a faded Gap denim work shirt. The pants were snug. It was time to work out or pray Levi's came out with a sedated-fit.

Befitting my mercurial mood, I slipped on a pair of black sweatsocks, a thick black leather belt and a black J. Crew work shoes. In my shirt pocket, I placed my weathered wallet, the one I'd had since college. Here's a crimestopper tip, kiddies: if you are a person of color, it's always smart to carry some form of identification. (Just don't pull it out unannounced in front of them coppers....that way it can't be mistaken for a loaded weapon....eh, folks??) Anyhow, if you have ID, then when the Finest find your body, they can readily identify the corpse. Hoo-hah. I took a deep breath, I really had to lighten up.

I looked out my window. There it was, El Barrio - or to be more precise, Lexington Avenue between 116th and 117th street - teeming with life. The block was busy with people meandering from one corner to the next; aware of each other's existence but too paranoid to acknowledge each other's presence.

Glancing straight down, I saw two sallow-faced middle aged Latino men in beat-up, three-quarter black leather jackets stumble into my uncle's downstairs tavern. It wasn't even two in the afternoon and these defeated men already needed libations just to make it through to the end of the day. I peered up at the sky. Overcast. Touched the windowpane. Cold.

Last Christmas, my mother gave me a black V-neck sweater. It was my favorite gift of a bad season, warm and loose enough to hide my holster. I wasn't in a strapped mood, however, so I decided to leave the gun harness home. A risky proposition, to be sure, considering the current state of the New York City streets but I didn't care. I was just so fucking happy I was leaving my apartment.

I put on the sweater, a black baseball cap - without an insignia - and a black-double breasted raincoat. (Just color me the brown Bogie.) From atop the TV, I snatched a reporter's notebook left from bygone days and pen I'd swiped off the desk of my unemployment counselor. I stuffed the mightier-then-the-sword duo in my right raincoat pocket.

My keys were in the left one. I pulled them out and stared at them. I couldn't believe it. After countless weeks of self-pity, I was stepping out.

Slowly, I opened the apartment door. I peeked in the hallway. It was dark and had that wonderful combination smell of beer and urine. No one was around.

I walked into the corridor, closed the door behind me, turned and placed the key in the lock. Afterwards, I could swear the echoes of the cylinders turning followed me down the stairs.

FIVE

I STRODE OUT onto the cracked sidewalk. The traffic had become heavy, covering the parallel streets in clouds of carbon monoxide. Just a yard away from me was an unmuffled city bus, with its windows obscured by urban dirt, loudly belching clouds of fetid smoke. Welcome to the filthy breach of freedom. Chopping five years off my lifespan, I inhaled deeply. Pollution never smelled so good.

I checked my pockets for money. Nada, nunca, nadie. This meant one thing: I had to see my uncle Chubby. I took, a quick three steps to the right, passed a blackened window with a flashing neon Budweiser sign and entered the Barcelona Bar.

The name was a misnomer. This was no bar; it was a watering hole. The place was a dimmed-out mahogany-paneled cavern complete with shadowy figures only discernable by the glint of their half-filled glasses or the red ash of their cigarettes.

Oh yeah, the place had rack lighting. Only my uncle's conception of rack lighting was two exposed 15 watt crimson light bulbs placed in the middle of the ceiling. (I've seen freshly ironed rayon blouses which gave off more illumination.) The lack of a floodlight scheme was purposeful. The drinking world is one set to a permanent midnight. The darker it was, the easier to drown one's sorrows.

I took a couple of steps in and felt the breeze from the heavy steel-reinforced door closing behind me. The tavern had three tables with four matching chairs arranged to the right. All were black with red trimming.

Stationed in the furthest corner from the door was a jukebox with an enviable collection of Latin 45's. (This was a vinyl-only establishment. To my Tio, digital only referred to a certain sexual act that you only allow a wife to do to you.) It was unplugged. Only on Tuesday and Thursday evenings - Ladies' Night - did the box get the electrified treatment. This was my uncle's idea. The rest of the days he wanted his customers to drink up not sing along.

Left of the entrance was a wooden counter. It was oak, painted black, with six aluminum stools facing it. All were occupied by rather intense, brooding men. This area was designated hombre country where manly men sat to guzzle, chain-smoke and kvetch from time to time about their wives, children, bosses and mistresses.

Behind the counter, serving this rum-soaked jury their drinks, was Papo Nariz. He was my uncle's best buddy. They'd met in grade school detention and had become true amigos forever devoted to each other. As Chubby told it, some bully and his crew were picking on Papo. Their verbal target was Papo's big hook-shaped nose. My uncle - a rather rotund but energetic fellow who took no shit from no one - stood up for Papo. The two of them proceeded to beat the hell out of all concerned. (Because the number of assailants proportionally grew with each retelling, determining the exact number of bad guys involved is forever impossible to discern.)

Papo and Chubby had gone through the army, the penal system and multiple wives together. Their bond was deep.

Papo was about five foot five, bearded, one-hundred-fifty stocky pounds and preternaturally quiet. Chubby told me in the near-half century they've known each other, Papo had spoken to him, in both Spanish and English, about a thousand times. I believed that tale a lot more than the one about detention's last stand. In my experiences with Papo, he'd rather point, grunt and roll his eyes than gab. My uncle called him ' a bilingual economist.'

Papo spotted me as he was putting a bottle of Ronrico rum away. He smiled and, with a subtle nod, pushed a hidden button. The button was located under the counter, just out of plain sight, right next to the cash register. It was a signal to my uncle Chubby that a VIP had entered the establishment.

About two feet beyond the far end of the counter and carefully obscured by a stack of liquor crates was a door. It opened and a plump man, wearing a powder-blue sweatsuit with a matching ascot, bounded out. Except for the flesh basketball a-masquerading as his stomach, he had the same height and build as Papo. It was none other than my beloved uncle Chubby, the owner/proprietor of the Barcelona Bar. He rushed to greet his loving nephew Freddie. His gut preceded him by five seconds.

As he headed towards me, I got a closer look at his sweatsuit. It was covered in zippers. About twenty of them. The damn thing looked like a kangaroo safety deposit box section. I had no doubt he could set off an airport metal detector from three miles away.

"Holy shit, Sherlock," Chubby yelled as our eyes locked, "you mean King Farouk had finally decided to depart from his womb?"

"I believe it's King Tut from his tomb, Tio"

"Tomb, womb," he said, "it's still a fuckin' hole in the ground, ain't it?"

There were some scattered chuckles from the barflies. I needed some bank so I did the right thing. With a grin, I changed the subject.

"Como esta, Tio?"

"Bien, Freddie, bien. What's going on?"

I shrugged and pointed to his office.

"Chubby, we gotta talk."

He gestured to me to follow him in. I did. Before closing the door, he poked his head out.

"Papo," my uncle said with a pregnant pause, "hold my calls." I could hear the customers tittering as he shut the door.

Uncle Chubby's office was a crowded affair. It was about five-foot by five foot with cardboard liquor boxes lining the walls. In the center of the room was an ancient golden brown desk picked up from a Board of Education scrap heap, a yellow faded folding chair and a rotary phone. (We were not a pushbutton family.) There was also, behind the Bacardi boxes on the right, a secret exit into the hallway - my hallway - next door.

It appears that the previous owner of the Barcelona - and the adjoining building - was in the pharmaceutical business and, due to some disgruntled customers, found himself in need of a quick getaway. While on the lam, about four years ago, he offered Chubby the place - through some intermediaries - at a dirt-cheap price. Now, my uncle was a legendary devotee of Barrio nightlife. Even three marriages, six children and a plethora of jobs couldn't keep him out of the East Harlem social set. This bar was his dream come true. Somehow, between support payments, he managed, with Papo's help, to scrape up enough moola to purchase the Barcelona.

My family disapproved of Chubby's endeavor. My father went so far as to predict total disaster for the Barcelona within the first year.

"I'm not bailing you out when the shit fails, Chubby, " he told him. "And don't come crawling around here for cash."

It's funny how things turn out. My uncle's business thrived, my dad got laid off for eleven months and I got taken in by Chubby. I gathered my uncle liked that.

"Once again, nephew, what's going on?"

"I got a gig."

"A regular j-o-b or this private-eye shit?"

"The private-eye shit."

"Coño. I'm impressed. Who're you're workin' for?"

I told him the whole story. While I was talking, he began to vigorously massage his chin, I kept thinking of Aladdin rubbing his lamp hoping to find a genie. When I finished gabbing he cut to the chase.

"So, basically, you need up front money."

"Basically."

Chubby unzipped his upper left sleeve and pulled out a wad of bills. I prayed it wasn't a hustler's roll. You know, a hundred singles framed between a couple of fifties. T'wasn't. My uncle was packing the real deal. He peeled off seven twenties and gave them to me. I proceeded to distribute the money around my person, as my father had taught me, by putting a single bill in a different pocket.

"When you can, nephew, when you can," he said.

I thanked him. He flicked his wrists to shoo me away.

"No sweat, Freddie," he said. "Do you need a piece?"

"Got one. Licensed. Upstairs."

"Well," he said sarcastically, "isn't that a safe, effective place to keep it?"

"Just for today, Tio. I'm going to the two-five for info, then to Mayra's downtown. After tonight, I promise I'll stay packed."

"Do that," he said I nodded and turned to leave when I heard him whistle.

"What is it?" I asked.

He spoke slowly.

"Be careful, Freddie. This shit may sound simple but, trust me, it rarely is."

"Okay, okay. Anything else?"

"Yeah, smartass. Don't forget I believe in you."

I had to crack up. I told Chubby I appreciated his backing but he just frowned at me.

"Now, all we have to do is get you to believe in you and we're all set," he said.

SIX

IT WAS A quick job in the cool weather to the two-five. The station was off a Hun-eighteen between bustling Lex and the shadows of the elevated Metro-North track on Park Avenue. Unlike the rundown Hill Street stereotype so prevalent in television's inner city, the two-five was a fairly modern facility built in the early '70's. (Wow, disco and the two-five. You hadda love the '70's.) Except for the thirty blue-and-whites parked outside, the two-story yellow brick structure could've easily been mistaken for an intermediate school. Except this building was well attended.

Frankly, I always hated walking into the place. In a neighborhood which was 50% Latino and 40% African-American, the racial makeup of the two-five was 90% White. And 99% of that 90% didn't even reside in New York City proper. They lived in "safe" communities located far away from the big town sleaze. Of course, this meant that El Barrio was being policed by a suburban occupying force. Not a comforting thought, to say the least.

Perhaps it was my admitted paranoia but I always felt each time I set foot in there each cop looked at me as either a potential perp, a probable perp or, simply a perp. I could see their eyes glaze over while they flipped through their mental criminal files and sensed their disappointment when they came up empty. This didn't make for the most pleasant chitchat. If you weren't a criminal then you were a pain-in-the-ass complainant. This meant paperwork. That took time. This was a very bad thing.

With my finest innocent-taxpayer strut, I stepped inside the station. The desk sergeant on duty was a balding, baggy-eyed fellow with a nameplate that read Skumbeaux. (Poor guy probably was tortured so much as a child he had to become a cop to regain some self-esteem.) He was arguing with a little old lady about some type of summons she received. I prayed it wasn't for hooking and just kept strutting to the back of the house where the detectives were located.

At the front desk was a detective I'd met before named O'Reilly. In his fifties, he was about my height with a shock of white hair and an elfin face. Solidly two-twenty, he was also a fourth-generation cop with a disposition of a bee trapped in a can. He eyeballed me as I approached. Flip, flip, flip. How predictable. In a stationhouse, a person of color was guilty until proven...guilty.

I turned the charm on.

"Good afternoon, Detective O'Reilly."

Like a neat carnival trick, his blue eyes narrowed and the bags under them rose.

"Do I know you, Bub?" he growled.

Oh no, I thought, not the dreaded 'Bub.' Like a prizefighter hit by his wife's jab, I shook it off.

"Yeah, you do," I said. "Last year, Cary Branson introduced us during the Christmas party at his old house." O'Reilly relaxed. Sort of.

"O yeah," he said. "You were the only civilian there. A scribbler. Worked with an ad agency."

"I was a research librarian at a weekly newsmagazine."

He waved his left hand dismissively.

'Whatever, scribbler, whatever. What'cha doin' now?"

"I'm a private detective."

O'Reilly laughed uproariously. "C'mon," he said, "really."

"Really, O'Reilly."

He ceased laughing.

"You making fun of me?"

I pointed to my chest.

"Me? Of you? Never! Say, is Branson around?"

He started to smirk. "I heard there was some bad blood between youse," he said.

I smirked back. "You've been misinformed," I said.

O'Reilly reached for his desk phone.

"I'll page him," he said.

I thanked him before turning my back. I scanned the station. Ruddy pink faces clothed in dark blue uniforms or suits on pitch-black phones at shit-brown desks. Each facial expression ranged from violently unhappy to vaguely annoyed. It reminded me of the first time I entered this place some fourteen months ago.

I'd left my job late that evening. Due to some White House mess, the issue closing was held up a few hours. I was tired and wanted to go home to C.J., my ladylove. But Cary insisted I stop by the station to talk to him. Important, he said. He had to talk to me.

The magazine was located at Fifty-third and Park. I figured I'd hop a cab there and take a run uptown. Should have taken me fifteen minutes tops. Stupid me. I'd forgotten New York City taxi etiquette. No pickups of - now here's a word I despise - 'minorities' heading uptown after dark. Didn't matter I was wearing a suit and tie. Cab drivers don't care about fashion. Be he garbed in tuxedo or fatigues, a colored person was just a colored person and he ain't getting no taxi after the sun sets.

After a half-hour of watching the canary-yellow parade pass me by, I glanced at my watch. Ten thirty. Running late. I decided to hop on the Lexington line to 116th Street. It was a stop I knew well. Hell, the street staircase was right at the corner of my uncle's bar. No sweat.

I ran to Fifty-first and Lex. Luck was with me. The local pulled in just as I swiped my Metrocard through the turnstile. I jetted on, copped a squat right by the conductor - the A-list seat in the New York Transit Authority travel survival kit - and began to read my magazine's latest issue.

Engrossed in the mag, I almost missed my stop. When I noticed we were leaving the One-sixteen, I threw myself through the closing doors. A blur in pinstripes, I barely made it.

After taking a minute to compose myself, I headed through the only unshackled exit door, made a left at the token booth and headed up the stairs towards the street.

Today I'm aware what that minute cost me. Not only was I the last one to get off the train, I was also the last one to leave the platform. My mind must've been preoccupied cause I just never noted just how dark that staircase was.

I was halfway up the garbage-strewn steps, absentmindedly groping my way through the shadows when I heard the click and felt the ice-cold steel pressed against the back of my neck.

"Gimme your wallet," a voice whispered.

It's strange what pops into your head during stressful situations. My life didn't flash before me. I didn't think of Clarice Jean or my parents or any other family member. All I kept hearing in my pounding skull was that Curtis Mayfield song from the Superfly soundtrack, "Freddie's Dead." Over and over and over, like a demonic loop, I heard Curtis crooning "Freddie's Dead," followed by that descending bassline lick: do do do, do do do, do do do, doo doo do.

Man, I hated that song as a kid. (What child wants to be reminded about his mortality?) Of course, my classmates teased me with it from the moment it came out; unleashing it whenever I'd screwed up in gym or got a word wrong in a spelling bee. It took me years to relax and appreciate Mayfield's artistry. Years not to take the tune personally. Years. And all it took was one click and some chilled metal at the nape of my neck to bring all that fear and resentment flooding back.

"Gimme the fuckin' money, bitch."

His voice was a little louder. The timbre sounded high-pitched. Oh shit, I realized. I'm being stuck up by a kid. He pressed the weapon deeper in my neck. Ah, the impatience of youth. By the tone of his voice, he couldn't have been older than eleven. Twelve, tops. No matter. I was still terrified.

"Inside left suit pocket," I whispered.

"Get it."

He tried real hard to talk tough but couldn't. Slowly, I reached inside, pulled out my billfold and held it up. He snatched it, then did nothing. I wondered what was going through his head. Was he debating whether to off me or not? Should I make a move? I hadn't even finished the thought when I heard the trigger being pulled.

You know in the movies, there's always a scene in action comedies when one of the protagonists is shot at or, more often, thinks he's being fired upon. His reaction - it's always a guy - is to clutch his chest, moan, groan and tell somebody, anybody, it's curtains and inform his wife/girlfriend/steady lady that he truly loved her. Then he pats his chest and, after not feeling any bullet holes, raises his hands and examines them for blood. Having not seen any, he briefly smiles before realizing the extent of his cowardice. He has broken the male code: he has acknowledged his fear. His lone response is some type of lame explanation to his skeptical onlookers. Too late. All respect is long gone. Of course, this is a classic film formula which produces some socko laughs. Of course.

In my case, the kid pulled the trigger. I screamed like a woman and pissed my pants. A split-second later, I realized I wasn't shot, bleeding or hurt. (Just wet and smelly.) The little bastard's gun had jammed. Embarrassed and livid, I wheeled round to clock the fucker. He anticipated my move and, as I turned, whacked me on the left side of my noggin. This time the gun went off. As I went airborne down the stairs, I heard my assailant running up towards the street. I landed so hard on my right shoulder I tore the corresponding seams on my jacket sleeve.

After a good three minutes spent a-writhing and a-rolling, I managed to pull myself up into a semi-kneeling position. Aching, and bleeding, I crawled up the steps to the street. I was so oblivious to my surroundings I went past the Barcelona and staggered the couple of blocks to the station. The first face I saw when I crashed through the precinct doors was Cary's. He caught me an instant before I hit the floor.

"Here comes Branson, scribbler," said O'Reilly.

For a moment I was disoriented, lost between past and present. O'Reilly's next comment brought me all the way back.

"Wow, check out that suit," he said.

I glanced towards the stationhouse rear. There was Mr. Cary Branson, rank of detective, hair slicked back Pat Riley style, striding towards us in a mega-expensive blue-black double-breasted suit, black shirt and blue and black tie. You'da thought he was on a model's runway by his strutting walk instead of an East Harlem cop casa. I confess: I was hoping the high-yella Regis Philbin would trip. He didn't.

"What do ya think, scribbler?"

"About what. Detective?"

O'Reilly jabbed the air with his right index finger as though he was a champion dart thrower.

"About the suit," he said. "Nice, ain't it?"

"It should be," I said.

"Why's that?"

"It was mine," I sighed.

O'Reilly actually seemed rueful.

"Sorry, bub," he said.

"No offense taken," I said. "The fact the fucker's wearing my eight hundred dollar suit doesn't bother me. The thought he's wearing my ex-girlfriend's panties does."

O'Reilly laughed.

"Which do you miss more," he asked, "them or her?"

I looked him in the eye.

"Both," I said.

"Don't sweat it scribbler," O'Reilly said as he punched my left arm. "I should inform you, however, that when I saw Branson in the locker room yesterday he was wearing a brassiere."

"That's a relief."

"Why?"

"My ex doesn't wear a bra."

Cary reached us just as O'Reilly started to crack up. His green eyes narrowed.

"Been talking about me, Freddie?" he asked.

"Just admiring the duds, Cary," I said.

He ran his hands down the line of the suit.

"You know, Freddie, I had to have it let out in the crotch," he said.

I waited a beat before answering.

"Yeah, I hear those hemorrhoids can be a bitch."

O'Reilly went into hysterics when Gary's face reddened.

"Branson," gasped O'Reilly, "quit while you're ahead."

"You mean behind," I added.

"Let's go talk business," said Cary gruffly.

"Sure," I said, "are you hungry?"

Branson nodded so I suggested cuchifritos on Hun-sixteen.

"Okay," Cary said while glaring at the giggling O'Reilly. "I'm happy you're so amused," he stated through tightened lips.

"So am I," O'Reilly retorted before collapsing into a paroxysm of laughter. "See you at Branson's next party, scribbler."

"Sure thing, O'Reilly," I said. "I hear it's going to be B.Y.O.P."

"B.Y.O.P.?"

"Yep, Bring Your Own Plunger,"I said.

"Freddie, let's just go," said Cary.

"Is that your final answer, Cary?"

O'Reilly exploded laughing. Cary just exploded.

"Now!!"

I winked at O'Reilly who gave me a thumbs-up. Branson and I headed out. Cary angrily kicked the street door open. As it slowly swung shut behind me, we could still hear O'Reilly's howls resounding around the station. He sounded like Stan Laurel on helium.

SEVEN

AN OLFACTORY ORGASM. That's what I was having while seated in the back of the Cuchifrito Cottage, (To be precise, it's Pepito's Cuchifrito Cottage, nestled snugly on the south side of 116th between Fashions By Gloria and the Cosmo movie theater.) My eyes were tightly shut and - after finally fading out the bullshit of Gary's faux-friendly drone - I could actually hear the sizzling of the various meats (pork, chicken, beef and mystery) on Pepito's yard-long, yard-wide grill.

Slowly, steadily, I practiced my breath control. Deeply, joyfully, I inhaled then exhaled. The scent was truly intoxicating. It was also overpowering. Winter, spring, summer or fall, an El Barrio resident could sniff Pepito's multidirectional cooking within a twenty-block radius. (The military could not produce a nerve gas with such strategic precision.)

It was like a quick snort of blow. I mean, you'd come out of the subway on a Hun-sixteen, hit the pavement running and right there to greet you would be the smell of Pepito's grill. One breath later, you'd be left semi-paralyzed on the sidewalk with a most definite buzz.

It was such a sweet aroma that it could even pass through brick walls. The best was when you were catching a double feature at the Cosmo. The local moviehouse - and Pepito's next-door neighbor - the Cosmo was a big old balcony-less theater with damp seats that creaked when you parked your carcass in them, floors so sticky you felt like you were jogging on flypaper, a dust-encrusted, marble proscenium and stone faced ushers who'd look more comfortable standing stock-still against a plain white wall while holding up a set of numbers for a police photographer.

In addition, the motion picture fare that the Cosmo specialized in programming was a variety of exploitation fare for the non-discriminating. One film distribution rule-of-thumb for Nueva York seemed to be that if a movie contained wall-to-wall-to-wall violence and great, goodly gobs of T& A, it played at the Cosmo. As a result, the theater was a holy grail for cineastes who preferred the shout of "loose joints" reverberating through a cavernous auditorium then the insidious whir of a VCR or the electronic hum from a DVD.

Well, when Pepito really started cooking (usually halfway through the first flick), the theater patrons would start to shut their eyes at the onscreen scenes of onslaught and murmur sighs of contentment as the fragrance of acapurrias, pasteles, tostones and maduros would ever-so-slowly waft their way through the vast, musty moviehouse. (Even the occasional rodent running down the center aisle would pause out of odorific respect.)

The effect was positively Pavlovian as Cosmo customers by the row load would rush out between pictures to satiate their stimulated taste buds. As my uncle Chubby once put it: "A bite of morsilla, a cold cerveza and a women-in-prison twin bill, who could ask for anything more?" Who indeed?

But such a reaction was routine to Pepito himself. In the eyes of many, the proprietor of the Cuchifrito Cottage had lived a charmed life. In fact, Pepito himself would be the first to admit it. A slight, bespectacled, shy individual, Pepito Malave had been the first Latino businessman - at a very young age to boot - to break the East Harlem color line.

Back in the '30s, Harlem was a blueprint for segregation. Take 116th Street for example. The Blacks had Harlem from the west side of Fifth Avenue on. Heading east towards the river, the Puerto Ricans had the opposite side of Fifth, Madison Avenue, Park Avenue (home of La Marqueta, the world's largest supermarket... at least, that's what the sign says) and the west side of Lexington. The rest of the way, from Lexington to Third to Second to First to Pleasant Avenue was Italiano. (Of course, with the exception of a candy shop here and there, all of the major businesses in Harlem were owned by Whites.)

Naturally, there were turf wars. A wandering fellow from group A could get severely fucked up if'n he wandered into Group B's territory and vice versa. Add in the various street gangs and cliques hanging around these areas of restriction and you had a pretty volatile mix.

Enter one jibaro named Pepito Malave. Barely sixteen, he had emigrated from La Isla Puerto Rico with his expectant bride Inez. Pepito wanted a better life than slaving away as a farm worker on a coffee plantation in the town of Yauco. Oddly enough, Pepito wanted to be a cook.

It seems that even as a kid, when he was knee-high to his mama Paula's apron, Pepito felt most comfortable inside a kitchen. The eighth and last boy out of a litter of eleven, Pepito was a chef savant. Once he saw someone prepare a dish, he never forgot it and could duplicate it exactly- (Whenever Pepito was asked if he ever used a recipe book, he'd always shake his head and then, with a dramatic flourish, tap his left temple with the ever-wrinkled tip of his right index finger. It's all up here, that gesture would say, all up here.) At the age of eight, Pepito was making dinner for the entire clan. At ten, he was creating his own dishes. At twelve, when he began work at the coffee plantation, he was selling little treats to his fellow laborers. (Needless to say, Pepito was very popular.)

At fourteen, at a co-worker's house party, Pepito was helping somebody carry in a block of ice when he spotted the raven-haired Inez Rosado. Awed by her beauty, he dropped his side of the block. The ice shattered; his heart didn't.

Evidently, the feeling was mutual. Inez would later confess to her friends, she too was instantly smitten. Just in case, Pepito wooed Inez with specially prepared dishes all named after her. There was "Carne con Inez," "Pollo con Inez" and so on. Pepito would tell her each one was 'cooked with love' and they were. About a year to the day they'd met, with blessing from their respective families, they were wed.

Eleven months later, Inez informed Pepito that she was expectant. Emboldened by the news, Pepito made plans to leave Yauco.

"I want my children to be born in America," he told his wife. "A land of opportunity for them and we."

Inez agreed so they practiced their English and cabled a cousin of a cousin of Pepito's who resided in New York City. The cousin of a cousin secured them a room in the building he lived in on 117th and Park. They packed up their meager belongings, kissed their families goodbye and came over to New York on an overcrowded boat called the Marine Tiger. They hugged each other when they saw the Statue of Liberty in the harbor. America, at last.

The bloom was off the lily less than two hours later. The subway ride uptown was unpleasant with a cadre of Blancos making snide remarks about the smell of immigrants. When they reached Harlem, they noticed the blocks were jammed with poor folks with exhausted eyes. Pepito's cousin had done the best he could on such short notice but the room he'd secured, with a window facing the street, was dark and roach-infested. That first night - a hot, noisy eve - Inez and Pepito did not, could not, sleep. They simply held on to each other and wept.

Within a month, Pepito had found work. He was a stock boy in a Coney Island butcher shop. Coney Island, Brooklyn. He'd rise at 3 AM, cook the day's meals for his wife and then dress. At 4 AM, he was on the subway to Coney. He'd begin work at 5:45, get a 15-minute break at noon and then hustle straight through until 7 PM.

Thirty minutes later, with a small loaf of bread in his pocket, Pepito would catch a Manhattan-bound train home. At 9 PM, he'd open the door and see his wife sitting at their little table waiting for him. There, while they nibbled on the loaf, Pepito would hear about his wife's day. Afterwards, he'd listen to the ancient spare radio his cousin had lent him. At midnight, four hours before the cycle would begin again, he'd finally fall asleep in Inez's arms. His luck changed with an accident. Pepito was on his way home from an exhausting day at work when the train he was riding stopped suddenly on 110th Street. He was just one station away from his usual departure point when the conductor announced that due to mechanical difficulties, the train was going out of service. Rather than wait for the next train, Pepito decided to walk home. And so he did.

Normally, Pepito was always somewhat oblivious to his surroundings - only Inez and food had ever fully captured his attention - but that night, he was abnormally alert. And anxious. The streets were empty and quiet. This unnerved Pepito. Swiveling his head back and forth like a weather vane on a windy day, he approached each oncoming tenement with the caution of a gunfighter walking down a dirt-swept road. There's danger in them there stoops, pardner, he told himself.

Coming down a stoop on 113th Street, about a half-block ahead of him, Pepito spotted a tall, thick white man wearing an ebony 3- piece suit. He had a derby in his left hand, silver hair with a black streak down the middle, spats and a deliberate walk. He was flanked by two broad-shouldered young men wearing identical brown double-breasted suits. They were each doing an impersonation of Napoleon Bonaparte with their right hands at rest inside their jackets. The trio would stop in front of every storefront on the left side of the avenue, go in and then, a mere millisecond later, come out with the man in the middle holding a large white envelope which quickly disappeared into the inside pocket of his suit. Pepito thought they must be bill collectors.

The three bill collectors were about to cross to 114th when Pepito heard a noise behind him. It was a black sedan with the headlights out and two windows on the left side rolled down. It creeped along the road slowly. As they passed a streetlight on 113th, Pepito noticed twin glints of steel flashing from the left hands of the driver and his backseat passenger. (Years later, while serving as a cook on an aircraft carrier during World War II, Pepito would recall that glint whenever he was standing on the ship's deck and saw offshore SOS signals.)

Pepito tensed. A hit just like in the Jimmy Cagney peliculas, he thought. He wanted to freeze, stop, scream, blend in with the limestone steps. But what Pepito ended up doing instead, was crouching low and, moving quietly behind the avenue's parked cars, he slowly picked up his pace.

It didn't take long for the action to start. A second before the sedan revved its engine, Pepito broke out into a full gallop towards the bill collectors.

"Get down," he yelled, "get down!"

Pepito later recalled he was moving so fast that he was already on top of them as his warnings reached their ears. The two brown suits turned around with their revolvers suddenly at the ready. Their guns were aimed at Pepito.

"Get down," Pepito said.

The double-breasted duo shared a quizzical look which was quickly erased by the splattering of gunfire from the sedan. As their bodies spasmed from the ferocious impact of a bullet barrage, Pepito leapt between them and landed on top of the ebony-suited man. He shoved him to the ground as the gunfire shattered the windshields of the parked automobiles around them.

For what seemed like an eternity, Pepito and the silver-haired man stared into each other's eyes as the bullets cascaded above them. Then the barrage stopped and they heard the sedan screech to a halt about a car's length ahead of them. They're coming back to finish the job, thought Pepito.

The silver-haired man wriggled around the pavement to the dead bodies of his former companions and yanked their revolvers out of their lifeless hands. Then, while taking special care not to slip in the spreading pool of blood surrounding Pepito and him, he pivoted around, with a gun in each hand, towards the spot where they'd heard the sedan stop.

It was over before it began. When the two assassins came strolling through the parked cars, the ebony-suited man already had the guns cocked and the targets zeroed in. Involuntarily, Pepito closed his eyes. He heard each trigger pulled twice. When he opened his eyes there were two new dead men lying in front of him. The armed silver-haired man stood up. He beckoned Pepito to do the same. Pepito did. The ebony-suited man stared at Pepito a long time before putting the guns in his jacket pockets.

"What's your name?" he asked softly.

"Pepito, Pepito Malave."

"Where do you live?"

"117th and Park."

The silver-haired man smiled then cocked his ear as if he'd heard something. He had. There were sirens in the distance.

"Pepito," he said, "go home. Say nothing to no one. I will be in touch."

Pepito found himself nodding uncontrollably before asking the gentleman who he was.

"Your benefactor," laughed the silver-haired man. "And now, you must go. Run!"

Pepito ran as he never had before. He ran all the way home, bounding up the four flights to his apartment and when his wife opened the door, he hugged and kissed her as if it were the first time.

"If she hadn't been pregnant at the time, I guarantee you we would've made another baby that night," he told me many years later.

Pepito read about the killings in the paper the next day. A Gangland Shootout, the headline blared. The article, written by a Jeffrey Scott, claimed the police were seeking eyewitnesses and were following every lead. Mayor LaGuardia said that these random acts of killing must stop. It didn't but nobody bothered Pepito and that was a good thing.

A month later, Inez was ready to deliver so Pepito had his cousin upstairs - who had the building's only telephone - call for an ambulance from the closest city hospital: Metropolitan. Gently, Pepito helped Inez down the stairs. When they reached the street, Pepito was surprised to see a brand-spanking-new ambulance. (Inez was in too much pain to notice.) Leaning on the car, wearing glowing ivory uniforms, were two young white attendants.

"Pepito Malave?" one asked.

"Yes," he cautiously replied.

"Come with us."

Inez got in the back with one attendant while Pepito rode shotgun upfront with the other one. The siren was screeching loudly as the ambulance whizzed downtown. The driver took Park Avenue all the way down, honking his horn at a pretty redhead as they passed 96th Street. Pepito was alarmed.

"Isn't Metropolitan Hospital on 96th?" he inquired.

"You're not going to Metropolitan," said the driver.

Pepito's protestations were cut off by the attendant in the back of the car.

"For God's sake, Harry, floor it! She's due any minute!"

Harry floored it and thirty seconds later, Pepito found himself and Inez being rushed inside LeRoy Private Hospital on 62nd Street and York Avenue.

"There must be some mistake," Pepito said as his wife was wheeled down some corridor.

"There is no mistake, sir," assured the driver. "Now, just go to your left and follow the blue arrows into the waiting room.

Pepito, a flounder out of water, did what he was told. The hospital staff stared at him as he headed towards his destination but no one stopped him.

He went inside the room and sat down. With his nerves shot, Pepito was literally holding his head in his hands when he smelled fresh coffee. Squinting through his fingers, he looked up. The sight sent shockwaves straight down to his aching feet. It was the silver-haired man holding a cup of java in his hands. He was wearing a white 3-piece suit. Pepito thought he looked like an avenging angel as he sat next to him.

"Here have some cafe'," he told Pepito.

Perplexed, Pepito took the cup. After a sip, he grimaced.

"Yeah, I know," chuckled the silver-haired man. "It's not espresso or bustelo."

"Why are you here?" asked Pepito.

"You did me a favor," said the silver-haired man as he placed his left hand on Pepito 's right shoulder. "You saved my life and you kept quiet about it. I owe you much and I wish to return the favor. "

"Who are you?"

"I am Don Vincenzo," said the silver-haired man. "I sort of run things in the neighborhood. I was out collecting the returns on my local investments with a couple of my... employees when some of my former competitors sought to unseat me from my position of respect. You prevented this and now I wish to help you."

"You want to help me?"

"I am not against the Spanish people," said Don Vincenzo. "They are some of my favorite customers. As long as they know their place we can exist together. Now, what would you like the most of all?"

Pepito thought hard before he responded.

"I would like my own place to cook. A restaurant."

Don Vincenzo rubbed his hands together before patting his hair down.

"A restaurant which serves Puerto Rican food and such exotic delicacies?"

"Si."

"I have a place, a millinery shop, next to the Cosmo cinema which is not performing up to standards. Would that location do?"

"On the other side of Lexington?"

"Yes, between Third and Lexington."

"Is it safe for me to go there?"

Don Vincenzo laughed.

"It is now," he said.

"Then, yes," said Pepito.

"I will take care of the rent, garbage pickups, health inspectors, electricity and all the supplies," said Don Vincenzo. "The split will be 51/49 and you will pay your people out of your 49%.

"Ask me no questions," he said in a lowered voice, "and tell no one anything. Do not steal from me and all will be well. You have seen the alternative."

Pepito nodded and they shook hands.

It was a deal.

Just then, the door to the waiting room opened and a hefty

blonde nurse came in holding two hairy brown children. Enthusiastic, she wasn't. That is, until she spotted Don Vincenzo. Then she straightened her spine, threw out her sizable chest and smiled as though somebody behind her had yanked her ears back.

"Mr. Malave?" she asked.

"Si," waved Pepito.

"You have twins,' she said. "A healthy boy and girl."

With tears in his eyes, Pepito thrust his arms out and lightly touched the crowns of his two children.

"And my wife?" he sobbed.

"She's doing fine," said the nurse. "You can see her in five minutes. I'm bringing the children up to her now."

"Thank you," said Pepito.

When the nurse left, he turned to Don Vincenzo. Pepito had a grin he felt would never leave his face.

"Don Vincenzo, it would be an honor to my wife and to me if you would consent to be godfather to my children."

"Pepito," said Don Vincenzo as he gestured towards the door, "I already am."

And so that's how little Pepito Malave Jr. and Pepita Inez Malave came to have Don Vincenzo (Deadeye Vinnie) Gianelli as their godfather. It is also how Pepito Malave Sr. became the Jackie Robinson of his day at the age of seventeen and got to open his Cuchifrito Cottage on the 'wrong' side of Lexington Avenue.

In fact, Pepito, under the auspices of his new best friend Don Vincenzo, was welcomed to the area by the surrounding merchants. As did the various area hoodlums. Open from 6 AM to 2 AM, seven days a week, Pepito's place became the prime meeting spot for criminals and certain high-ranking police officials to converse about life, sports and the general conducting of business. It was where 'the criminal elite meet to eat,' claimed the reporter Scott in an expose of Mob hangouts.

None of this bothered Pepito. Not even the birth of eight of his children, 16 grandchildren and 32 great-grandchildren (there's an exponential factor to Latino families) worried him. Nor the plush Long Island estate he purchased just a few towns away from Don Vincenzo. Not even the fact that the complexion of the neighborhood grew progressively darker.

See, in nearly sixty years of proprietorship, Pepito had the only business in El Barrio which never experienced a robbery attempt. Not even one.

Hell, the restaurant was even designed to be raid-proof. The front windows were opaque. Customers could see out, passersby could not see in. (At best, they might be able to make out a few anamorphic shapes.) The chairs at the tables were placed side by side and faced the door. Even the counter seats were angled towards the door. The one window, which opened to the street, allowed only a view of the grill and the steam-drenched worker behind it.

The very best table was placed smack-dab-middle against the rear wall of the joint. It offers a panoramic view of the backs of the other customers and the door. Dubbed Don Vincenzo's Throne, it is solely reserved for special guests like police, brass, top racketeers and friends of the family. (Not to forget, Don Vincenzo himself whenever the spry nonagenarian decides to peep out some uptown action.) Which I guess I was since Pepito, personally, sat me and Cary here. As he had told me himself at the bar of the Barcelona when he told me this tale late one night:

"America, Freddie, can be a wonderful place. I only hope you can fulfill your dreams as I have."

EIGHT

"...**DREAMING? WHAT THE** fuck..

Freddie, are you listening to me?" I opened my eyes and there was the impatient Cary Branson looking all perturbed as he sipped his glass of mango juice.

"I don't get it," I said as I rubbed my eyelids. "I closed my eyes, clicked my heels three times and yet you're still here. I am outraged. I think that witch sold me a false bill of goods."

"Very funny, smart-ass," he said. "You know, after all I've done.. "

It was tune-out time again although this time I made sure to give Cary my glassy I'm-really-here-listening-to-you-really-l-am look, the one that I'd long since perfected at my parents' house.

Besides I knew the litany. Cary and I had met our first day in Stuyvesant High School. It was freshmen assembly in the two-tiered auditorium and there we were sitting side by side in adjoining wooden seats. I was five-foot-two, a Nuyorican nebbish in mismatched plaid-on-plaid clothing. He was an even six feet, a light skinned Joe Cool in a three-piece plush denim suit. I was reading a comic book. He asked me who was the super-villain. Whammo, we wuz pals.

I guess I had what Seinfeld comically referred to as a nonsexual crush. For the little guy I was - a school brainiac consistently shunned by his fellow classmates - Cary was the big brother/best bud figure I never had. So we both played our roles to perfection. I wisecracked and idolized. He laughed and preened.

He and I hung out tough throughout high school. We shared our hopes, our dreams. I wanted to be an editor - never really had the balls to be a writer - and he wanted to be an attorney. On our day of graduation, we pledged mutual devotion to each other in our yearbooks.

Even when we attended different colleges in the city - me at NYU, Cary at Fordham - we made it a point to get together each and every weekend. We'd catch a ballgame or a flick or do something.

On those days. I'd bare my young soul to Cary. I remember how proud he was when I told him I'd finally lost my virginity. It was early in my NYU freshman year. I was in this study booth at Bobst Library with the heated, horny Nancy Veloz. I tried to be cool; I wasn't. It was a stumbling, bumbling, fumbling affair. The sex act just about ended before it started. I just thank the Almighty I had had the sense to use the blue-colored condom Cary had given me.

Cary's response was a classic: "Ohhhh, yeahhhhhh, welcome to the other side, Freddie."

(Well, at the time, it made me feel like I had been inducted to the mack-daddy Hall Of Fame.)

Now, sex was nothing new for Cary. He'd been knocking them boots - while I'd been knocking my knees - since he was twelve. In high school, he ran through damn near the entire female student body. (No pun intended.)

Me? Well, I was a slow starter. (Perhaps the clinical term sexual retard would be more exact.) I was lucky enough to steal a kiss here and there and that's all. That's why I lived vicariously through Cary's conquests. By the virtue of his incredibly intimate descriptions, I felt I knew these women personally. And when I did meet these women personally, Cary would make sure to point out - silently and surreptitiously, of course - their 'hot spots' of passion. The true joke, he was saying, was on the women and I was privileged to be in on it.

I literally started to grow up in college. On my high school graduation day, I was five-four, a hundred and thirty pounds and wore a thirty-four regular jacket. By my junior year at NYU, I was five-nine, one-eighty and a thirty-nine regular. (Now I'm five- eleven, two-twenty and a forty-six regular. A quick view of my belly confirms that only 35% of it is fat.) As I got closer to Cary's height, I noticed he got a bit more standoffish and competitive. And when we played ball against each other, a win for him wasn't automatic. In fact, the older we got and no matter the sport we played, I began to beat him quite regularly.

Scholastically, I also began to pull away from him. I was racking up grades of B + with appalling consistency. I wasn't sure what was going on with Cary in Fordham's 'Land of the Jesuits,' but I knew this: it was going to be awfully hard to get into law school with a C average.

Also my self-confidence had zoomed with the arrival of Ms. Clarice Jean Austin into my life. Honey-brown skin, five-five, 36C-26-37, short auburn 'fro, sweet hazel eyes, a medium-sized nose with a bump on the bridge and a full-lipped smile that stopped traffic, Clarice was an A student with a major in Political Science, a minor in Philosophy and an inexplicable interest in me.

We met in junior year in a Philosophy of Life class. I was seated in the row next to the window. She'd come in late and scrunched those mighty hips into the chair behind me. I turned to casually check her out, she looked at me and I was gone. The attraction was immediate, kinetic. I couldn't concentrate in class. Just couldn't. My grades were slipping. I was a mess. So one nerve-wracked day I asked her if she'd help me out by studying with me. Thank the Lord, she said yes.

We went to a study room at Bobst. (No, not the Nancy Veloz suite, I didn't need that kind of pressure.) The first hour we studied. Then we looked up from our books and kissed the next two hours away. We were inseparable after that.

It was thanks to Cary that Clarice and I finally got to make love. It was the beginning of our senior year. Both she and I lived with parents who never vacated the premises. (It's like they were rooted there.) Cary had, however, converted his folks' garage into an ersatz-bachelor pad. (A place where a lube job held an entirely different meaning.) I told him how special Clarice was to me. A library cubicle just wasn't going to cut it, dry humping - a misnomer if you know what I mean - was taking years off of my life and so I begged him to let me borrow the place.

A week later, he gave me his key. When I opened the door with Clarice, the place was pristine. There were flowers lining the windows, candles beside the bed and the Isley Brothers on the stereo.

"What a thoughtful and attentive man," Clarice said.

She was half-right.

That afternoon was magic, I told her I loved her and never wanted to be without her. She said she felt the same way. We resolved we would be together forever.

Flash-forward five years later. Clarice and I were living together in the East Village. I started working at the magazine. Clarice was a year away from her doctorate in Government Studies.

I thought it was a happy time. Cary'd come over often. He couldn't get into law school so he decided to get into law enforcement instead. He'd regale us with tales of car chases, kicked-in doors and free lunches. Perks of the job, he'd say.

Another perk was women. They just love the uniform, he claimed. (I thought it was the license to kill they loved but that's a different story.) Clarice would tell him that's because he hadn't found the right woman.

Maybe so but Cary was racking up astronomical numbers of poon. He was nailing models, singers, actresses, doctors, nurses, flight attendants, dental hygienists, bankers, fellow police officers. You name it, Cary was banging it.

Yet Cary would always confess to us he had a 'problem.' He hadn't found a woman 'high-class' enough to escort to the big brass occasions.

"You know, Freddie, somebody like Clarice," he said.

"Few men do, Cary," I said with a grin.

"Who you telling? Hey....wait a minute!"

Yep. He asked if he could take Clarice. I thought about it. He was my friend. She was my lady. Sure he was a dog but he'd never dog me out. Besides, I could always at least trust Clarice.

What a dumb fuck I was.

"It's okay with me if it's okay with her," I said.

"I don't mind," she said.

"Great," he said, "I'll pick you up at eight next Friday and have you home by..."

"8:02," I joked.

We all laughed.

That Friday night, Clarice strolled in at midnight and told me she had a great time.

"That's nice," I said.

It had begun. I'd come home late from work and Clarice was on the phone. I'd put down my briefcase, take off my coat, jacket and tie and then she'd hand me the receiver.

"Who is it?" I'd ask.

"Cary," she'd say. "He just called."

"Hey, hey buddy," he'd say. "Good timing, huh?"

And then the bullshit would flow.

But did I suspect anything? Fuck no. These are two people I love, I respect. Then one evening I go to meet Cary at his job, get fucked up and collapse in his arms.

I woke up that night in Harlem Hospital. There were footsteps in the hall and Cary by my bed.

"How long have I been out?"

"A couple of hours," he said. "What happened?"

"You were shot in the head. Just a graze actually. You were lucky.

"My head was full of pounding jackhammers.

"Why don't I feel lucky?" I asked.

"Well you should," he said.

Cary glanced around before pulling a Polaroid out of his pocket. He showed it to me.

"Do you know this guy, Freddie?"

It was the kid that held me up. Correction. That shot me. He looked no older than twelve. He'd get no older either. He was lying in the middle of a project entranceway with a gaping bullet hole in the center of his forehead. He had a red Adidas T-shirt on. I didn't think red was the original color though. Yep, he sure was dead.

"That's him," I said.

"Thought so," Cary said as he put away the photo - the snapshot - in his pocket. "Had trouble with him before. Stickup kid. Recognized his Em-Oh. Found him in front of the Jefferson projects over on Third Avenue. Sitting on a bench rifling through your wallet. Counting your money. Ran towards the building when he saw me. Capped his ass right then and there."

Cary put his hand on my chest for a moment.

"You'll be okay, Freddie. I took care of everything."

The door to the room opened suddenly. It was Clarice. She came in and went directly to Cary.

"Are you okay?" she asked.

"Yeah," he said. "Here's his wallet."

It was then that I finally realized what the fuck was really and truly going on. Why it was so 'urgent' for Cary to see me. To talk to me. When she took the wallet from his hand, I saw how their touch lingered and I wished right then and there that little bastard's bullet had found its mark.

NINE

"...**DONE FOR YOU**," said Cary.

"Cary, you asshole, stop the bullshit. You broke my heart and stole my woman."   "I saved your life!"

"Only after you took it away first!"

"You simply cannot come to face the reality that Clarice wasn't happy with you. That she needed a change."

I had to laugh.

"Oh so now you're some kind of sensitive masked avenger who rescues unhappy maidens from long-term commitments. Homeboy, you're fucked up," I said while shaking my head. "Besides, she never told me she was unhappy with me until she kicked my depressed ass out of my apartment."

"Maybe you frighten her."

I glared at him as hard as I could.

"Knock off the Oprah shit, fuckface," I said. "You took my lady. Plain and simple. You betrayed me and our friendship. You may think offing some punk motherfucker mugger may square things with me, bitch boy, but it doesn't. Or, maybe you figure, jeez, I fucked up Freddie's old life so let me assist in getting him a new one."

"I helped you get a PI's license so you could go play Sherlock, didn't I, butt nugget? I even got you a legit gun permit for that Sig Sauer cannon you wanted, didn't I?"

"Uh-huh."

"Well, doesn't that count for something? Cutting through all that red tape?"

"It means you've got a guilty conscience for getting a suicidal, depressed agoraphobic out of an apartment you wanted to move into."

"If you hate me so much, Freddie," sighed Cary, "then why did you accept my help?"

I was silent for a couple of seconds.

"Because you're the only friend I have," I responded.

"Now, that's fucked up," laughed Cary.

"I know. Anyway I need your help on this thing I'm working on."

"Sure. Shoot."

"Don't tempt me, Branson."

I repeated to him everything Mayra had told me about her brother. (He seemed particularly interested in her apparent prosperity.) Cary said he'd get the missing person report, nose around a little, make a few calls and get back to me when he had something, I thanked him when the meal came and, thankfully, we ate that meal in silence.

As we were leaving the restaurant, Pepito stopped me by the grill. He sounded as if he were pleading.

"It's real good to see you, Freddie, real good. Don't be a stranger, huh?"

"I'm trying not to, Pepito. I'm trying not to."

I thanked him and then we left.

TEN

IF MAYRA SIMPLY lived in an 'apartment,' then homeboy here has been living in a hamper. The whole place was like a vast mesa. By that I mean, she's got a spacious den, a spacious parlor and a spacious dining room separated from a spacious gourmet kitchen by a wraparound counter with a grill and sink. (I think the key word here is spacious.) Next to the kitchen was a spiral staircase. The floors are bare, burnished wood. The walls are ecru-colored. Each room was expensively, minimally decorated. Wow, I thought. Money does talk.

The effect was disorientating. Not an hour before, I was standing on a cramped number 1 train, practically shoehorned to get into the car. Now here I was, after wolfing down dinner, sitting on a half-court-long black leather couch in the middle of a palatial duplex with somebody 1 have known since pre-puberty.

"Well, Mayra, you've come a long way from Bushwick," I said.

"I know," she responded. "Is there anything else I could get you?"

"Yeah, this apartment. If not, I'll take a Coke."

Mayra laughed then slowly shrugged. "You like the place, huh? It's okay but since Junior's disappearance ...it doesn't feel

56

right."

"The spirits are out of whack."

"Si, Chulito. Like the place's tainted."

"How are the folks dealing?"

"Badly.... oh, shit. I forgot your drink."

Mayra rose and hustled off to the kitchen It gave me a grand opportunity to enjoy the sights. Her sights, to be exact. In my mind's eye, her shimmy to the fridge was a slo-mo one. I could hear the music from The Bionic Woman with her every step. Her face was still breathtaking - and not one sign of surgery! - and the body had finally caught up.

Sure, she had gained some weight but yo soy un Latino. I like a woman with meat. Besides, the poundage was distributed to all the right spots. Her back was to me as she opened the icebox. She bent over to grab a soda from the bottom shelf. I lifted my head a tad so I could get a better view over the obstructing kitchen counter.

What a sweet sight.

"Can okay?" she asked.

"I'll say."

Mayra wheeled around, slightly flushed, with a dazzling smile.

"Hey now," she said, "I'm a married woman."

"So I hear," I said. "And I'm a semi-respectful single guy who enjoys the fruits of his 20/20 vision."

"Well, just keep your eyes and your hands put."

"Trust me, honey, every appendage's a-staying put."

She threw the Coke can at me. I've got pretty good reflexes. I caught it, popped it open and took a guzzle. All in one motion.

"Sheer poetry," said Mayra.

"Yeah," I belched. "Like 'there once was a lady from Nantucket.'"

"Chulito!"

I drained the rest of the soda and flicked the can on the counter. Perfect landing.

"Okay, okay ..show's over," I said as I got up from the couch. "Time to work. Show me the room."

She beckoned me to the staircase. We sprinted up. Mayra was first - whoa, buddy! - and me so very close behind. The top level was laid out simply. There were three doors about ten feet apart. Each door led to a bedroom. The first was for guests, the second Junior's and the third one was Mayra's. Each room was, according to Mayra, equipped with their own bathroom. Junior's, the one in the center, was right in front of the stairs.

I gave the door my best narrow-eyed stare.

Yep, I thought, seems like a door to me.

I'll confess I didn't really know what I was looking for - probably some police tape and a chalk outline - but I thought it prudent to appear intensely attentive.

I signaled Mayra to open the door. She did. The shades in the room were drawn so she flicked on the overhead light switch. The putrid smell was overpowering. There were dozens of pizza boxes, cookie boxes, candy wrappers, ice-cream sandwich wrappers, soda-pop bottles and Styrofoam containers with half-eaten Chinese food strewn all over the unmade bed, the floor and the dresser. It was a room even Oscar Madison would have been disgusted by.

My first thought was our little Junior was a major-league junk-food junkie. My second was maybe I'm only half-right. The kid certainly had a serious sugar habit. That much I was sure of.

"I'd cleaned up the rest of the apartment but I decided to wait until you had a chance to go through everything before I overhauled this room," said Mayra. "You know, in case you were looking for clues or something."

"I concur on the 'or something,'" I said as I kicked away some of the wreckage. "I'll be happy just to find the wood on the floor."

"Chulito!"

"Just joking."

I rolled up the shade and opened the window. Fresh air at last. I spent a few minutes waist-deep in the big messy and found...zippo. That's right. I found a pizza-greasy Zippo lighter which I which I wiped clean with a nearby napkin before I slipped into my pocket.

"Mayra, did Junior smoke?"

"Never. At least not around me."

Once I realized I'd probably just destroyed an important clue I was ready to give up the hunt when I spied a pizza box in a corner move. First it shimmied slowly and then quite emphatically.

"Mayra, honey," I asked calmly, "do you have a rodent problem?"

"No. Why?"

"Cause that Ray's Original Pizza Box in the corner is doing the macarena."

"I wonder if it's a .." she said as she strode towards the gesticulating cardboard.

"Careful, hon, if that's a rat.. ..they will fight back if they feel cornered."

"That's no rat," she said as she lifted the lid. "It's a kitten,"

That it was. A baby calico cat - to be precise -with cheese plastered against its whiskers. Mayra made a move to grab it but the cat leapt past her, bounced on top the bed and into my outstretched arms. It started licking my hands. I was incredulous.

"You mean to tell me that this gato has been in here all this time?"

"I guess so," said Mayra.

"How could the police miss him? Even la policia from Mayberry could find this cat."

"I don't know."

"And you didn't hear any noise, any purring at night?"

"No."

I sniffed the air. The open window had cleared out most of the funk. I didn't smell any cat urine or see any droppings. Then again, I hadn't been looking for any before.

"The window's been closed all this time?"

"Si, Chulito."

"Anybody else, besides you, me or the Keystone Kops been in here?"

"Maybe my husband but I doubt it."

"This is so fucking weird."

"Isn't it though? Oh look, the kitten's got a collar."

It sure did. A thin little gold chain one. I hadn't seen it at first. Wait a minute. There was a little tag on it.

"You've got good eyes, Mayra."

She smiled and winked at me,

"Always have. How do you think I spotted my husband? What does the tag say?"

"Macha, 320 East 124th Street, New York, New York."

"El Barrio."

I cradled the kitty. Cute little thing.

"I know. I'm kinda familiar with the neighborhood."

She walked towards me. It was almost as good seeing her from the front as from the back. Almost.

"Are you going to check it out?"

"When a clue leaps into your hands I think you better. It's in the detective handbook."

I took the tag off the collar and put it in my pants pocket.

"Mayra, do me a favor. Can you keep little Macha here for the time being?" The cat purred.

We had a love connection going on.

"Sure."

Mayra reached for the kitten. Macha swiped a paw at her and nicked the wedding ring on her left fourth finger. Had it been any of the other bare digits it'd have been deep slice time.

"Macha!" I yelled. "Be good. Go with Mayra."

Macha looked at me for a second then ever so gingerly jumped into Mayra's arms. I could read that kitty's mind like a subway advertisement. I'll be good, she was thinking, for now.

"You do that," I told Macha.

The kitty-cat gave me a nod.

"Do what?" asked Mayra.

"Oh, just something between me and Macha."

"You sure hit it off quick with this cat," said Mayra, "I'm impressed."

"So am I," I said. "Lord knows this is the closest I've been to a pussy in fourteen months."

"Chulito!!" admonished Mayra.

I left soon after. I had a Zippo in one pocket and an address tag in the other. I decided to forego my usual evening fare of self-pity and try to get some rest. Tomorrow was going to be a busy day.

ELEVEN

WHEN I DECIDED to become a private detective, I wanted to make sure of a couple of things: that I got a real big gun and I knew how to use it. I was a victim of crime once in my life and I never wanted to go through that bullshit again. So I got me a nine-shot Sig Sauer P220 nine-millimeter automatic handgun - originally, I wanted the fifteen-shot P226 but I figured I'd have to work my way up - and took lessons in self-defense and sharpshooting. I found that the Sig gave me the luxury of not having to be dead solid perfect with each shot. It had enough power that when I hit something, that shit stayed hit. Granted, the recoil can be a bitch at times but, then again, so's the result.

I needed all the power I could muster, I'd spoken to Cary the morning after I saw Mayra. He told me he'd gotten his hands on the missing person report. It had a photo of Junior which Cary was circulating amongst his junkie lackeys for a possible ID. I told him what I'd found in Junior's room and the address on the cat's collar tag. He recognized the place as being a serious crack house and advised me to wait for him to get off his shift that night before I checked it out. Trust me, it didn't take much for me to agree to that plan so we made plans for him to pick me up about eight o'clock that evening.

Unfortunately, that gave me the rest of the day to ponder the mystery of my irrepressible insecurities. Part of me wanted to get into bed, pull the pillows and covers over my head and stay there until the end of time. Using my professional powers of deduction, I sensed this was the beginning of a big-time anxiety attack so I whiled away the afternoon oiling my gun and blessing my bullets just like any other mentally disturbed potential assassin.

At seven that evening, I finally got dressed. I was feeling darkly blue so that's what I wore; blue boxers, blue pocket-T shirt (so I could hide my wallet), blue Levis (relaxed, of course), blue cotton turtleneck sweater, heavy blue cotton socks, thick black leather belt and black hightop Nike sneaks. I put on my black leather shoulder harness, slipped in the Sig, put on my black pea coat, my black Isotoner gloves and topped it off with a black New York Yankees cap.

When I was through I ran to the bathroom to sneak a peek at myself in the bifocal bathroom mirror. Man oh man. What a disappointment. I wanted to look like Schwarzenegger. Instead, I resembled some neophyte politician looking for an undercover buy-and-bust photo op. I was toying with the idea of changing into an all-military motif when the downstairs buzzer went off. I raced to the window. It was Cary wearing a black knit fisherman's cap, a black leather motorcycle jacket, a black sweatshirt, black stovepipe jeans rolled up at the cuffs and black combat boots.

Just great, I thought as I closed the apartment door and headed down the stairs. Instead of New York Undercover, we've got Chips meets Mr. Smith Goes to the Ghetto. Sartorially speaking, we were not off to a scintillating start.

TWELVE

"**...SO NOT ONE** hour goes by after I pass around that flyer with Molina's photograph before I get a jingle from one of my ace snitches - Ernie Pescador they call him and believe me you don't want to know why - and he, Ernie, tells me that he knows this guy named Junior who looks like the Junior in the flyer I gave him, who hangs out in front of some mostly-abandoned building on One-Twenty- Fourth between Third and Second Avenue."

"Yeah, that block is the local turnoff to get on the Triboro Bridge."

"C'mon, Freddie. Don't interrupt the master when he's rolling. Anyway, then you called me with that address and I put two and two together and got.."

"320 East 124th Street."

Cary cut his eyes at me. He really did despise interruptions. Especially when he was on a gab roll. It's one of the reasons he'd have made a lousy lawyer; he'd shot the opposing attorney the first time he heard an objection.

To keep the peace, I shifted my gaze to the windshield and watched the Third Avenue traffic play stop-and-go and buck-and-wing in front of us while Cary prattled on about the strategic joys of police recon. That, at least, explained why we were driving in a circular pattern from 116th and Third, making a right on 125th, another right after passing a garage onto Second and then straight up and back to 116th. Yes sirree, there we were in Cary's latest sports utility vehicle, a white Ford Bronco, engaging in a little road-round-robin, Yippee-ki-yay, motherfucker.

For some reason, Cary had become enchanted with the notion of owning a white Bronco ever since - what else? - the O.J. car chase on television. We were in a bar watching the Knicks playoff game when they cut in with that surreal scene. While half the bar erupted into chants of 'Go, O.J., Go,' and the others screamed 'Lets Go Knicks,' Cary just kept repeating 'that's a bad car,' Well, who would've guessed that a few years later he and I would be doing traffic loop-de-loops on a case in his very own O.J, mobile. I prayed that if real trouble broke out, the Bronco would show a lot more pickup than it did for the Juice. Forget Steve Austin a.k.a. the Six Million Dollar Man, I'm telling you that night Lee Majors playing himself could've caught the Juice's car in mid-gallop.

After our fifth pass around, there was a lull in Cary's self-congratulatory soliloquy so I took full advantage.

"So what's the plan, hombre?" I asked.

"We park the car, get out, go inside and look for Junior."

"That easy, huh?"

"That easy," he assured.

"No people posted at the door?"

"None that I've seen and so what if there are? You are chillin', my man, with Cary. "

"Oh, excuse me, Mister Brash Branson. I just find it unusual that a serious crackhouse wouldn't have any guards, lookouts or enforcers."

"We raided that place three days ago, Freddie. I'm sure they want to lay low for awhile. Besides, I've got a rep in these streets. Not too many people in this neighborhood want to fuck with this top cop."

"Well that's just a Jim Dandy news flash. I only hope that the guys stationed in this building know you and your rep. Otherwise, you're simply gonna be a nosy asshole trespasser doing a very bad Erik Estrada impersonation."

We pulled into One-twenty-fourth. Cary parked about three yards west of the building on the right side of the street. The whole block was deserted expect for the occasional passing auto. Nobody was around, I mean, nobody.

"I don't like this," I said.

"Have faith," said Cary.

"I might have faith," I said while pointing to the building, "but do they?"

"If a tree falls in a forest while no one's around, does it make a noise?"

"Gee, Cary, I don't know but more-to-the-point, if a body falls in a crackhouse, does it make a sound?"

He glared at me and then opened his car door. With the exception of the glare, I did the same.

"Only one way to find out, Freddie," said Cary.

Simultaneously, we closed our doors then strode towards the building entrance. There were no windows on the first floor then two apiece thereafter. Otherwise, at least from the outside, it was your standard six-floor-high slum tenement fixer-upper.

Cary walked on the sidewalk edge, I strutted on the inside. I looked around. There wasn't a garbage can on the block. These are some neat crackheads, I thought.

I stared at Cary. "You know, it takes a real risk taker to walk on an empty block, bro."

"You just realized, Freddie," he said while glancing over his right shoulder, "that I am the man."

"Hell yeah, you are! You park a brand-new car on a dark, dangerous street without putting on The Club or even a car alarm.... shit, Mr. Man, youse a fuckin' daredevil!"

Cary stopped, pulled his keys out of his leather jacket pocket, wheeled around and pressed the little electric-eye gizmo on his key ring. The Bronco squealed its appreciation.

"Oooh...a practical daredevil," I said as we reached the building's entrance. "I think I love you."

The entranceway was a single closed steel door painted bark-brown. The doorknob had been broken off. You had to shove your way in.

"Let's go inside, Chulito." smirked Cary.

That sure knocked the smile off of my face.

"Don't ever call me that," I said. "You haven't earned the right, tu hijo de schmuck."

Cary put his hands on the door.

"Alright, already," he said. "You coming?"

"Not yet, but give me a rubber doll, a dollar and a dream."

I held my breath, counted one-thousand-one, one-thousand-two and slowly exhaled through my mouth. Then I looked Mister Branson square in the eye.

"Let's go, motherfucker," I said.

He shrugged and opened the door.

THIRTEEN

CARY STEPPED INSIDE first. I followed. I heard the door behind us slowly creak shut before we were completely enshrouded in blackness. Even with my gloves on, I sensed I could actually touch, feel the darkness so I reached out and did. It felt damp.

There was a stiff breeze blowing in our faces. It seemed to career throughout the narrow hallway like a juiced pinball in a lively machine. An involuntary chill raced up my spine. It sent my shoulders spasming clear up to my earlobes. A waterfall of sweat was making its way down my back while the wind blew with greater force.

"Must be broken windows from the back yard," whispered Cary.

I nodded but I tend to doubt he saw it.

"Did you bring a flashlight?" I softly inquired.

"Yeah but I'd rather flick it on when we get up the stairs," He said in a confident voice "Don't want to be no easy target. Just give me a nudge when your eyes get accustomed to the dark."

That took only thirty secs but, guaranteed, it was the longest half-minute of my life so far. Finally, I started to make out shapes. For example, about seven yards ahead of us was a staircase which, after a couple of steps, angled sharply to the left. About four feet from the staircase, on the right, I saw there was an alcove. I reached inside my coat with my right hand and took out the Sig. Quietly, deliberately, I slipped the safety off. I snuck a peek at Cary. He'd done the same with his nine-millimeter. His gun was in his left hand. Great, I thought, we look like a matched set. I nudged him in the ribs with my left elbow.

"Okay, let's go," he said.

Like conjoined twins, we goose-stepped mighty carefully down the passageway. When we got to a foot from that pesky opening on the right side, Cary put out his right arm to stop me. I stayed stopped. He leaned against the right wall, gripped his gun with both hands, tucked in his elbows, drew his forearms up to his left shoulder, breathed in and jumped into the alcove with his arms extended and ready to fire.

Nothing happened but it was a good show anyway.

Cary, still wired, took two large steps into the opening. Still nada. Snapping his wrists, he motioned for me to join him. I did.

"What's up?" I asked.

"Looks like where they kept the garbage."

I squinted. It looked like an upside-down wall grave. (Wait a minute, ain't that a tomb?) Six foot high, wide and deep. Only there wasn't any caskets or cans. Just shards of glass from broken crack vials and three Cheez Doodles bags on the floor. All were covered in roaches.

"Also looks like a good place to stash a gunsel," I said.

"Oh yeah. ...okay, Freddie, let's start heading up. I'll take the point. You hang close by."

"Ay-ay, mon capitan."

Gun at the ready, Cary assumed his G.I. Joe position. I had to hold back from asking him if he came with kung-fu grip. Instead, I did the same. He ignored the banister on the left, preferring to slink against the right wall. (He used it as a guide.) Once again, I followed. I was getting real good at that.

Cary was two paces ahead of me. He went up the staircase with extreme caution, swinging his left foot over his right on each step as if doing the electric-slide at a wedding. With my finger on the trigger, I willingly joined the dance, aping Rambo's every move.

"Please do not shoot me in the butt, Freddie," said Cary.

"But it's such an inviting target," I replied.

It took us five long-ass minutes, forty jumbo steps and three sharp lefts to get to that first floor landing. Once we got there, Cary stood motionless. Gripping his handgun tightly in his left, he listened carefully for any unwelcome residents. When he heard nothing, he pulled out a mini-mag flashlight from his left jacket pocket with his right hand.

"Be ready for anything," he advised.

Well, that remark tripled my heart rate. I stretched my arms out. The edge of my sleeves were dripping with perspiration. (After this, my pea coat was making a pit stop at the dry cleaners.) Gun out, my left hand held my right wrist steady.

"Okay, sluggo, go," I said.

Cary put the flashlight on. Like a hot knife through oleo, the beam sliced through the darkness. My eyes narrowed once again as they followed the beam's arc. Cary swung the light around. There were two doors. One faced street side. Facing that door, to our immediate left, was another staircase. Behind us was another door. I looked at the floor in front of it. There was a three-inch gap between it and the door's bottom.

"There's your breeze," said Cary.

"Let's take the back one first."

"Oh, really. " he mocked. "Would you like to open it yourself or in tandem."

"Forgive me, ol' swami," I replied. "I am not planning to challenge your paramilitary authority."

"Then follow me, peasant," he said.

Cary headed to the door by the staircase in front of us. Once again, he placed himself on the right side. I went left between the stairs and the wall.

"What do you think?" he whispered across the door frame. "

"Six-and-a-half feet high, two strategically placed hinges on the left, a peephole in the center, a doorknob belt-high." I paused. "Sure looks like a door to me."

Cary sucked his front teeth.

"Cut the shit," he said, "and take your position."

One bunny hop to my right later, I'd drawn a bead on whoever, whatever was behind that door. I hoped that if trouble happened I was ready to take them out. Meanwhile, Cary wedged his ass in the gap between the door frame and the right outer wall. He tucked his flashlight under his neck, held his gun across his body in his left hand and cradled the doorknob in his right.

Like a safecracker with the bank vault's dial in hand, Cary carefully twisted the knob until we heard a click, the door opened inward about an inch. Cary looked at me. He stuck his chin out and swung it towards the door. Homey wanted Freddie boy to lead the way. I guessed it was a dare. And so, like a typical male Neanderthal, I accepted.

I nodded in agreement, took a skip and a hop and kicked the door wide open. The sound reverberated throughout the building. Weapons out, we scampered inside as the door slammed closed behind us.

"Well, that oughta wake the dead," I said.

Cary gave the place a fast eyeball. It was a one room apartment. There was a sink on the right wall and an exposed well- used commode on the left. All the comforts of home, I thought. Facing us, in the middle of the wall, were two windows with drawn black vinyl shades nailed shut to the sill. Now, what held this MTV kid's attention is what was in front of those windows.

Garbage cans. Fifty of them. Lids down. Carefully arranged in rows of ten. It looked like The March of the Sanitation Soldiers.

"Did your people do this?" I asked.

"Not that I heard of," Cary said.

"Kind of takes street sweeping to a new level."

"Yeah," said Cary as he lifted the lid of the can nearest to him. "Hey, anus, check this shit out!"

I trotted over. Inside the can were thousands of brand-new unfilled crack vials. In the glare of Cary's penlight, the vials glimmered like the jewelry on the Home Shopping Network. Yep, I thought to myself, zircon diamonds of death.

I opened the can next to me. Same thing. Cary opened another, then another, then another. The same thing all the way down the row.

"What is this, Cary? Krack-Mart?"

"I don't know…..wait a minute…."

Cary shone the light on the side of one of the rear cans. The furthest one to the left and right under the window, had a red stain on it. It looked fairly wet and fairly fresh.

Dumbfounded, we looked at each other. Then we rushed to the can. Cary lifted the lid and I thought I was going to throw up.

There was a guy in it. A dead guy. The left side of his head above his eyebrow was missing. Just blown off. His blue eyes were wide open. What was left of his brains were taking their sweet time sliding down the side for his cheek. It looked like he was crying mental matter. The brains were steadily dropping off his stubbled chin into the can. The drip didn't have far to go; the blood in the can was up to his Adam's Apple. It was like the poor fucking guy was swimming in it.

"Is. ..all of him there?" I asked.

"I.. don't think so.. looks like the legs could be missing," said Cary.

He wiped his brow and gestured down the last row of cans.

"Something tells me we'll find them there."

"I ain't that curious, Cary."

"Well, don'cha at least want to know who he is?"

"Sure I do," I replied. "But I'm not sticking my hands into that mess to look for a wallet or a telephone bill."

"Oh, you don't have to," Cary said flatly. "I already know his name."

I was shocked.

"You know who he is?"

"Yes, I do."

"Personally??"

"Uh-huh."

"Well, then, who the fuck is he?"

Cary looked at me. He was shaking his head.

"Freddie Perez, meet what's left of Ernie Pescador."

FOURTEEN

A TOTAL BRAIN freeze. Take it from me, it's a most unpleasant moment to endure. I pointed to the can.

"You mean this pickled herring's your snitch?"

"He was."

"Then what the fuck are we doing here? Waiting for a eulogy? A séance? Let's call the cops..."

"I am the cops."

"No, you are 'the cop'. Singular. I'm looking for cops. Plural."

"I tell you I am the fuckin' cops., plural."

"Then, Sybil, let's call backup for the other cops," I screamed. "I mean, for God's sake Shaft, don'tcha get it? We are in the midst of a most fucked-up situation here. This could be - and I humbly defer to your encyclopedic knowledge of police procedure - a fucking trap! The Molina kid's missing, your ace coon boon Pescador's sleeping with the fishes... I mean, wake up joy boy, somebody's severely fucking with our minds!"

"See, see, Freddie," said Cary. "That has always been your major problem. You've always looked at the glass as half-empty instead of acknowledging it as half-full."

"No, no, my brother," I interrupted. "That is a very bad example." My voice seemed to leap an octave towards Marc Anthony-land as I jerked a thumb towards the remains of

Senor Pescador. "Because this time I perfectly realize the can here is three-quarters full and that golden nugget of info ain't doing anybody any good. Now cut the cut-rate philosophy and call in the troops, the coroner, the criminalist, Quincy, Matlock, O.J., Johnnie Cochran, Rudy G, Judge Judy, anyone who knows how to handle this shit!"

"Uh-uh," said Cary. "You think I'm gonna miss out on the prize and glory? No fuckin' way. This case's a titfuckin' oil well, my Boricua baby. We're going to go through this entire building, nab the mo-fo who did this, find the Molina kid, collect the reward, become heroes, legends, get medals, write a book about our experiences, sign a Hollywood movie deal starring Denzel as me and whoever-can-approximate-that-lack-of-steelo-quality-you-have-mastered-so-effortlessly as you and I get paid!"

"What earth are you from, motherfucker?" I asked. "Hello! We've got a murder victim right in front of us! Dead body here! And you're talking feature films? Are you just estupido, hombre? You know, Cary, with your low-slung set of smarts, a studio head would offer you major gross points and you'd bargain him down for a percentage of the net. And you'd swear you'd won!"

"You think I want to be a cop all my life," Cary said defensively. "Well, I don't, I've got ambition, I've got plans. And solving this case will help them."

"No, Cary," I corrected, "What you have is Clarice, She has ambition. She has plans. You have zero. Cero, Zippo, Bupkus, The law firm of nada, nunca and nadie. All your chumped life you've taken the easy way out. You've coasted on your charm, your badge, your pretty-boy looks. You're a card-carrying member of the Fucking Lucky Club but your payment of dues is coming up. See, Cary, luck has a nasty way of running out on glamour guys like you and, my man, you're pushing the little you have left to the limit. Now leave the 'I am somebody' speech for the right Reverend Jesse and let's get the fuck outta here."

We were turning to leave when we heard a thud right above us. A few plaster flakes shook loose, floated through the air and landed in the new sunroof in Pescador's head.

"Second floor," Cary whispered. "Let's go."

It was lights-camera-action time. We rushed to the door. With pistolas ready and penlight out, we opened it and made our way up the facing staircase single-file style with Mr. Branson in the lead. It was tippy-toe time as we grimaced with each squeak our Flintstone feet coaxed out of the wooden planks.

The ascension took ten minutes. By that time, I was a complete nervous wreck. There was, however, good news and bad news. The bad news was my sweat glands were working overtime so now my pea coat was so wet I could get a job in a circus as a human sponge. The good news? Well, I was leaving a liquid trail a cub scout could follow.

The second floor was a carbon copy of the first. A door in front, one in the rear. The one in front of us was the one above us so that turned out to be the one we were gonna check out.

Deja vu.

We assumed the same positions as rapidly as possible. Me on the left side. Sig steady on the door. Cary wedged in the slot on the right. Head against the wall, nine in his left across his body, flashlight held chin-high, right hand on the doorknob.

Slowly, he twisted the knob. First to the left and then to the right,

Nothing.

No click.

Nothing.

"What's wrong?" I mimed.

"She won't open," he mouthed.

"Let's get backup," I mimed.

"We don't need it," he mouthed.

Cary pulled his hand away from the door. I thought he was going to signal me to kick it down when we heard this loud click. It was one of those oh-shit moments. Startled, we both stared at each other. Big mistake. I heard a second click just before I saw the wall by Cary's face explode.

His head blew apart like a dropped pumpkin.

In place of his skull was a crimson geyser which spewed

ceiling high. Poor Cary had finally struck a gusher only this time it was him.

His blood spattered all over me as his headless body lurched towards me like a glass pitcher pouring cherry Kool-Aid. The blood made a nice base for the plaster debris which cascaded through the air and stuck to my body. I had read once that a tar-and-feathering could be quite a traumatic experience. Believe me. I'd take that any day over a plasma plastering.

Suddenly, I hulked out. My rage kicked in and took on over. I fired a couple of rounds into the jagged hole in the wall and then a few through the door. I heard something fall hard. Nailed the fucker! I had to make sure so I balled myself up and went shoulders first through the center of the door.

Snapped it in two. Splinters sprayed the room. But I'd hit the door too hard - I was so pumped up - that I'd lost my balance. I fell flat on my face and banged my head on the floor.

Dazed, I glanced to the right. There was some light coming from the hallway. It was from Cary's mini-mag rolling on the hallway floor. There were specks of blood on the bulb. It made the room look like a kaleidoscopic slaughterhouse.

My focus started to kick in. There was an object a couple of feet away from me. I crawled closer to get a better view. It was a body. Some guy lying face down. Was this the one I nailed? I put the Sig in my left, crept closer, reached over and lifted his head up by his hair to get a good look.

"Junior," I gasped.

There was a sudden stirring behind me. I swiveled my head, glimpsed a glitter of green, followed by an explosion of stars and then everything went black.

FIFTEEN

MURMURS.
VOICES.
WORDS.
Sentences.
I was coming back in sections.

This much I could discern: I was lying down in a bed with my aching head and shoulders propped up at a 45 degree angle. I took a deep breath and shuddered. Oh yes, the unmistakable odor of stale antiseptics. I had to be back in a hospital. The thought of it gave me the creeps.

"...I believe Mr. Perez is regaining consciousness now, detectives."

"Is he alert..."

"..and aware?"

"I believe so."

I opened my eyes. It wasn't easy. They hurt. My eyelids felt like they were pumping iron. My throat was dry and my head was throbbing. The flood of light momentarily blinded me. When my peepers finally focused I saw there were four men in the room. There was a doctor (at least I assumed he was one by the white cotton jacket he was wearing with a St. Luke's Hospital insignia on his breast pocket) to my left, a curly-haired guy in a sport jacket and jeans to my right and, in the middle, two guys wearing gray suits right out of the Sears catalog with their backs to me.

Everyone in the room had a golden haze to them. For a second, I thought they were all sporting halos.

"Are you angels?" I croaked.

The sport jacketed cop leaned over me to speak.

"How you doing, scribbler?"

I hadda smirk.

"I've been better, O'Reilly."

"Mr. Perez, I'm Doctor Murrabi."

I turned to look at him. Ouch. My head hurt. Doctor Murrabi looked like an East Indian version of that model Tyson. Great, I had a matinee idol for a physician. I could easily grow to hate him.

"Wow, a swarthy, well-toned medical practitioner. I'm doomed."

He laughed. Heartily.

"I'm quite competent, I assure you," said Dr. Murrabi. "Now, sir, you have suffered a severe concussion. It is not life-threatening but we are going to have to keep you overnight for observation. "

"That's real nice, Doctor Love, but I can't exactly afford these swanky accommodations."

"Not to worry about, Mr. Perez. Miss Molina is taking care of all your expenses."

Oh shit. Mayra. Fuck. I wondered if she knew it was me who shot Junior. Fuck.

"Well, can we..."

"..talk to him.."

"...now, Doctor,

Impatience in stereo? Had to be the gray suits. I looked at the foot of the bed. Two white-button-down-shirted, thin-black-tied, short-blond-haired White guys. Make that the same White guy twice.

"Great, it's the Doublemint twins," I said.

"This is not the time..."

"..for jesting.."

"...Mr. Perez, not..."

"..with the death.."

"...of one of New York's..."

"..finest occurring.."

"…this…"

"..evening. "

"You did know..."

"..Detective Branson.."

"...was dead, didn't..."

"..you, Mister.."

"…Perez?"

"I had a notion the second I saw his head disappear in a cloud of dust."

"Scribbler," said O'Reilly in a conciliatory tone, "these are Detectives Tod and Tad Trimble. They're from Homicide. They've been assigned - as have I - to work this case."

"Tell us..."

" ..what happened.. "

"...in your own..."

"..words. Mister.."

"…Perez."

So I did. I told them about Mayra hiring me. About Cary's help. About the tip he got from the snitch. About investigating the thud upstairs. About Cary getting killed. About my response. About everything. Well, almost everything.

"Why didn't..."

"..Detective Branson.."

"...call for..."

"..backup?"

Now, I could've told them the truth. Detective Cary Branson wanted a book and feature film deal so fuckin' badly he got careless and got himself killed. He was yet another casualty of the tireless pursuit of fame, fortune and finance. I instead told the detectives Siamese a tiny untruth. Just color me a political consultant.

"There wasn't any time," I explained. "We rushed in, found Pescador's body, heard the thump above us and then bim-bam-boom. All hell broke loose."

"Why was ..."

"..Branson.."

"...in such..."

"..a rush?"

I became indignant. On a large scale.

"Gentlemen, we had reason to suspect Junior Molina's life was at stake."

"About Molina..."

Oh shit, here we go.

"..did you know.."

"...he was dead..."

"..when you.."

"...shot him?"

"What?" I exclaimed.

"That is.."

"...correct..."

"..Mr. Molina.."

"...was about…"

"..two weeks dead."

"You killed a cadaver, scribbler," said O'Reilly.

Madre de Dios, I was soooo confused.

"But, O'Reilly, I touched him. He didn't feel cold or smell bad or have a picture of Pat Buchanan in his hand."

"He was well preserved," interrupted Tad Twin.

"Very well preserved," added Tod.

"Somebody kept a body well preserved for fourteen days?" asked Dr. Murrabi.

"Yes, doctor," said O'Reilly.

"Gosh, I haven't heard about something like that since medical school."

"What are you gabbing about. Doc?" I asked.

(I get so informal so quickly.)

"Well, sometimes in school, we get a fresh cadaver it tiptop condition. The body's not mangled or burnt.."

"You're making me ill. Doc."

"..or diseased. There aren't any gaping wounds or excessive damage so we try to maintain it."

"Maintain," said Tad.

"Keep on ice," I said.

"For what?" asked Tod.

"Practical jokes. We might put it in a shower stall or on top of a toilet seat to simply scare the heck out of someone."

"Ah, our leaders in action," I said.

"You'd be surprised how much fun you could have with a corpse," said Dr. Murrabi.

"Not me," said O'Reilly. "I've been married."

"Doc, I want to party with you," I said.

The supermodel doctor laughed.

"One time we took Harry - we always named them Harry for some forgotten reason - to the main university's Friday midnight movie one Halloween. It was Night of the Living Dead."

"Once again life imitates art," I said.

"Boy, we cleared out that theatre," said Murrabi wistfully.

"Hang on a sec. Doc," I interjected. "How did you guys find me?"

"You were…"

". . extraordinarily fortunate."

"…Mr. Perez."

"Please, Bobbsey Boys, call me Freddie."

"It appears someone was driving down 124th Street, heard the shots and dialed nine-one-one," said O'Reilly. "I knew we had cleaned out a building on that block a week or so ago and I remembered Branson that morning asking about it so I put two and two together and put a rush on the call."

"Two and two," I mumbled. "I guess I am fortunate."

"You are," said Tad.

I ran my fingers through my hair. It was still damp from the perspiration.

"I mean," I said, "how often does a passersby driving through a demi-deserted block call in the sound of shots?"

Light bulbs went over everybody's heads at the same time.

"Tod, check the…"

"..call? I'm on it. Tad."

I caught O'Reilly's eye and motioned him closer.

"What did you guys find upstairs?"

"Garbage cans, crack vials and Cheez Doodles."

"Cheez Doodles?"

"Bags of them."

"That's weird. Cary and I spotted some empty bags in the ground floor alcove. Is it possible the building's pushers were serving them as some sort of post-crack aperitif?"

"Could be, scribbler, could be."

"Tod, Tad," I said. "We could be looking for some rail-thin yellow-fingered criminals with a Cheddar after-odor here."

"We?" they said.

"You chime so well in unison."

"We?" they repeated.

"Don't you think that I want to find the murderer of my best friend?"

"Didn't he…"

"..steal your girlfriend?"

Boy, word gets around quick.

"Then that's even more of a reason to find the killer," I said. "I want the asshole who turned my ex-girlfriend into a widow to pay."

"But they..."

"..weren't married."

"All right, Barbi boys. Prospective widow. Besides, I'm sure they were wed in their hearts."

"Well, you aren't investigating anything tonight, Mr. Perez," said Dr. Murrabi with a glance at his watch. (A Rolex at that.) "You've got to get your rest."

"Okay, Mr. Perez..."

"..we'll be in touch."

"Why don't you leave your number at the desk?" I asked. "Or should I just look in the phone book under the thing with two heads?"

Tod and Tad shook their displeased identical craniums and followed Dr. Murrabi out. O'Reilly faked a step towards the door and then doubled back to my bed.

"I think the twins like me," I said brightly.

"I don't," he replied. "Listen, the Trimbles would kill me if they knew what I'm about to tell you..."

"It'll be our little secret. Cross my heart..."

"...and hope to die? Okay, scribbler, we found one more thing in that wreck that we're keeping mum about. Officially."

"And that is?"

"An operating table."

I bolted upright. Shouldn't have. Couldn't help it. My cabeza was pounding but I needed some clarification.

"A surgical operating table?"

"Yep. We're dusting for prints but we aren't finding a thing. Do you know of any surgeons?"

The name Oswald Velleto sprang to mind.

"Not yet, O'Reilly, but I will."

"Let me know," he said. "Oh by the way, we're holding your gun at the station. Had to because of the continuing investigation. When you get out of here, give me a call. I'll pull a few strings and get you your cannon back. You should see the hole it blew in Molina."

"Stationary target."

"Yeah."

"How'd his sister take the news?"

"Like a champ. We explained to her the bullet hole in the body was accidental on account of you shooting it out with the bad guys. She said she'll try to see you soon."

"Thanks."

"Keep in touch, scribbler."

"I will."

He feinted a right cross, smiled and headed out. I eased my head back onto my pillow. A middle-aged nurse popped her wizened noggin into the room.

"Lights out," she croaked about a millisecond before she knocked them off.

I nodded in agreement in the dark. I closed my eyes and heard her gently shut the door as I began to weep thinking about the second time I lost the only friend I ever had.

SIXTEEN

I ENDED UP spending more than a night at jolly ol' St. Luke's. Instead I had three glorious evenings spent musing about the joy of bedpans, the freedom of changed sheets and why nurses are either homely or comely. The first night, Doc Murrabi stopped by. He said he kept me for a longer period because he wanted to make sure that my scrambled brains weren't permanently scrambled. I told him that's a mystery only the Big G in the sky could solve. A couple of days later, the Doctor set me free.

My hard head still hurt after I left the hospital but I don't think it was due to the blow. I believe it had more to do with my folks visiting me the day before my discharge. My mom kept crying about what happened to her sweet baby - that would be lil ol' me - while my father loudly ruminated as to what fuckin' manner of fuckin' idiot would fuckin' work as a fuckin' private detective. (See where I inherited my poetic soul?)

I feared Da-da might have been referring to me so I spent most of their visit feigning unconsciousness. This seemed to cut short their St. Luke's sojourn so I was a happy fuckin' clam when I was at last fuckin' discharged, picked up by fuckin' Chubby and fuckin' Papo and returned fuckin' home to fuckin' recuperate.

The recuperation took but another day. As bad luck would have it, both Junior's and Cary's funerals were scheduled for the same day and time. (But not, alas, the same place.)

In terms of proximity, Junior's farewell soiree was closer. His viewing was in the city on Eightieth and Amsterdam with the burial in the Bronx. I decided to go to Cary's in Brooklyn. It felt like the right thing to do

The service was in Cary's old stomping grounds, Clinton Hill, at Figaro's on Atlantic Avenue. Chubby drove me in his new sky-blue 1985 Monte Carlo with the leather bucket seats and the new, near-nuclear, souped-up engine. The hood burbled ominously every ten feet on the downtown FDR Drive.

"Coño Tio," I said. "What's the horsepower on this thing?"

"Five hundred something."

"Jesus. Just imagine if Ben-Hur had this kind of power in front of his chariot."

"He 'da crushed the shit out of Marsala!"

I craned my head to look at him. The speedboats in the East River seemed to whiz out of Chubby's head like thought balloons.

"Chubby, he did crush the shit out of Marsala."

"Not really. Marsala still managed to taunt him a bit with that fucked-up shit about his mom and sis in that leper colony. Now, if he had been driving this baby, Ben woulda pulverized him. There wouldn't have been any taunting, there wouldn't've been a body. Just some Marsala dust."

"But then he wouldn't have found his mother and sister in the leper colony."

"Sure he would've," said Chubby as he navigated the hairpin turn onto the Brooklyn Bridge. "You forget he had God on his side. They'd been buddies since Ben was Moses in a previous life."

"But He sure did abandon him when he landed on the Planet of the Apes."

"Well, nephew, common sense tells you not to be fucking with those apes. Don't yell fire in a crowded theater, don't accept gifts from strangers and don't fuck with no monkeys."

Traffic was light all the way to Atlantic so we got to the funeral parlor in record time. Chubby found a parking space directly across the street and I waited patiently while he went through the rigmarole of owning an auto in Nueva York. First, he put the Club on the steering wheel. Then he hit the hidden choke switch under the dashboard. This was followed by hiding the pullout radio/CD player under the driver's seat. Finally, the coup-de-grace, he placed the scuzziest blanket in existence on top of the box.

"Ready?"

"Almost," said Chubby before putting on the car alarm. "Now, my baby's safe."

We crossed the avenue. Except for a few black sedans and a cop car out front, the street was deserted. I had on a black three-button suit with medium lapels, black wingtips, a white button-down shirt and a thin black poly-silk blend tie. Chubby was wearing a black two-button suit with a low-slung break, lapels the size of an airport runway, cuffed bellbottom trousers - he told me this has been his fave funeral suit since the disco '70s - an off-white shirt with a tab collar, black bubble-toed shoes with a Cuban heel and a wide silk black tie Don Cornelius would've envied.

"You know we look like an outtake from a Tarantino film," I said as we daintily straightened out our suits.

"Then we look like movie stars," replied Chubby.

"I once went out with a girl who said I look like a movie star."

"Which one?" he asked as we stopped in front of Figaro's. "Godzilla?"

"I believe she said Ghidrah."

"Aha, the three-headed monster."

"Well, I am a Gemini."

"You're still a head short."

"Am I really?"

"My last old lady use to claim I reminded her of King Kong."

"Before or after shaving?"

"After sex."

"You're a grunter?"

"Nah, that's Mighty Joe Young. I'm more of the chest-thumpin' bellowin' type."

"There's an image."

Chubby pushed open the funeral parlor's double-door entrance.

"When you get my age you use whatever works," he said. "Verdad?"

"True that," I said.

Figaro's was like every funeral parlor: full of the smell of cedar wood, air conditioning and death. The announcement board in the lobby said the Branson funeral was taking place in Room C so we walked over there. Standing in front of another set of double- doors, by the guest book, was O'Reilly sneaking a smoke. We nodded to each other while my uncle signed in. When Chubby was through, he offered me the pen to sign in. I refused. My theory is one signs only into hotels. Funerarias were more like roach motels: guests check in but they ain't gonna check out.

"I feel the same way, scribbler," said O'Reilly.

"Scribbler?" asked Chubby.

"Nickname," I told him.

He nodded.

"It's a cute one," Chubby said.

"I don't see any of your brethren around," I told O'Reilly. "Where's the brass?"

"Branson's family wanted to keep everything low-key. They didn't want their grief to be a TV photo op. The brass came early, paid their respects and vamoosed. Some of them and the stationhouse crew will be at the burial. Evergreen, right? Off the Jackie Robinson?"

"Yeah. Off the ol' Interboro. In Bushwick."

"Anyways, they'll be there. I....I heard the family wanted you to speak but you turned them down."

"Yep. I didn't want to break down in public."

"Understand. How's the head?"

"Intact, but I'm picking up some weird broadcasts in my left ear at night."

"As long as they're FM, you'll be okay. Better fidelity. Doesn't break up under overpasses like AM"

"True, but the playlists still suck."

"C'mon, nephew," interjected Chubby. "Let's head in."

"That's right," I said. "I forgot to introduce you guys."

"That's okay," said my uncle. "How's it hanging, O?"

"Low, Chubs, low," responded O'Reilly.

"You guys know each other?"

They sized each other up with knowing grins.

"Let's just say we've been acquainted," said O'Reilly.

My uncle laughed and then turned to me.

"Let's grab seats," he said.

I agreed and told O'Reilly I'd see him later. He and my uncle wished each other well and then he split while Chubby and I went through the doors. There were rows and rows and rows and rows of empty pews. Decisions, decisions. I looked at my uncle.

"So you know O'Reilly?"

"Sure thing. From the neighborhood. He used to live on Ninety- sixth and Second. The other side of the tracks. Had a thing for a Latina on a Hun-twelve. Used to chase his ass home all the time. That Irish bastard could run."

"No shit?"

"None."

There were about sixty people spread out in Room C. The place was eerily quiet with the occasional muffled sob slicing through the silence. In the front of the room underneath some ruffled black satin curtains was a mahogany casket. It was closed. On top of it was a eight-by-ten photo of Cary. In the picture, he was smiling like he didn't have a care in the world. Well, he didn't.

Chubby and I sat down in the back row, a few chairs away from an elderly couple. They made small talk with us. Turns out they were relations of Cary's mother. Cousins. I really didn't pay much attention to what they were telling me. I was too busy looking upfront where Clarice was sitting.

She was in the front pew, to the right of the casket, seated next to Cary's parents. She was wearing a simple black dress, black stockings and had a sensible pair of black flats on. Her face was obscured by her veil. Didn't matter though. I swear, when she glanced at the back of the room and spotted me, her eyes were a- blazing.

It was the same look she'd given me when she kicked me out of the house and asked for my set of keys.

"I need a real man who 'll take care of me, support me and not some depressed little child," she had told me back then.

Head bowed in shame, I gave them to her.

"You mean like. ..Cary?" I asked.

"Yes, like Cary."

It was so matter-of-fact. So cold. It was also the last thing she'd ever said directly to me. Since then we'd spoken through intermediaries, through her mom, her dad, Cary, but never to each other. That scowl she was giving me kinda guaranteed the streak would remain intact.

Seated on her left was Cary's mother who sensed Clarice's rage. She turned around too to see who and what was agitating her almost-daughter-in-law. When she saw it was me, she gave Clarice a surprised sideways glance before giving me a warm smile. I gave her a little wave, a fond how-de-do from the guy who helped get her only child killed.

Cary's mom nudged the man to her right. He joined the emotional carousel and swiveled around also. It was Cary's dad. His face was a mask of repressed agony. Somehow, through all of his grief, he managed to contort his features into a pained grin. I did the same as his wife comforted him by lightly brushing his chin with the tips of her fingers. This time, Cary's dad's smile was genuine. He extended his arms around her and pulled his wife to him as close as he could, I looked away as I heard them weep in tandem.

"Where's Clarice's parents?" asked Chubby.

"They don't get along much," I said. "I'd be surprised if they showed."

It was true. Clarice never felt close to her folks growing up and the feeling was vice versa. She'd come from Pittsburgh where both of her parents were teachers in the public school system. They'd been together for nearly twenty-five years -

they'd met as teenagers - and were childless until, as the saying goes, late in life. In fact, her mom was 38 and her father 39 when Clarice was born. They seemed to regard the birth of their only child as an intrusion into their ordered lives and so raised their daughter in a perfunctory, proper, passionless manner.

I'd met them a couple of times and while they may have both been fine educators, I found them to be atrocious communicators. In fact, dinner with the Austins contained silences you could 've pulled the continent of Asia through. This lack of discourse truly disturbed Clarice who felt rudderless without a strong sense of family.

(It didn't bother me any because let's face it, from a guy's standpoint, the only thing better than a woman estranged from her family is a woman that's an orphan. Think about it: no meddling in-laws, nobody to impress. To an insecure male, that's heaven on earth.)

I guess that's why when Clarice committed to me I honestly thought it would last forever. We were going to start our own family. We'd overcome our backgrounds. We'd be touchy-feely parents just bursting to smother our kids with mucho love and affection. But we never got that far. And Clarice proved to me that DNA does matter with her refusal to tell me about the problem she felt existed in our relationship. And so she reverted to her parents' suppressed, secretive ways and conducted a clandestine affair behind my back with my best friend. Not once did she betray a whiff of insincerity to me. Once an Austin, I guess, always an Austin.

Anyway, the service itself went off without a hitch or an emotion explosion. (The mourners were obviously conserving that tearful display for the burial.) Cary was a lifelong Sunday-church-attending-Methodist so his regular preacher, the Reverend Lorenzo Louis Lipton delivered the eulogy. It was a stirring from-boy-to-man-to-friend-of-the-public-trust-policeman-to-hero-to-martyr speech which the Reverend delivered with grand gusto. The audience ate it up. They laughed, they cried, they got their two bucks worth. So what if fifty percent of it was bullshit? So what if Cary really wasn't that nice to people? Or cared much about them? So what if he loved the pubic much more than the public loved him?' So what? The eulogy gave the folks a chance to honor the deceased and that's all that counts. See, we want to always think the best of our dead. We want to believe they were *good* people who *deserve* our tears and sorrow. We want to think they were worth *something*. It's our self-cleansing process which gives us hope and perhaps even a reason for living.

After the eulogy and the obligatory moment of silence, Cary's dad announced that the service was over and the hearse would be leaving for the cemetery in fifteen minutes. This gave the mourners ample time to go to the restroom, wash up, get out those keys and start up their cars. My uncle and I did all of the above and were copping a squat in his Monte Carlo when the casket was brought out of Figaro's by a half-dozen squatty cops.

By arrangement with the department, the six pallbearers - two White, two Black, one Hispanic, one Asian - were plainclothesmen from the two-five. It was a publicity-oriented stunt rather than a heartfelt gesture of true brotherhood. Not one of the handle carriers had been close to Cary. That's not to say they didn't care. The police are a fraternity with a gun permit and a member of the frat had been slain in the line of duty. But, truth to tell, the six of them looked more uncomfortable then bereaved. The sextet knew, in a city as volatile as New York, any of them could be the next dead cop carried out.

Now parked in front of Figaro's were two police cars, a hearse and a big black limo for Gary's folks and Clarice. At the foot of the steps were two camera crews and a photographer.

"Must be a busy news day," said my uncle. "Normally, it looks like the Beatles at Kennedy when a cop's killed."

"Or the Backstreet Boys in Times Square," I said, "But not for cops of color."

"You got a point."

Slowly, the Rainbow Coalition came down the steps with the casket. In fact, they came down so damn slowly, it gave the lone tabloid photoflasher time to click away from every single angle. I'd swear, with each whirring click, I heard 'c'mon, feel it, baby, feel it' echoing somewhere in the distance.

Five rolls of film later, they finally got Cary in the back of the hearse. Then the assimilated six ran into the two waiting police cruisers, Cary's parents and his/my ex got into their limo and the game was afoot.

"Another day, another funeral procession," my uncle muttered.

Chubby gunned the engine, switched the lights on and we were off. In a line of twenty cars, we were fourth, right behind the limo. As the Monte Carlo cruised up Atlantic, I thought about all the good times Clarice and I shared. I was still daydreaming when we made a right onto Eastern Parkway and another on Bushwick Avenue where Evergreen Cemetery was located. We were in the Brownsville/East New York section; home to some of the highest murder rates in the world. The sidewalk denizens paid us no mind. They'd seen far too many processions to give a damn.

The gates of Evergreen were open. We drove up the winding roads and gazed at the thicket of headstones surrounding us.

"You know, Chulito, folks are just dying to get into this neighborhood," said my uncle.

"All the time," I grunted. "All the time."

After a fifteen-minute ride, the police cars upfront slammed on their brakes. I rolled down my window to have a look-see. Up on a hill, about two hundred feet ahead of us, was a throng of blue uniforms and television cameras.

My uncle and I got out of the car. He started to lock it up.

"The show begins, Tio," I said.

"It never ends, nephew."

The burial was a blur of tears. The mayor spoke as did the commish. I can't tell you a single word that they said. I kept listening to all the voices in my head. My mind was an unending tape loop of all the discussions, arguments, laughter I had shared with one Detective Cary Branson.

A mournful trumpet playing some sad blues cut through the brain hubbub and snapped me back to the day's proceedings. It was a series of horrors. The casket lowered into the ground;

Mother Branson screaming to the heavens to bring back her murdered boy; Mother Branson trying to hurl herself on top of the casket; her husband restraining her; Clarice standing stock still while glaring at me.

I returned the frosty favor. I'd been through too much to deserve such a look from the woman who wronged me. So there we were, the former lovebirds glowering at each other over an open grave, like rival gangs bumping into each other on the IRT.

What's going on here, nephew?" whispered my uncle.

"Showdown," I replied through clenched teeth. "I'll meet you in the car after Clarice and I speak."

"You're going over there?" "No need," I said.

"She'll come this way just as soon as the last bit of dirt is tossed on Cary."

"You sure?"

I licked my lower lip.

"Oh, yeah," I said. "I know my baby."

And that's just what happened. She waited until everybody around us - the cameras, the cops , the crews - had left. She waited until they dragged her poor one-time-prospective-mother-in-law kicking and bawling into the waiting limousine before she started walking towards me.

It was an unhurried gait designed to make me wait, make me nervous, make me cower, make me sweat. Would have worked a year ago. Maybe even a week ago. But not today. Not any more.

She stopped a foot away from me. It was a favored distance of mine. I used to love to pull her close to me, kiss her deeply and then hold her up to the sky before we made love. Man, those days were long gone.

She stayed silent while we maintained the unfriendly eye contact. I gather she was expecting me to break the ice. Not a chance. She finally spoke first.

"Freddie," she said in a soft, strangled voice, "I cannot believe you showed up here. Today."

"Why not?" I responded evenly. "He was my friend. Once."

"Why not?!!" she semi-screamed before regaining her

composure. "Why not? Because you put him in that grave as sure as you once buried our relationship. You could have gone to that building with anybody else just as you could have told anybody else about this stupid-ass case. But no. Not you. You involved Cary because you knew he felt guilty about what had happened between us. You knew his weakness and you played on it. You exploited it. You knew that building was dangerous, a deathtrap, and you sure as shit set up the man I loved to die in it. You couldn't face the fact that it was over between us. That what I had with Cary was real. Was true. That he loved me and I loved him. That he was good to me and for me. That Cary was everything you weren't. He was genuine. Cared about the community. He was confident. He took care of me. He didn't let the common daily bullshit of life bring him down. No, no, he was a man and you couldn't handle that. Just like you couldn't see past your neuroses how unhappy I was with you and your pettiness. It was right in front of you and still you couldn't see it. Look at yourself, Freddie. You had no real ambition, no real prospects, nothing. You would 've been content just to maintain in the White man's world. But not Cary. He wanted to go places, be somebody.. "

"Go places?" I asked.

"Yeah, go places!"

"And look, Clarice," I said as I pointed to his grave site. "Look just how far his 'ambition' got him."

"Fuck you, Freddie. Fuck you! You and your P.I. fantasy ruined my life! You deliberately ruined my happiness!"

"You think I wanted Cary to be killed?" I said incredulously. "So you'd be unhappy?" I laughed. "Let me tell you something. ..You know I used to wish the most horrible things would happen to me just so I could get your attention, your sympathy. I imagined myself shot dead, watching from above, peeping through the clouds just for a glimpse of something that proved to me you cared. These same emotions, tears, you're now shedding for Cary were the ones I wanted. But I never got them. Not even when I was shot in the head, Not even when you kicked me out after backstabbing me with my best friend... "

"Well..."

I put my palms up.

"I'm not finished," I said. "Then my anger turned outward and I wished those horrible things would happen to you. That I would be there to see you suffer like I did. I wanted you to know the agony of betrayal. How it harms you. How it changes you. How it infects your spirit. How I'm afraid to love someone freely again. Deeply again. How I'll never trust anyone again. How, I...."

I stopped and looked down at my shoes. They were slightly muddy. I guess a thousand acres of buried rotting dead bodies would make any ground damp. The soil of lost souls.

"Oh, fuck all this bullshit, Clarice. Plain and simple, I did want to see you in pain once but that period ended a long, long time ago. It ended long before Cary's demise. Long before I took this fuckin' case. Long before I moved to the barrio. To be frank, honey, I simply don't care about you anymore. I don't care what happens to you now. I don't care where you go from here. I don't care about your future or about our past. As far as I'm concerned, you and Cary fucked me over and on that issue, our relationship is as dead as he is. I am going to find out who killed him but it ain't because of our former friendship or anything that has to do with you. I'm doing it because it's damn good business to do so and that's that."

I turned to leave, took a step and then turned back to talk to Clarice.

"I'd wish you well, hon, but I'd be lying, so fuck you and goodbye. "

She looked stunned. I didn't care. I walked away and never looked back. If Clarice said something, I didn't hear it. Didn't want to, either.

My uncle was sitting in the driver's seat. His window was down and he was gabbing with O'Reilly when I got to the Monte Carlo. The look on my face cut their conversation short and O'Reilly walked towards his jalopy without saying another word.

I opened the passenger's side door, slid into the seat, buckled my seat belt on and turned to my uncle.

"Ready?" asked Chubby.

I nodded vigorously.

"Oh yeah," I said.

"Bueno."

He turned the ignition key, the engine roared and the car was on its way back to Manhattan, back to El Barrio and back to my new life.

SEVENTEEN

WHEN I RETURNED home from my graveyard therapy session, I noticed the orange light from my newly-purchased-right-off-the-corner-knockoff-of-a-clone answering machine was a-blinking. None too eagerly, I hit the play button. (After all, up to that point, I couldn't think of anybody who had any good things to say to me.) The male voice on the line was unfamiliar to me: high-pitched with an over deliberate enunciation and a real reedy tone. The message he left was blunt and disdainfully friendly.

"Hi Freddie. This is Oswald Velleto. Mayra's husband. I truly hate to disturb you but I was wondering if you could possibly clear your busy schedule so we could meet tomorrow afternoon, about twoish, face to face, for a beverage in the lobby of the Algonquin Hotel. It's located on West Forty-Fourth Street between Fifth and Sixth Avenue but much, much closer to Sixth. I'd like to talk to you about this whole ungodly mess and what we can do to resolve it. In person, that is. It's always better to talk about ugly matters in person. Anyway, I hope you can make it. Thanks a lot, sport, for all you've done so far. Nobody here is the least bit angry with you and I truly appreciate you taking the time to see me. Oh yes. And let me add my deepest, sincerest condolences to you, your family and all of your loved ones. See you tomorrow, I hope!"

I hated him even more now. Not only had the punk-sounding bastard used up my entire answering tape but he'd done so with the combo bedside manner of an used-car salesman from New Jersey and the Reaper himself. Where was Jumping Jack Kevorkian when you needed him? . Oh yeah, 'sport.' I just couldn't wait to meet homeboy up close and 'face to face.'

I prepped for Velleto like a fighter training for a big bout. Hookers, drugs, forty-dogs, opera socials. Just kidding. I went to bed early. Actually woke up at a reasonable hour. Laid off the talk shows. Exercised some to relieve any excess tension. Ate a sensible breakfast devoid of bran so to minimize the chance of a shall-we-dub-it colonic revolt. Took a long, lukewarm shower to gather my thoughts and carefully cleanse my glands.

Afterwards, utilizing my hot iron and some leftover club soda, I gingerly pressed my black suit of the day before, this time, I added a black mock turtleneck to further convey the seriousness of my hey-do-not-fuck-with-me-buddy mood. (In a continuation of the exploration of what method actors term 'their character's inner life,' I made sure to wear a black T-shirt, briefs and socks. I felt I needed that sepulchral edge.)

After lacing up my black wingtips, I peeked out the window. Looked like another dank, gray day. To be certain, I flipped on the radio to the all-news station to hear the weather report. It took four murders, six assaults and two tales of possible dot-com financial ruin before I got it: chilly with cloudy skies and an eighty percent chance of afternoon showers. Perfect, I thought as I snapped on my shoulder holster and jammed in my gun, just perfect for my New York state of mind.

I snuggled into my suit jacket and rummaged through my closet. Pulled out my black double-breasted raincoat. Clarice had given it to me a couple of years ago for Christmas. (Before the governmental studies student had issued her decree against working for the White man…..man, that line still pissed me off!) I topped it off with a black fedora Chubby purchased for me on a Hun-sixteen the other day.

I tried real hard to give my hat a rakish Bogey tilt but it just t'wasn't happening. With my melon head, it looked more like I was hiding an anthill lump on the side of my skull. (Which, come to think of it, I probably was.)

So I simply pulled the fedora off, held it square over my head, dropped it straight down and then gave it a slight tug on the brim. I rushed to the mirror to sneak a peek. Didn't look half-bad. (God, I loved playing dress-up.)

I put on the black faux-designer watch Chubby had gotten me last year, grabbed my keys and the black leather gloves I'd swiped from my dad last Father's Day. As I stepped out of my place I pulled up my coat collar a tad. I just knew I looked good. Had to. It was time to rumble.

EIGHTEEN

THE LEXINGTON LINE local got me to Grand Central Station in such a hurry that I didn't have time to perfect my solemn game face. I ended up slidestepping my way through the crowded refurbished terminal with my head swiveling back and forth looking for any reflective surface that I could practice my mean motherfucker look in. Finally, as I headed west up the great marble staircase which leads to Forty-third Street and Vanderbilt Avenue, I found a stern countenance I liked while glancing at the black vinyl handbag of a twenty-years-too-late punk rocker two steps ahead. My eyes were slightly narrowed which accented my Taino Indian cheekbones and my lips were pursed with my chin lockjaw tight. Although my Mr. Meanie mug didn't show it as I trotted up Forty-third past Madison Avenue, I was suddenly the happiest man in New York.

(Forty-third Street has always amused me. The office buildings haven't any architectural flair. In fact, their entrances resemble emergency fire exits rather than welcoming portals. It's almost as if the edifice designers themselves were ashamed that their work wasn't being seen on the far more prestigious then-haughty-naughty-bawdy Forty-Second Street.)

The temperature was dropping rapidly. The air had a

clammy chill that you felt in your bones. I tugged at my coat. It was, at long last, winter. I crossed Fifth Avenue and made a sharp right. For mid-midday, there wasn't much foot traffic. Most of the area's working stiffs, I guessed, decided to call out for their fast food or java fix.

Perched on a ten foot high black pole, in front of a bank on the southwest corner of Forty-fourth, was a gold-encased clock. It had a white face, spindly black hands and roman numeral lettering. I looked at it. The time was X to II. I took this to mean 1:50. Either I was early or hideously, prehistorically late. As I turned the corner, I hoped it was the former.

Located some fifteen yards from Sixth Avenue - Avenue of the Americas for foreigners - the Algonquin Hotel has a storied reputation in the annals of New York's literary circles. First and foremost, it was the hallowed home of the Round Table, a fabled collection of wits, storytellers and raconteurs. (In other words, a bunch of pish-posh drunks who got together to wisecrack and play the dozens.) To this day, many of Broadway's (and the magazine world's) best commiserate there to exchange ideas, hammer out a business deal, catch up on the latest gossip or see a cabaret show. Or so the legend goes.

There was one disbeliever outside the hotel, bobbing and weaving around the Algonquin's awning. (In New York, a hotel ain't a hotel if'n it ain't got an awning.) It was a middle-aged bag lady; one who looked like she'd crammed in seventy-five years of hard-knocks in about a half-century of living. Five-five, about two hundred pounds - most of it coats - she was wailing at the top of her lungs in a cracked, pained voice that the end was near and that people have lost their capacity to care.

In agreement with her hypothesis was the hotel doorman, a squat, ruddy-faced, medium-sized man in his early thirties. He was a man who wore a uniform - a brown double breasted one with gold buttons and matching epaulets - so he was accustomed to some type of respect. All of which, he felt, this screaming homeless creature was not giving him. And so the doorman grabbed the now-struggling woman by her first two layers of overcoats, lifted her off her rag-swabbed feet and was in the midst of flinging her out into the path of the oncoming traffic when your intrepid shamus arrived on the scene.

Now, I confess, I was going to ignore the entire incident and stroll into the hotel and go on my apathetic merry way like a good New Yorker should when I made a big mistake: I looked into the woman's eyes. They were sad and defeated; she was simply putting up a fight out of animal instinct and nothing else. Those eyes reminded me she was a human being. In addition, I saw the zestful glee in which the doorman had seized her. It was the fucked-up merriment of a bully kicking the shit out of someone even lower then them on the social scale. It's a sadistic joyfulness I've seen in fast-food cashiers, department-store security guards and token clerks. It's a look I have grown to hate.

So, just before the homeless lady got the road heave-ho, I reached out and put my right hand on the doorman's left shoulder. Right on the epaulet.

"Don't do that," I said, "do *not* do that."

His ruddy face got ruddier. It was the look of shock.

"What?" he gasped. "Are you..?"

"I told you to get your hands off the woman."

"But, why?" he asked before regaining some mental balance. "I mean she's causing a disturbance here, in front of my hotel."

"You don't own this place, you proletariat bastard," screamed the woman. "You're a fuckin' worker wombat, you know."

I leaned real close to the doorman's ear.

"You are fucking up our undercover operation, asshole," I said as I opened my coat up so he - and only he - could see my Sig Sauer. "This is important government business. Now let go of my operative, stupid."

Startled, he dropped her like a hot greased trench fry. She fell to the ground, rolled and bounced back up ready to punch him out when, hands up, I stepped in between.

"All right now," I said, "let's keep cool."

I swiveled to the doorman and asked through clenched teeth if he had done that on purpose. His quick head shake convinced me it was an accident. There was an embroidered name on his jacket: Al. I used it.

"Al," I said, "we are looking for a major, major, drug courier who has been using this hotel as a drop."

"The Algonquin?" he replied in horror.

"That's right, fruitcake, even the home of Dorothy Parker isn't immune to the war on drugs."

"But.."

"But, nothing." I went all out Bogie. "This courageous woman is here staking out this place trying to get the info that'll keep this establishment out of the tabloids and save your miserable job, bub. And all ...all you do is treat her with rampant public disrespect. I oughta have you arrested right now for treason and sedition."

"I didn't know," he said with widened eyes.

I raised my voice a derisive shade.

"You didn't know? That's the problem with America today. Every one of you idiotic drones don't want to know. Well, goddamnit, you better know."

I turned to the woman. She'd been listening carefully the whole time.

"Agent 12?"

"Yes?" she smiled with - surprise, surprise - a full set of white teeth. (Funny, the things street people seem to take care of.)

"Al here says he wants to help." I looked at her directly. "Should I believe him or take him uptown?"

Her eyes narrowed.

"If the wombat brings me a couple of meals every day I'm ...undercover, here, looking for..."

"Drug couriers," I said, "dangerous drug couriers."

"Yeah, them fellas... then I won't press for arrest."

"But won't I blow your cover by feeding you," asked Al.

"Well, we'll just pretend you're undercover too as a kindly doorman," I said.

He tugged at his uniform jacket like a petulant child. I gave him an authoritative nudge to which he nodded his assent. I extended my hand. He shook it. I welcomed him to the war on drugs.

To the left of the Algonquin was a windowed coffee shop with a two-headed fire hydrant sticking out of its edifice. A New York stool. I motioned the recently appointed Agent 12 to have a seat. She did.

"Don't run this game too long," I cautioned.

She nodded and pointed to my watch.

"You better get where you going because......because the end is near, you know."

I had to smile.

"Thank you," she added.

I headed towards the hotel entrance. Al, his face a ghastly pallor, nervously opened the door for me.

"You're meeting somebody..here?" he said.

"That's right so earn that uniform, soldier. Look alive, be alert, keep quiet and get my co-worker something to eat."

"Yes sir," said Al.

He even saluted. I knew all of those viewings of Patton finally would pay off.

NINETEEN

I WALKED INTO the lobby. Lots of wood paneling. I was heading to the information desk when I heard my name being called. I wheeled round and there, eureka, smoothing out his wine-colored cashmere turtleneck which was framed by a most expensive single-breasted dark-blue pinstriped suit was Dr. Oswald Velleto.

He was about six-one but looked even taller because he was so lean. Velleto must've been 130 pounds, tops. Obviously, this was a guy who missed many a meal in his younger days. He wouldn't have lasted a month in my household. My father would've shot him the first time he refused to eat my mother's cooking.

"Can't be one of mine," Pops would've said just after patting his full belly.

Not that Velleto wasn't handsome; he was. (That is if you've got a hankering for pasty-complexioned white boys.) He had medium length salt-n-pepa hair parted down the middle; aqua-blue eyes bisected by a sharp, longish nose; prominent cheekbones offset by a finely coiffed, slightly curled mustache and pointed beard. Another thirty pounds and he could have easily been a fashion designer's dream model. As it was, he reminded me of an anorexic Mephisto.

In greeting, he extended his right claw. I shook it noticing there were tufts of black hair peeking out of the cuffs. Mark of the beast, I thought.

"Nice to meet you. Doctor," I fibbed.

Velleto waved his paw.

"Please, Freddie, we're almost like family. Call me what my friends call me."

"What's that? Oswald? Osvaldo? Osvaldito? Ozzie?"

"No," he laughed. "Nothing so formal. Just call me Oz."

"Okay.. .Oz."

"Good." He looked around the lobby. "There's an empty table by the window. Shall we?"

"Sure thing. ..Oz," I said as I removed my hat. "I must thank you for paying my hospital bills. I really appreciated it."

"It was my - and my Mayra's - pleasure."

We ambled over to the table. Oz took the good seat - the one not facing the sun - and left me in the catbird's seat to squint to my heart's content. It really didn't bother me much, I thought as I flung my fedora against the window sill. I always wanted to be Clint Eastwood.

"So ..Oz, what did you want to see me about?"

He gestured to a tuxedoed waiter who was passing by. The penguin came running.

"Just a second, Freddie. ...I 'Il have the usual, Dick, and as for my friend..."

"Excuse me ..Oz," I said, "the waiter's name is..."

"Dick. Why?"

"Oh, just checking. "

I looked at Dick and ordered a cola. He hurried away from the table. I hoped it was nothing I said.

"A soda pop, huh?" said Velleto. "Are you a teetotaler?"

"Well, it is the early afternoon and I am on a case.."

"That's right," interrupted Velleto, "and how is that going?"

"It goes."

Dick returned with my cola and placed a rather large - three olives worth!- vodka martini in a saucer in front of Velleto. In the saucer were red toothpicks. We murmured our thanks as Formal Wear Dick sailed into the sunset and, for the moment, out of our lives. Oz slurped down a quick swig and let out a satisfied sigh.

"Now, that looks like a stiff drink," I said.

Velleto replied that it was as he grabbed a pick and stabbed at an olive. He grinned as he pierced it right through the heart. Oh, those surgeon hands. He gobbled one down then quickly speared a second. I wondered whether I was sitting with a plastic surgeon or Captain Ahab.

"Where are my manners?" he said as he pointed the olive at me. "Would you care for one?"

"I'll pass."

Velleto ate the second, then the third and polished off the rest of the drink with a mighty gulp. After a stifled belch, he slammed the glass down and began scanning the room.

"Looking for Dick?" I asked.

"Why, yes I am and here he is."

Sho nuff, Dick had returned with another martini. He had placed it on the counter barely a second before Velleto scooped it up for another taste.

"Would you care for another soda, sir?" asked Dick of me. " No thanks, Dick, haven't had a chance to touch this one yet."

"I see," said Dick as he strode away.

"Don't forget me, Dick," said Velleto after him. He had already made two olives and half a glass disappear.

"Somehow I don't think he will, Oz. Now what did you want to talk to me about?"

Another swig. The glass was nearly empty. Velleto took a moment to compose himself, drained the rest of the vodka and, in a smooth bedside-manner voice, spoke on without a single slur.

"Freddie, I know you've, we've, had our share of tragedies lately and I want to show my - and Mayra's - appreciation. I want to give you this for all you tried to do for Junior."

Oz reached into his inside suit pocket and pulled out a piece of paper. He handed it to me. It was a cashier's check for ten thousand dollars. It was my turn to gulp. As coolly as possible I asked him what was the check for. He said it was for services rendered.

"All I did was find your brother-in-law dead," I said.

"You assuaged our tension. We were, in an admittingly strange way. Now we're just happy that the whole horrible saga had an ending."

"What ending? Oz, baby, don't know if you know it, but a cop is dead. I'm not - and I'm quite certain the New York City Police Department is not - going to rest until Detective Branson and Junior's killers are found."

He gave me a conspiratorial look.

"But I thought we knew who slayed Junior."

Somehow, I kept my temper and voice under control.

"If you mean me...well I'm sorry to re-inform you that ballistics, the coroner, everybody agrees that I shot a dead body. But you knew that, didn't you?"

Velleto gave me a smug, little smile. He had tiny teeth. Just like a fuckin' rat.

"That's right, you have been cleared by police personnel. Forgive me, I forgot for a moment. Must have been the vodka talking."

I doubted it but that didn't stop me from pocketing his check. "So what's this money really for?"

"Consider it a retainer," sighed Velleto, "and advance payment for that glorious day you nail the killers of our friends and family. "

"Or killer," I corrected.

"Or killer," agreed Velleto.

Just then we heard a high-pitched squeal go off. Oz threw open his jacket and snatched a tiny lime-green piece of plastic off of his belt.

"My beeper," Velleto said apologetically as he pressed a side button and peeked at a number on top. "I have to leave," he announced.

"Medical call?" I asked.

He nodded his head vigorously. I remembered the two martinis.

So did he.

"Don't worry, Freddie, it's nothing that a semi-in-the-bag

surgeon could botch," Velleto assured. "I'm more of an observer, a consultant in this case."

"I see,"

We stood up. He shook my hand, told me not to worry about the check - I wasn't cause I wasn't paying it anyway - and ran out to a waiting taxi. An old checkered one, at that. I quickly scribbled the cab's license plate number - NYC 6869 - on a nearby napkin, picked up my cola and, finally, drank it.

All finished, I put the glass down, grabbed my hat, waved to a puzzled Dick and walked out the door. Holding it for me was my latest recruit for the Untouchables, Al.

"So that's the guy you had to meet, huh?"

"Yep," I said.

I scrunched on my fedora and looked towards Sixth Avenue. Seated on the water pump was good ol' Agent 12 halfway through a hero sandwich wrapped in wax paper. It looked pretty tasty.

"I should have known something was fishy with that guy," said Al.

Now that got my attention. I turned to Al and asked him why.

"Because I see him in here maybe a couple of times a year and he's always meeting with the same couple of Spanish guys."

Spanish? I thought of Velleto's in-laws, Mayra's kin. Junior. So I started to describe them to Al. He shook his head.

"Nah, they're not Puerto Ricans. I've lived in the Bronx all my life. I know what Puerto Ricans look like. Now, you look like a Puerto Rican ...except for the bad, I mean, kinky hair, pardon me... but you look at least mostly Rican."

"It's a governmental trick," I said as I rubbed my scalp. "Part of my cover, to confuse the enemy."

Al peered at the top of my head. What a moron.

"Yeah, I can see that now. Pretty clever. Anyways these guys were pretty sharp in a gaudy way. Lots of tone-on-tone shirts and ties. Look like those South American dealers on - what was that show? - Miami Vice.

" South Americans?

"You mean, Colombians?"

Al slapped his hands together.

"That's the fellas. I didn't want to come right out and say it on account I don't want you to think I'm a racist or something. For example, I didn't believe it was them fellas that did that to that Simpson woman.."

"That's funny, I did."

Al's eyes opened up wider then the Suez Canal. "Really?"

I leaned closer and whispered to him.

"Keep that quiet, Al. Government secret, ya know?" He nodded while I continued. "I want you to do me a favor though, I want you to go home tonight, get a blank piece of paper and write down everything you remember about how those 'fellas' looked. How they dressed, how tall they were, how they smelled, everything. "

"Sure, sir." He paused. "Is there any money in this? For me, that is."

Hard stare time.

"If you consider the fact that I'll personally implore the Internal Revenue Service not to investigate any of the tips, gifts or gratuities you no doubt receive a doorman at a major New York hotel, well, then. I guess you can say there is money in this for, you. Do you understand?"

Al looked a bit on the pale side. Could be a stroke coming on. Tsk tsk.

"Yes sir," he croaked.

"Good, I'll be by to pick up your recollections some time tomorrow now if you don't mind I'd like to speak to Agent 12 in private please."

Al nodded and stepped inside as I gave him one last admonition to keep quiet about our little chat. The second he left. Agent 12 waved me over.

"I saved you some of my sandwich," she said as she held it out to me. "Don't worry, it's still clean. I haven't touched it."

"It's not that," I smiled, "I'm just trying to see what kind of a sandwich it is."

"Salami and swiss cheese with dijon mustard, lettuce, tomato on whole wheat."

"My favorite."

I grabbed my half, sat on the sidewalk next to Agent 12 and started chewing.

"Do you want to know why the world is coming to an end?" she asked me.

"Why not," I said between chews.

She smiled and told me why. It led to a rather interesting discussion and debate. Hell, she even complimented my hat. The two of us talked for a long, long time.

TWENTY

I STOPPED BY the hotel the next day - after depositing Velleto's check, of course - to collect Al's homework assignment, He was cordial, courteous and just a wee bit chickenshit. No matter. I thanked him brusquely and took the single piece of paper he gave me with a disdainful snatch and crumple. He was in the midst of a mid-sentence apology when I started my step-away. I had one eye peeled for an Agent 12 sighting. No such luck. She wasn't around. I silently hoped she'd made it through another night on the wicked pavements of Manhattan. I really did.

Heading back uptown on the subway, I unwrapped Al's book report. Unfortunately, whatever talents Al had as a doorman didn't extend to the descriptive arts. Basically, the writer's rendering Al gave me easily characterized half the residents of Jackson Heights, Queens: two medium-sized, - and I'm paraphrasing now - swarthy-skinned Latinos with jet-black hair in their 20's or 30's. (Sounds like a typical police bulletin, doesn't it?)

When I got off the Hun-sixteen stop, I was feeling mighty frustrated. Going up the subway stairs, I growled at everybody going down. It wasn't until my feet touched the cracked sidewalk and I took my first deep breath of cuchifrito-injected city air that an idea entered my thickening skull.

Pepito.

I chugged over to the Barcelona, flung open the door - which startled the shit out of Chubby and Papo - and called out my uncle's name. He ran to me asking what was wrong.

"I need you to do me a favor, Tio."

"What is it?"

I whispered 'it', in his ear. He closed his eyes for a moment then inquired if I was sure. I nodded yes. He held his right palm up, nodded back and hustled into his office. I sat at the bar until he came out. The counter was dusty.

"Okay?" I said.

Chubby smiled and exaggeratedly shook his head up and down. I had to laugh.

"When, Tio?"

He pointed down at the counter and scribbled out '4:30 AM Tomorrow' a split-second before Papo wiped it clean with a towel.

"Bueno," I said.

"I hope so, nephew," said Chubby, "I hope so."

TWENTY-ONE

TOMORROW CAME QUICKLY so at 4:20 AM in the morning, I was sitting in a closed-down Barcelona Bar listening over-and-over to a Tito Rodriguez bolero with Chubby and Papo while waiting for a the-coast-is-clear phone call from Pepito. Not a lovely way to spend an evening.

"Listen to the pain in that man's voice," said Chubby.

"Listen in the pain in mine from listening repeatedly to the pain in that man's voice, uncle."

He just igged me.

"That man is singing his heart out about the pain of losing the woman he loves," he said.

"Been there," I said, "done that."

"We all have, nephew, it's part of being a man. It is as essential to us as our penis."

"Been there," I said, "doubt that."

"I'm sure you do. You'll see the light one day, Freddie, you will."

Praise the deity the phone rang. Twice. It was Pepito's signal.

Time to go.

"C'mon, Freddie," nudged Chubby, "Papo and I'll walk you over there."

"No problema," I said.

I patted my Sig side and asked my uncle if I should take my little friend.

"Why not," he stated, "it's not like you're gonna use it anyway."

At the time, I assure you, that answer made perfect sense to me. Really.

We put on our coats, buttoned them up and stepped out into the brisk moonlit evening as Papo locked the bar's front door.

"Don't pull down the gate, Papo," said Chubby, "we won't be gone long."

Papo bobbed his head and moved quickly to my curbside right. Instinctively, Chubby shifted to my left leaving yours truly dead center.

"Jesus, guys," I said, "I feel like I'm flanked by the Secret Service."

"The way things have been going for you, you'd be lucky to be flanked by a car service, wiseguy," opined my uncle.

"Especially in this neighborhood," I said.

We crossed One-sixteen towards Pepito's. The joint was lit up like a Christmas tree. At this hour, it was probably the only semi- legit business opened up for miles.

Papo elbowed me. Right out front was a conga-line of brand-new Black Lincoln Town Cars. About ten of them.

"Looks like the Man's here, hub, Papo?" said Chubby.

"And he got a hell of a deal from Ford."

Papo grunted in concordance.

"Well, at least he buys American," I croaked.

"That's not all he buys," cautioned my uncle.

Just before we reached the restaurant's entrance, Pepito stepped out. He must've been watching all the time.

"Ola', hombres," he said. "This is as far as you can go. Only Freddie's allowed to 'come in."

Chubby didn't look too pleased but didn't look surprised either as he turned to me.

"Well, nephew, it's your call."

"I'm going in."

"Okay, but be careful, hub?"

"I guarantee his safety," said Pepito.

My uncle turned to him. "Pepito, mi amigo, that's a given. Isn't it?"

There was a trace of malice in his tone.

"Of course. Chubby, of course."

"Bueno," said Chubby as he tapped Papo on the shoulder. "C'mon, loudmouth, we'll wait for Freddie in the bar." He looked at Pepito again.

"You will call when he's ready to return?"

"Of course, of course."

"Deja vu," Chubby said absently.

He threw me a wink and walked off with Papo into the darkness. I wheeled towards Pepito. He beckoned me inside. I thanked God for my predilection for black underwear. This was shaping up to be a mega-stain night.

TWENTY-TWO

THE DOOR CLOSED behind me with the ringing finality of a death sentence. My knees started to knock. Pepito sensed this. He placed his hand on my left shoulder to steady me. It would 've worked except I was in optical overload. In front of me, strategically seated at every stool, chair or table was an armed platoon of gentlemen who looked to be of a certain Mediterranean extraction. I felt as if I were at a Scorsese casting call.

"So that's the young man that wants to meet me?"

The voice was aged but still full of power. I looked straight to the back of the restaurant. There, seated regally at the table dubbed his throne, immaculately attired in a dark gray double-breasted suit was the now-completely silver-haired Don Vincenzo Gianelli. And he was beckoning me to him.

An ape with a duck-tail pompadour and wearing a shiny knockoff of the Don's suit sprung in front of me, blocking my path and all the surrounding light.

"You want that I should frisk this fucker, Don?" he snarled.

"No," said the voice from behind the human eclipse, "and watch your language."

"Sorry, Don," grunted the gorilla as he moved out of the way.

"Thank you, Magilla," I said as I passed him, "and my best to

117

Mr. Peebles."

"Now, now, young man," chided Don Vincenzo, "I understand you may feel the need to wisecrack to release your considerable tension but I guarantee you they are as welcome here as that Sig-Sauer P220 handgun beneath your buttoned coat."

The old man had either done his homework or old Deadeye had graduated to X-ray eyes.

"And I guarantee you, Don," I said, "my wisecracks and my handgun will remain under wraps for the rest of this visit."

"Good," said the Don who pointed at the chair in front of him. "Now, come sit down."

I did so. All of the Don's boys were facing the door doing their best to seem inconspicuous. Only to Stevie Wonder, I thought. Pepito went behind the counter to rustle up some grub for the troops. Smelled like sausage.

I pivoted towards the Don. The years had added their wrinkles but the hair was still thick and the eyes - the eyes! - were as coldly crafty as I'd been told.

"Pepito has spoken highly of you, Freddie," he said. "It is because of my respect for him - and nothing else - that I have agreed to this meeting. So, I ask you young man, what is it that you would like to talk to me about?"

I made sure my voice was low and respectful and my gaze direct and steady. (I hadn't spent four years of Catholic religious instruction for nothing.)

"Don Vincenzo," I said, "I'm sure you have heard about the fatal shooting of my friend. Detective Branson.."

"You mean, the scoundrel - if you can forgive me for speaking ill of the dead - who stole the woman you loved," the Don interrupted with a smile. (Oh yeah, he'd done his homework. As for 'speaking ill of the dead,' why not, he'd had generations of practice.) "Yes, Freddie - if I may call you Freddie - I've heard about him and that nasty little fracas you two had on a Hundred and Twenty-Fourth." He leaned forward. "I promise you that our people had nothing to do with your tragedy."

"I realize that, Don Vincenzo, and let me assure you that

thought never entered my mind."

"Then why did you wish to meet?"

A deep breath moment.

"I want the names of the people who are involved," I said.

The Don burst into a loud laugh. Alarmed, his men turned quickly toward us. With a flick of Don Vincenzo's liver-spotted hand, they just as quickly turned back around.

"Young man, Don Vincenzo is not, by any stretch of your feeble imagination, a stool pigeon," he chuckled.

Rapidly I jumped in. I wanted to defuse any misconception.

"And I have not - or would ever - call you one," I said.

"I mean, you have seen The Godfather, haven't you?"

"One, Two and Three, Don Vincenzo."

He shook his wrist again.

"Three, I wasn't too crazy about but One and Two are classics of the cinema you would agree."

Of course he would love the first two, I thought. They were practically recruiting films for the Mafia.

"I too agree they are classics, Don Vincenzo," I said.

"Then you may have heard of a little something we in my business call omerta," he said. "In your world it can be translated as keeping one's big mouth shut!"

"Allow me to postulate a different theory on omerta, Don Vincenzo."

The Don had a bemused look on his weathered face.

"Go ahead," he said.

Another deep breath.

"I believe omerta - a fine and honorable policy, by the way - should only apply to those in your organization, in your direct sphere of influence."

"Meaning?"

"Meaning, Don Vincenzo, the law of omerta should only apply to people who are members of the Cosa Nostra. If they're not in it, then they are not - and should not deserve to be-be covered by those right and just laws."

"So, you are telling me, if these people who did this to your friend are not part of my business or in my direct sphere of influence, and I know who they are then, because, according to you, I am not bound by the strict rules of omerta, I should tell you their identities."

"Something like that."

"That's ludricious, Freddie. Cleverly convoluted but ludricious."

"Is it really, Don Vincenzo? Listen, sir, I don't know if you do any sort of business with these people and I don't really care. All I do know is these animals have, by executing a New York City police officer, brought a lot of unwanted and unwelcome attention among a number of independent proprietors, yourself included."

He nodded so I continued.

"All I'm asking for is a name, a clue of some sort, that will lead me to the culprit or culprits involved. If their disappearance should happen to benefit, in any way, big or small, you or your compatriots, then so be it. I can sleep well at night knowing you are in control of whatever situation you see fit as long as those evil creatures are punished for their actions."

"You are willing to swear to me," said the Don, "that you will never interfere in my operations, no matter what they are, for as long as you live."

"No," I corrected. "I am willing to tell you that as long as your actions do not harm me or any of my loved ones in any way that I will not interfere in your operations for as long as you live."

The Don grinned.

"There are a lot of loopholes in that contract."

"And there are a lot of bullet holes in yours," I said. "I'm a man of my word, Don Vincenzo, please help me."

He stroked his chin.

"I hope so, Freddie, I hope so."

"This may sound like a stupid thing to say to a great man such as yourself but trust me."

"It does and I will."

After a pause, the Don beckoned me closer. I leaned in.

"The name you are looking for is the Wizard," he whispered.

"The Wizard?" I repeated. "What Wizard?"

"Close, but no cigar," said the Don.

He sprang up, snapped his fingers and began to walk away.

"Remember, Freddie, life is not always linear," he said.

His minions quickly surrounded him in a protective cocoon. The last words I heard him say just before he left the restaurant was a reminder for me to keep my word. Then, I heard a gaggle of engines start, rev and peel out. It sounded like the Indy 500 or a Friday night on the Belt Parkway.

Pepito came from behind the counter and placed a heaping plate of sausage in front of me.

"I'm gonna call your uncle and Papo to come over and eat," he told me.

"Great, Pepito, thanks for everything," I said distractedly.

He tapped me on the noggin. I looked up. Pepito was beaming.

"You did good, Freddie, the Don really liked you. I could tell."

I thanked him again as he handed me a fork and then walked towards the private telephone he had stashed under the counter. What Wizard? I wondered as I dug into the chow. And what about the Don's crack about life not being linear? What could he mean? Life is crooked? A crooked Wizard? I shrugged. Start from the beginning, Freddie. A non-linear Wizard? A non-linear Wizard of what?

Wait a second. Not what Wizard, but Wizard of what? I dropped my fork onto the table. Of course.

"Well, fuck me silly," I said. "Wizard of motherfucking Oz."

Fucking Oswald Velleto. I picked up my fork and started to stab at the sausages with a vengeance, I shoveled three or four into my mouth. They tasted great. Good, I thought as I chewed, I was going to need all of my strength. Tomorrow night, Freddie Boy was going to be off to see the Wizard.

TWENTY-THREE

TURNED OUT THE Wizard wanted to see me. And so did Mrs. Wizard.

After my meet with Don Vincenzo, Chubby, Papo, Pepito and myself had hung out till the wee-wee small hours of the morning, at first, shooting the breeze in the Cuchifrito Cottage, then moseying over to the Barcelona for a spirited round of philosophical exchanges and uninterrupted libations. (In truth, we needed the booze to cut the prodigious grease intake from Pepito's sausages.)

At 10:00 AM, after the four of us had bid each other our woozy good-byes, I managed to stagger upstairs to my apartment. No sooner had I locked my door behind me when the telephone rang. My motor reflexes weren't at their best so it is with no small measure of pride that I'm proud to say that I was able to fling off my coat, navigate my path to the phone and pick it up on what was either the third ring or the twentieth. Anyways, with my eyes blinking like an entrant in an optical Morse code contest, I managed to croak out a hello when the honeyed voice on the other end spoke.

"Chulito? Did I wake you?"

"No, Mayra," I said while silently slapping myself in the face to remain lucid, "long time no hear."

Her tone was apologetic.

"I know, Freddie, it's just that...after Junior's death, may God have mercy on his soul, I just didn't feel like talking to anyone."

I rubbed my temples.

"Yeah, I know."

"Listen, Chulito, I'm feeling a little better and I want to see you and I want you to have dinner with us tonight."

"With 'us'?"

"Yes, you, me and Oswald," Mayra said. "It's about time that the two of you met."

Met? So she didn't know about me and Velleto's little hotel assignation the other day. What about the ten G payoff? I made a mental note to call the bank right after I got off the phone to make sure that check cleared. The last thing I needed was some financial funny stuff.

"Yeah, Mayra, I agree," I said, "it is about time that we two met."

"Oh, Chulito," Mayra said excitedly, "that means so much to me. You know with the exception of my father, you two mean more to me than any other man in my life."

Oh God. The Molinas.

"How are your parents dealing with this?"

"It's so tough for them to understand. They feel they've done something wrong. They just don't realize that Junior was a grown man who chose the wrong path in life."

That got me a little curious.

"What do you mean 'wrong path'?"

"Drugs! What else? Drugs."

"Yeah but the autopsy was inconclusive so there's no evidence - real evidence - that Junior was a long-time user or simply got caught in a bad situation."

"Like what?" Mayra challenged, "Like what?"

"I don't know but it's something to check out. Maybe your brother wasn't a bad guy but got into a predicament he couldn't control. "

"No, no, no," said Mayra. "He had to have been doing bad things for a long time and that's why he was punished."

"Jeez, Mayra," I said, "That's kind of harsh, isn't it?"

Man, I was losing my buzz quickly. I hate when that happens.

Meanwhile, Mayra spoke like she never even heard me. She was too busy riding a wave of indignation.

"He was probably using drugs for a long time and I never even noticed him. And to think I entrusted him with this apartment."

"Wait a minute, hon. It's not like he ever stole from you, right? You never had any jewelry, rings, necklaces, bracelets missing?"

"No," she said after a pause.

"Nor did you ever come home to find your television or stereo gone. So maybe, like I said, Junior was a victim of 'wrong place, wrong time.'"

"No, I am convinced he was using."

God, she was stubborn.

"How could you be so sure?"

"Well, Oswald pointed out to me all the telltale signs.,"

"Oswald?!"

"Yes, Oswald."

"Well, I'd guess he'd know," I said bitterly.

Too bitterly.

"What makes you say that?"

Shit. She'd picked up the nasty sound in my voice. I had to shift gears.

"Mayra, honey. He is a doctor, isn't he? He'd have to know."

She seemed to buy that.

"Yeah..yeah, you're right."

"Listen, sweetheart, why don't we save the rest of the chit-chat for din-din. That way you'll hear my theories, I'll hear your theories and we'll all get to hear Oswald's."

"Great, Chulito," she said. "Have you ever been to Yolanda's over on Canal Street?"

"East or West?"

"West."

"Over by the Lincoln Tunnel?"

"That's right."

"No I haven't but I hear the food is great."

And expensive, I wanted to add.

"Oh it is," gushed Mayra, "and the pasta is to die for."

Interesting choice of words, I thought.

"Yeah, I think I read about it."

In some snooty restaurant column, no doubt. What a great job that must be. You get to eat for free and still blast the owners. Some people have all the luck.

"Informal, right?" I asked.

"Yes," she said, "and, of course, Freddie, dinner will be on us."

And my luck just picked up.

"Well, I know it's fruitless to talk you out of it so I'll just thank you in advance."

God, I hated my false humility but I had a stomach to replenish. Priorities, you know.

"What time would you like me there?" I asked.

"About eight."

"No problem."

"Good, you know Oswald told me the other day he can't wait to meet you."

"I feel the same way," I said as I patted my holstered two-twenty. "I'm just glad the two of you decided to invite me along."

"Actually, I guess there's no harm in me telling you, I haven't told him yet."

I took my gun out of my holster.

"No? Really?"

"See, he's been after me to get out the house and I figured this was the perfect time to get together ..so.."

I practiced my aim in the mirror. I made a nice target. Bloodshot but nice.

"Say no more," I said. "Sounds like a good little surprise to me and after all we've been through I know I'd like to have the chance to personally thank you and Oswald for all you've done for me"

"Oh, Chulito, any time. And, not that I've forgotten, I'll have your check for you."

"Check?"

"Sure, mi amor. A deal is a deal. You did your job and you deserve your money."

I had to smile. Benjamins a-plenty. Mo 'money, mo' money, mo' money.

"Mayra, I like the way you think."

"Sure, Chulito. Business is business."

And I hoped to take care of a great deal of it that evening.

"See you at eight, honey," I said.

"See you then," she said as she hung up.

I put down my gun and drew down my shades. I was going to need plenty of rest. After all, it was going to be a night of dinner, detecting and, quite possibly, a double-dealing doctor for dessert.

TWENTY-FOUR

WHEN I WOKE up about 6:30 that evening, I felt refreshed. Eight hours of uninterrupted sleep will do that for you. It helped I had unplugged the phone after I'd called the bank to see if the check cleared. (It had.) I didn't want to talk to Oswald before we'd met for dinner. I wanted the advantage of surprise.

The black suit had seen too much action the last couple of days - dusty and musty! - so I dressed cazz-you-al with some navy-blue corduroy slacks and a corresponding cotton-knit turtleneck sweater. (Hell, even my sweatsocks matched!) I do admit I was a little worried about the pants. With my rapidly expanding, junk-food addled thighs in a pair of cords, I could easily start a brushfire with a mere jog to the corner. But since tonight there wasn't going to be any undercover surveillance work, I figured a few sparks thrown wouldn't harm me or the case.

To hide the two-twenty I threw over a bulky black and blue windowpane plaid sport jacket I'd appropriated from Father Perez's closet on the sly. Purchased in the early '70s, the jacket lapels were a bit on the wide side but so what, anyway? The fit was cool. Besides, any evening with Mayra had a retro feel to it.

The weather was as cool and cloudy as it's ever been. I

wished the sky would stop threatening and simply let loose. New York was the sort of city that could use a perennial pissing from the gods. Not that a torrential downpour could ever truly cleanse the long-neglected streets but it certainly helped rearrange the dirt.

I shoehorned on my black work shoes, patted my growling stomach, flipped on my raincoat and thought about the fedora as an added touch. But another glance at the skies reminded me the theme of the evening was comfort so I yoked a New York Yankees cap over my hammer head and strutted out the door.

The Lexington local took its sweet time downtown and gave me a wonderful opportunity to share in the civic misery that is New York. First, from 96th Street on, there was the frenzied search for a seat as middle and slumming upper-class folk compete vigorously with the downtrodden for the pleasurable right to squeeze a thirty- four inch and up keister in a twenty-eight inch plastic crevice masquerading as a chair. So, instead of seven people sitting comfortably together, we now have ten angry individuals wedged like slaves in a galley ship. (All that's missing are the oars.) And that's not counting the furious hordes of people who didn't get a seat hovering and leaning and breathing above them.

Naturally, this invasion of one's personal space makes for the sort of sparkling conversation one would normally have to go to a prison to enjoy. (In fact, the only major difference between the subways and jail is the rate of sodomizing is lower on the trains. Although, with the Transit Authority in charge, even that's debatable.)

Then there's the never-ending festival of beggars, junkies, pleaders and the homeless who ask for just a couple minutes of your precious time to hear their tale of woe and contribute a few dimes, nickels, dollars or quarters to help them out. And as soon as one leaves the front of the car; another enters from the rear to tell their sad story.

By the time the train was pulling out of Union Square I was all saddened out. No fewer than twenty-four people had passed by me to recount the pitfalls of their disastrous life. (I felt like I was a judge on Queen For A Day.) Disgusted, I was debating whether or not to get off the train at the next stop and walk the mile or so to the restaurant when I spotted Agent 12, through the closed doors, on the platform. She was sitting on a bench gazing blankly into space looking mottled and agitated but remaining defiant and unbroken. Our stares met for a split-second. In her weary face, I was a brief smile of recognition before I - and the train - was whisked away in a blurry roar. Then I heard her voice in my head.

"There but for the grace of God, Freddie," she spoke to me, "there but for his grace."

"Oh my Jesus," I murmured to myself. "That could have so easily been me."

I doffed my cap and, for the first time in too many a year, said a novena. The woman seated next to me remained unconvinced. Eyeballing me nervously, she moved to the next car. Guess she was an agnostic.

TWENTY-FIVE

WHEN I REACHED Canal Street, the temperature had dropped. It was downright frosty with the heated breath of passing pedestrians as visible as smokestacks in the Midwest. The chill didn't really disturb me though. I just put my hands in my pockets and stepped livelier.

I'd always found Canal Street so interesting. A two-way, four lane main drag running east to west from the Manhattan Bridge to the Holland Tunnel, not only was it the commercial hub of Chinatown with hundreds of quasi-legal businesses and delicious restaurants lining its cramped sidewalks but it was also the unofficial borderline to so many neighborhoods. There was the rapidly shrinking Little Italy to the north, the foreboding courthouse area to the south. Heading towards the Holland, trotting past Broadway, there was the fashionable pomposity of Soho to the north and the always unseasonable blustering of City Hall to the south. And always, the incessant honking of horns from folks driving east to Brooklyn and parts unknown or west to New Jersey and parts nobody really wants to know.

Yolanda's was located on the south side of Varick and Canal, right at the beginning of Tribeca, not far from the Velletos' digs on Franklin. Specializing in neo-Italian-American cuisine, the joint was lackadaisically swank with a bare-bones decor in various shades of brown and taupe, tactically placed, understated hickory wood dining tables - each with their own Tiffany lamp - and surrounded, from entrance door to fire exit, by a large semi-circular bar topped off with a giant neon sign saying Liquors on the wall in the center, all of it facing a opaque street window.

The spot was just like the neighborhood - a series of lofts for prosperous baby boomers - casual and pricey. (Think of it as if Bijan's took over Conway's.) Packed with Gore-Tex, chinos, cowboy boots, running shoes and denim, Yolanda's reeked of Tribeca chic. (The sort of a site where all of the help wore black turtlenecks and jeans as if they were in mime school or something. Then I realized, oh shit, they dress just like me.) And there, sitting in the middle of it all, was Oswald and Mayra.

I'd stepped into the dimly-lit place, instantly confronted by an aggressive Pamela Anderson-clone hostess who demanded to know if I had a reservation. (Funny, how diligent these service people are in determining whether a person of color has a right to the service they are there to provide. Why, it's almost as if they ...don't want us there.)

It was only after I had dazzled the blue-eyed blond bitch with my convivial smile, pointed out the people I was scheduled to meet and suggested forcefully, mayhaps, she should send someone over to the Velletos' table to verify my identity since I was being treated as a Mexican at the Texas border, that she relented and allowed me to pass. But not without escorting me to the Velletos personally. From the rear route, of course.

"Thanks, sweetheart," I told her as we made our way through the maze of tables, "I'll tell my attorney Mr. Cochran to meet me here for dinner."

"Anyone's welcome here if they have a reservation, sir," she said bitterly, drawing out the last syllable like a serpent slithering after it's prey.

"Sure thing, darling, put us both down for 'Bring Your Own Sheet and Cowl' night."

"I don't know what you mean," she growled.

"Of course, you do," I said as we reached the table and the Velletos' backs. "Why, I bet you've got your own cross a-oiled and ready to burn."

She tried to ignore me but I could tell by her reddening ears my little jab got through.

"Excuse me, sir," she said as she tapped Oswald on the shoulder, "do you know this ..man?"

Oswald and Mayra both turned around. Their coats were on the backs of their seats. Mayra greeted me with a warm smile which, after seeing my face, turned into a scowl of consternation. She'd been around. She knew something was up. Oz, however, looked very surprised and very nervous. He knew this was a loaded question. After all, as Mayra said, he was dying to meet me. I guess that little ten grand in my bank came from the tooth fairy. He chose to stay dumbfounded and quiet. Not so his wife.

"Yes, I know this man," said Mayra indignantly, "he is my friend, my family and I certainly hope he has been treated with the respect a guest of mine deserves."

Blondie started to sputter.

"Certainly, ma'am, we were .."

"You were what?" Mayra said loudly. "Just making sure that a Latino male belonged in here?"

The diners around us got quiet.

"No.. you don't understand," said our now-embarrassed hostess.

Blondie began to look around the room. Her hands began to shake. Guess she really didn't want a scene. No matter. I took off my coat and pulled out my chair for the ringside view.

"No, nothing," said Mayra. "Let me tell you something, young lady, we are not trash nor do we expect to be swept out like such. I am the chairman of the board of the Carrington Foundation - the same foundation that has hosted a number of functions at this establishment - and I will not hesitate to mention this indignity to your employer when he asks us to return. Do you understand me?"

Blondie weakly nodded her head. She had nothing to say.

Neither did Oswald. Yep, this was the best seat in the house.

"Good," said Mayra, "Now where is the manager? I want to register a complaint now."

Blondie seemed to perk up a little. Like the manager was her final lifeline.

"He's not here right now but I'll send him right over when he arrives."

"Fine," said Mayra.

Blondie looked right at me.

"And I'm sure he'll want to talk to you," she snarled.

Sounded almost like a threat. I leaned in real close. Made her flinch a little.

"Good," I said, "bring him on."

"Oh I will," she said as she started to walk away,

"Yoo-hoo, peroxide lady!" I called out in my finest Jerry Lewis voice.

Stopped her dead in her tracks. She looked disdainfully over her shoulder at me. It was time for my best Barry White baritone.

"Be a good girl," I said suavely, "and fetch us a waiter and some menus."

Blondie snapped her fingers and a Black waitress appeared. The only chocolate one in the entire joint. Six feet tall tail, built like an Amazonian, she was hard to miss. With the trace of a smile, she handed us our menus as the crowd noise returned.

"Here you go, folks," she said. "Let me know if there's any thing I can do or get for you."

"Actually, there is," I said.

I gestured to her to come closer. She did.

"What's that?" she asked.

"Can you make sure nobody spits in our food?" I whispered.

The waitress let out a little melodious laugh.

"Not a problem."

"Really," said Mayra. "How come?"

"The cooks," whispered the waitress, "are all Puerto Ricans." (Well, we are legion.) "If anything, after I tell them what happened, they'll probably give you more food."

"Just as long as it won't contain any additional additives," I said, "the chow will be welcome and the tip big."

"You got it and how's about I give you a round of martinis on the house?"

I checked the nameplate above her enormous left breast. (Trust me, the right looked to be the same blessed size also.) The tag read Juanita. I was a little disappointed. With jugs like those I was expecting Pam Grier.

"That'll be fine, Coffy..I mean, Juanita," I said. "Thank you."

Her brow furrowed and she let out a lusty chuckle.

"My pleasure. Shaft ...I mean.."

"Freddie," I blushed.

"Freddie, huh?" She clucked her tongue against the side of her mouth. "I think I liked Shaft better."

"He is a bad mother shut-your-mouth," I offered.

"Yeah and we can dig it, " said Juanita.

"I think we're ready for those drinks right now," interrupted Mayra.

Juanita and I shared a look. God, she was cute.

"I'm sorry," she said, "I'll get those right away."

Mayra thanked her and she was off. Holy moley. Juanita was built like an R. Crumb drawing: a massive mocha brown gang of boobies and booty.

"I think she liked you," said Mayra.

"Nah," I said. "Really?"

"Oh yeah," said Mayra but she didn't sound too happy about the fact, either. Women. "What do you think, Oz?".

Oh, that's right, Oz. The Wizard, himself. And he sure had been mighty quiet. A deafening quiet, you might say.

"Oh," he said with a scratchy voice, " I think.....l believe Freddie made a favorable impression."

"Gee, thanks. Dr. Velleto," I said with a hard stare. "That means a lot coming from you."

Mayra looked perplexed.

"Dr. Velleto? Oh, that's right. You guys haven't met yet."

"That's right, dear," Oswald quickly said while extending his hairy paw. "Oswald Velleto, Freddie, call me Oz."

Deja mother-fucking vu. Man, he looked pale.

"I bet that's what all your friends and family call you." I said.

I glanced at the cutlery. Taupe forks? What had this world come to?

"That's right," he said, "and know that I consider you to be both."

Mayra grabbed his claw and held it.

"This is a special moment for me," she said with teary eyes. "Two men I love finally get to meet."

"It's a special moment for all of us, Mayra," I added. "Now let's eat."

I grabbed a menu and opened it just as Juanita returned with our drinks. I thanked her while admiring God for a job well done. Boy, she had a purty face. Kind brown eyes, high cheekbones, sensual mouth with a nice, wide smile. Looked like she had all of her teeth, too. That's always a plus.

"Any suggestions?" I cooed.

"Plenty," she beamed, "but unfortunately for you, they're all centered around that piece of cardboard in your hands."

Oh-mi-god, just the way I like them: big & sassy.

"There's nothing unfortunate about it," I said as I held up my menu. "Believe me, I know how to work with the materials on hand."

"I'm sure you've had lots of experiences with your hand, Freddie," she purred.

"You mean, hands-on experience and that's Mr. Freddie to you, missy."

I gave her the cocked eyebrow look. I look so cute when I do that.

"Was that Mr. Freddie or Miss Daisy?" asked Juanita.

"Depends, darlin'," I said while leaning forward, "on whether you want to drive or be driven?"

She and I were padlocked in some double-eye contact and I was loving it.

"I think we'll have the lasagna with a bottle of your best red wine," piped up Mayra.

Good thing she had. I'd forgotten there were other people at the table.

"You too?" asked Juanita.

"Oh, you know me, Juanita," I said. "I'm a follower."

Now it was her turn to lean forward. Mamma Mia, what a double-barreled delight.

"Only when I'm driving, Mr. Freddie," she said before walking away. It was a sway I felt in my nether region. I snatched my martini and gulped it while moving my legs further under the table. A mere napkin in the lap was not going to do the trick. (If anything, with my privates at full mast. I'd probably resembled an approaching pirate.) Yes, indeedy. Little Freddie was starting to stir.

Oswald laughed while sipping his vodka.

"You look a little....flushed, Freddie."

"And you look a trifle pallid, Oz. Feeling under the weather?"

"You do look pasty, Oz," said Mayra. "Is something wrong?"

"No, no, sweetheart," he assured. "It's all the hours I've been putting in at work."

"Really," I injected. "Where have you been working? Has there been a run on face-lifts or something?"

"Yes, truthfully," laughed Oz. "It's November. The well-to-do like to have their procedures done around this time so they're all healed up by the late spring and early summer."

"A winter tune-up," I said.

"Exactly."

He took another mighty martini sip. This was a boozehound incarnate.

"And where do you work out of? Your magnificent apartment? A brownstone, perhaps?"

"Not in the least." Oz turned to Mayra. "He is an inquisitive one, isn't he?"

"That's his job, honey," she said.

"So it is," he responded before turning to me. "I'm based in Darby Hospital on the Upper East Side."

"Never heard of it."

"I'm not surprised. It's a tiny, out-of-the-way private hospital which caters only to the one-time jet set. It's located on 90th and York."

"Right off the FDR Drive."

"You know it?"

"Just the area. My cousin David used to live around there. We used to play basketball at a playground over there."

"Yes, yes. We're located right across the street from that playground."

Velleto polished off his martini. So had Mayra. Funny, I hadn't seen her even take a swig. Maybe Oz ingested it by osmosis.

"Was your cousin any good at basketball?" he asked.

"David? Oh, yeah, very good."

"How about you?"

"Not really. I was cagey, though."

"How so?"

"Once I latched on to something I could use, once I found out my opponent's weakness, I never stopped exploiting it until the game was over."

Velleto fingered the stem of his glass. He didn't look up.

"Really, now?"

"Really Oz."

Just then Juanita arrived with dinner and the wine. As she predicted, the portions were the size of the Roman Coliseum. And just as beautiful. She passed around our glasses and showed me the bottle. (You'd think I was paying, hah!) It was a Midwestern wine: a 1984 Hoey. I read somewhere that they were good. She popped the cork, no jokes please, and put it under my nose. It smelled fine to me - but then again so does Robitussin - so I nodded as if I knew what the fuck I was doing. Then Juanita poured a little in my glass. I lifted it to my lips, slurped a little, rolled it around my mouth like some sort of grape mouthwash and then swallowed. As the Great One himself, Jackie Gleason would say: 'Smooth!' And it was.

"Is everything to your satisfaction, Freddie?"

"So far," I said as I signaled her to pour a little heaven for my hosts. "I'll call you later if it isn't."

She poured and simultaneously, surreptitiously slipped a card into my jacket's hanky pocket.

"Call me even if it isn't," she murmured before hip-gliding away.

The woman had me panting so heavily I was going to have

to buy a tank of O2 just to catch my breath. Thank God for food. I picked up my taupe fork and knife, readjusted my lap napkin - more height - and smiled at the Velletos. I stabbed into the saucy mound of meat and pasta and watched the steam rise to the ceiling.

"So Oz," I said before shoving a forkful into my mouth, "why don't you tell me how you kids met?"

"Well, it was my first day of my senior year at Harvard and I was walking across the square when I saw this lovely lady walk by."

That got a grin from Mayra. God, she was fine. I was going to nail this guy to the wall.

"Is that so?"

"Yes," said Oswald between chews. "I knew right that second this was the woman for me so I followed her around campus."

"A stalker, eh?"

"No, nothing that evil, Freddie," said Mayra. "Things were nicer then."

"What year were you in, Mayra." "Freshmen. "

"So, Oz, my man, you were seeking out the new meat, huh?"

"Nothing so vulgar," said Velleto.

He sounded disgusted. Good. I was getting under his skin.

"Freddie's just playing, sweetheart," chided Mayra.

"Oh, I know," recovered Oswald. "To make a long story short, she looked lost, so I offered to escort her around campus. Two weeks later, we were dating."

"Two years after that, we'd moved in together," added Mayra.

"We got married during my third year of Medical School..."

"Then we moved out west for his residency."

"The perfect place for plastic surgery," I said.

"Yes," said Oz. "Out there, everybody's obsessed with looking young. "

"It's the film industry," I added.

"Sure," said Mayra. "We can't even go to the movies anymore with Oz critiquing the stars' faces."

"You'd think, Freddie, for the prices they pay, they'd get it done right, "

"A lot of bad work, eh?"

"You'd think Freddy Krueger was the surgeon-in-residence."

"You seem to profit though."

"It pays to do good work. I do a turnaway SRO business."

"SRO?"

"It's a surgeon's joke," guffawed Oz, "SRO: Superstars Room Only."

"Not bad," I said. "By the way Oz, where do you come from? Where 'd you grow up?"

"Providence, Rhode Island."

"It's supposed to be scenic country there."

"That's the first time I ever heard Providence called scenic but compared to Brooklyn I guess it was."

"Any brothers or sisters?"

"No, I'm an only child."

"Oswald, is the only child of two parents who were only children," said Mayra. "I guess that's why he took to Junior."

We all let an awkward moment pass before I continued my gentle interrogation.

"So what did your parents do?"

"They," stammered Oswald, "they had their own business."

"Oh, sweetheart, don't be so modest," said Mayra. "Freddie, have you ever heard of the Angelo Pharmaceutical Company?"

"Yes. Aren't they the largest in New England?"

"Si, well, that's the company Oswald's parents founded."

"Angelo was my father's first name," Velleto said sullenly.

"Was?"

"Both my parents passed away a couple of years ago."

"Car accident," said Mayra.

"I'm sorry," I said.

Velleto looked down at his now-empty dish and reached for his wife's hand.

"There's been too much tragedy in our lives lately," he said temperately. "Too much."

I actually felt for him. Then Mayra excused herself to go to the little girl's room. Velleto watched his wife march all the way to a narrow door located next to the fire exit - what genius architect thought of that one? - and waited 'til she closed the door before speaking.

"Thanks for keeping your mouth shut, Freddie," he said. "You prevented a bad situation."

"Why didn't you tell her, Oz?"

"Because she's been through so much that I wanted to spare her. I just want this whole thing over."

"What over?"

"The investigation?"

"Whose? Mine or the police's?"

"Both."

"Well, that ain't happening. A cop's dead, a friend of mine to boot, and so's your brother-in-law. This just ain't going away, Oz."

He put his head in his hands.

"Oh God, I wish it would."

"Why? For God's sake, Velleto, what the fuck's going on?"

His voice was strangled.

"You don't understand the pressure I'm under."

"From who?" I demanded. "From Mayra?"

"From everybody!" he half-shouted before regaining his composure. "From everybody."

"What kind of pressure, Oz? Maybe I can help you."

His beeper went off. He reached around the back of his chair and picked it off his belt as if he were lifting a two-ton boulder. Warily, he glanced at the number on top. His features seemed to sag.

"I've got to make a call," he said.

"No cell phone?"

Velleto shook his head.

"Keep losing them."

A doctor who keeps losing his cell phone? Sure hope he didn't have the same luck with scalpels.

"I see."

"This place has to have a pay phone, right?"

I looked around the restaurant. There was a pay phone not too far from the bar, right where the kitchen was to the immediate left of the Liquor sign.

"Over there," I pointed.

"Thanks," he said.

He rose and put a hand on my shoulder as he went by. I felt a cold shudder shoot down to my ankles. I glanced at my watch. 8:46.

"Where's Oz?"

The question startled me. It was Mayra. I didn't see or hear her coming. Talk about stealthy.

"He went to use the phone."

"Again? You know Freddie I'm worried about him."

"How so?"

"He..hold up, Chulito, silencio, here he comes."

Man, Velleto was walking towards the table like it was the last mile. Whatever he was involved in was deep. Six feet deep.

"Sorry, people, but I've got to go." Oz said. "Hospital emergency."

"Tonight?"

"Yes, sweetheart. Some complications with a patient. I'll probably be gone all night. I am sorry to spoil your evening."

"That's okay," she said, "at least, I've got Freddie to keep me company."

"And take her home," I volunteered.

Oz smiled, kissed his wife and grabbed his coat.

"Thanks Freddie.. for everything. Don't worry about the bill, I've already paid for everything. I kicked in a little extra in case you want something else."

"Okay, honey," Mayra said, "and please lay off the junk food. It's no good for your complexion."

Velleto smiled, I thanked him again and he was off to the races. Mayra and I watched through the opaque window hail a cab. A checkered cab! License plate number NYC 6869! Hold up, I thought, this is way too convenient. Way to convenient.

"You know, Freddie, Oswald's always been able to catch a taxi like that," she said with a snap of the fingers. "It must be that non-New Yorker look."

"The one that says 'take me. I'm a tourist.'"

"Yeah," giggled Mayra, "that one."

"You were about to tell me..."

"Oh yes. I'm worried about Oswald, he hasn't been himself lately."

"How so?"

"He's nervous, overtired, running around. I know something's wrong."

"Well, there has been a lot of tragedy lately."

"It's more than that. I simply cannot put my finger on it but I feel it."

"Please forgive me for getting personal but do you think it's another woman?"

Mayra laughed. It was the laugh of the beautiful; the ones who know they are what mortals try to attain, not betray.

"Our sex life is fine, Chulito, Oswald's not going anywhere."

"Whipped, huh?"

"You can check the lashes on his back if you don't believe me."

Lord knows I did.

"Then what then? Business?"

"Oswald is the head of Angelo Pharmaceutical but he has good people who help him run it."

"Who are they?" .

"I don't know them all. There's Javier Canseco who we met at Harvard. Roberto Concepion, Tito Sabes.."

My alarm went up. All Latinos. I felt ashamed. Instead of being proud, I was thinking like a white racist cop.

"A lot of hombres there, huh?"

"Oh yes," Mayra said proudly. "It was Oz's idea. He wanted to break the white white-collar ceiling. I thought it was a great gesture."

I checked my watch and nodded. Almost 9:00. Time to leave.

"You ready, chica?"

"Almost."

She handed me a piece of paper. It was a check for $7,000. Made out to me. I surprised myself. I didn't jump up and down. This shit was becoming old-hat.

"What's this for?"

More motherfucking deja-vu.

"For all you done and ..an advance for what I'd like you to

do."

"Which is?"

She rubbed her palms together.

"I'd like you to find out what's bothering my husband. Now, I'm not your typical snoopy wife. I trust my husband. But I can't help but feel he's in something over his head. He's in trouble..I know it."

Women's intuition. Tough to beat it. And the seven grand.

"I'll look into it on one condition."

"Yes?"

"That the truth, no matter how painful it may be, comes out. Pardon my words, Mayra, but if Oswald's into something bad, I don't want a whitewashing. Nothing's getting swept under a rug."

She seemed confused but agreed.

"All I want is the truth," she said.

"Bueno, then let's go."

We got up from our table. While I helped her on with her coat, I scanned the scene. No Juanita in sight. Must have been her break, I thought as I put on my coat.

"Where's your girl?" asked Mayra as we headed towards the door.

"I was just thinking about her. I don't know."

"Hey, speaking of pussies, when are you going to pick up your cat?"

"Mayra! I'm aghast."

"What? I'm a happily married woman. I can be raunchy too."

"But to be so blatant.. it's like looking at the Flying Nun soaring above you and noticing she's wearing crotchless panties."

"Nobody told you to look up her dress."

"For a lover of the sky, such sights cannot be helped."

"Bullshit, Freddie, c'mon now, when are you going take Macha?"

"In a little while."

"Make it soon, will'ya, that cat doesn't like me."

"How could anyone dislike you?"

"I don't know but this gato from hell does and I want it out of my house."

Wow, she was serious.

"Soon," I pledged, "soon."

"Good," said Mayra, "Uh-oh, Freddie ..."

I looked at the door. There, in the shadows, was Blondie, smirking triumphantly next to an outline of The Incredible Hulk in what appeared to be a double-breasted suit. She had that lover's lean. I wasn't too worried, with my coat opened and my sport jacket unbuttoned, good ol' two-twenty wasn't far away.

"Thinkin' about that gun, eh, wiseguy."

I knew that voice. It was ...Magilla! Be respectful, Freddie, I told myself.

"Not anymore, Paisan, how are you?"

He stepped into the light, duck-tail pomp and all. No shiny suit this time. Guess he saved it for off-hours.

"Good, Freddie. I heard there was a problem."

He turned to a perspiring Blondie. She was shifting a brick. "You had a problem with my friend here?"

He made it sound like a threat.

"I didn't know it was one of your friends?" she pleaded.

Blondie appeared terrified. Good. I guess she thought fucking the big lug made her invulnerable. Wrong-0."

I'll deal with you later." He looked at me. "Freddie, please accept my apologies. It won't happen again."

 "Certainly, but..."

"But, nothing!" he thundered.

The place quieted down while he was shooting the evil eye at Blondie. I'd seen that look at Pepito's. T'wasn't fun.

"I guarantee you, Freddie, it will never happen again. You have my word."

That was plenty good enough for moi.

"Of course it won't." I tapped him on the girder he called an arm. "Thank you for your kindness."

"From now on, whenever you come here, your money is no good." He patted his massive chest. "Remember, you're always a guest of Jimmy Vee."

So that was his name. And he called me 'a guest." Looked

like the Boys were putting on the ritz in ritzy Tribeca.

"Thank you. Mr. Vee...," I started to say.

"Jimmy," he said with shrugged shoulders as he stuck out his hand.

I shook it. It was like picking up a cow with your pinky.

"Jimmy," I said, "I thank you sincerely."

"Anything, anytime."

"Thank you again and I'll be seeing you."

I led Mayra out, took a step before ducking my head back in. Jimmy moved close.

"And say hello to our special friend," I whispered.

"I will," he said as the door closed.

Mayra and I began heading to her place. She had an odd look on her face.

"You know that guy?" she asked.

I nodded.

"From where?" she demanded.

"University," I said.

"He went to NYU?"

"Uh-huh," I said before changing the subject.

It wasn't a complete lie. Jimmy Vee had schooled me on one thing; the Don must've really liked me or else he and I would have tussled. The respect he gave me was the sort a non-Cugine only gets if the word is out. It looked like Pepito was right. I had made an impression and, thank the Lord, it was a favorable one.

TWENTY-SIX

I WAS OUT and about early the following morning. When my bank opened for business at nine I was the first to step through the door. After I dropped off my seven grand deposit, I grabbed a quick cup of java and then headed over to the two-five to meet with O' Reilly.

We ducked into a broom closet of an office for privacy. We took no chances. Even with no windows and a locked door, we spoke in ultra-hushed tones. I told him about the returning checkered cab, gave him the license number and asked him to check it. I also hipped him about the 8:45 phone call Oz had made from Yolanda 'sand suggested a trace. (If, as I suspected, Yolanda's was a mob front, this wouldn't be too difficult. The cops would already have their bugs in.) Cursing myself for my own inherited prejudice, I asked O'Reilly to look into the Angelo Pharmaceutical Company. I didn't tell him to do it because of the heavy Hispanic involvement. Rather, I stressed the Oswald factor: a physician with a direct drug processing outlet.

"You think Velleto's dirty, scribbler?"

"I don't know."

O'Reilly gave me a wan smirk.

"You're lying," he said.

"If so, only to myself."

"Okay, I'll tell the Trimble twins to investigate this stuff. I'll call you to set up a meet to deliver the info. I don't trust talking about this crap on the phone."

"Gotcha,"

"Now what are you gonna do?"

"I'm placing a tail on Velleto,"

"Who, you?"

I flung out my arms. Ta-da!

"Who else?" I said.

O'Reilly gave me a headshake.

"That's dangerous, scribbler. One, he knows you. What you look like. Two, and no offense, you're a babe in the woods. Surveillance is an art. Takes more than one man. This is your maiden case. First time around the block. And your batting average so far ain't been all-star material."

"Granted but you gotta learn sometime."

"It can kill you when you learn on the job."

I thought of Cary.

"It can kill you when you have a degree," I said.

"The odds are better then."

"Look, O'Reilly. I don't have a death wish. I just want to follow him for a couple of nights to get a feel for the guy. I promise you I won't walk into any dangerous situations. In fact, if they come up you'll be the first flatfoot I call."

He chuckled. It was a sad chuckle. He reached into his inside jacket pocket, took out an old black leather wallet, opened it and pulled out a white business card. He asked if I had a pen. I did and gave it to him. He wrote on the back of the card and then handed it to me. I peered at it.

"There's my beeper, cell phone and home number," he said, "you get in trouble you call,"

I was kinda touched.

"Thanks," I said. "Now can I have my pen back?"

O'Reilly placed it inside his jacket with his wallet.

"When you call, you get the pen."

"Oh, the old police strong-arm scheme."

"What ever works, Freddie, what ever works."

TWENTY-SEVEN

O'REILLY HAD STRUCK a chord so I asked my uncle Chubby to join me for a night of watching. He dug the notion of playing Kato to my Britt so, after filling him in on the case thus far, we found ourselves at 7:00 PM up the block from Velleto's Franklin Street digs sitting and shivering in the dark in his sky-blue 1985 Monte Carlo's leather-influenced bucket seats with hero sandwiches in our laps. Cokes on the floor and the heater off. At least, the rocket- powered engine was silent.

"Coño, Tio, could you have picked a more ostentatious car?"

He took a big bite of a Ham and Swiss.

"No," he mumbled.

"I was being sarcastic, you know."

"I wasn't."

"Well, don't you think Velleto's gonna spot this car?"

I took a sip of soda. "I mean, Ronnie Milsap could spot this car."

"What is that? What's a Ronnie Milsap?"

"A sightless country singer."

"What's wrong with you? You're making blind jokes now? And worse than that, obscure blind jokes?"

"Ronnie Milsap is not obscure."

"He is to me."

"I dare say that if you mentioned the name over the airwaves over 85% of this country would know the name Ronnie Milsap."

"Doesn't mean shit to me." He took another bite. "Now if you said Stevie Wonder, I'd get it. Jose 'Light My Fire' Feliciano, I'd get it. Brother Ray Charles, most definitely but this Milksack guy.."

"Milsap," I corrected.

"Whatever. This guy doesn't influence my knowledge of him, therefore, he does not exist and, ergo, the joke, the attempt at humorism, does not work."

"I do not laugh, therefore, you are not a real person."

"Exactly, nephew. Now do you know any good cripple jokes?"

Thankfully, I saw Velleto exit his building. Wearing a single-breasted raincoat, he was carrying a briefcase in his left hand. Gucci, I'd bet. His head bobbed up and down as he inspected the street scene. Satisfied, he stepped into the street, right arm raised at a 45 degree angle to give any passing taxis the universal New Yorker 'cab heil' sign.

"That's the guy," I told my uncle.

Chubby snapped into action, wrapping up his sandwich, finishing up his Coke, flinging it out the window and turning the ignition key. The car engine roared with the decibel level of a gas-tank explosion. I prayed Velleto didn't jump out of his skin much less notice.

"Jesus, Chubby," I said while half-ducking under the dashboard. "The fucking thing sounds like a sonic boom."

"Yeah," he grinned. "Had my baby tuned up this morning. Doesn't she sounds special?"

"Special Ed, maybe. Remember we don't want to draw attention."

"Then get your fuckin' head from under the dash. You want people to think you're giving me head?"

"It wouldn't be a bad idea if a fucking brain came along with it. "

"Oh, shut the fuck ...hey, your homeboy just got a ride."

I took a peek. The heil worked. Usually did for white people.

"That the cab we're looking for, Freddie?"

I looked. This was a sleek 1996 Dodge not a beat-up checkered.

"Nah. This is a new one. Let's follow anyway."

"Gotcha."

The taxi took off with us right behind. Made a right on Canal. So did we. Traffic heading east was light. We were so close I could see Velleto in the back. He appeared to be reading.

"Think he's going to Brooklyn?" asked Chubby.

"Don't think so," I answered. "Let's hang back a little. I don't want him to spot us."

"Nephew," Chubby said with finality, "people only spot something when they're expecting it. Otherwise, they are some oblivious motherfuckers."

"Okay, okay," I said. "I trust you."

"You never could lie well," he said.

"Told you I liked your ex-wife."

"Which one?"

"All of them...watch it, he's turning."

The cab made a left on the Bowery then a quick right on Houston Street.

"I think this guy's heading for the FDR Drive," Chubby said.

He was right. They took Houston past the Lower East Side's Alphabet City and made a left on to the Drive.

"Going uptown," said my uncle.

I wondered if Velleto would be so stupid as to go to the Barrio. Then I remembered I had no proof he'd ever been there. At least not to 320 East 124th Street. But I could always hope.

Chubby carefully followed the taxi. He stayed about three car-lengths behind to allow for traffic and give us some flexibility in getting off an exit quickly. I gazed out the window at the East River. Even in the cold moonlight, the River's waves seemed inviting. I wished I could go for a swim and wash my hands of this case.

"Getting off, nephew."

I snapped to. We were coming up to the 96th Street exit ramp and the cab's right blinker was on. We did the same.

"Stay close," I urged.

"Not a problem."

The taxi eased off the FDR, hung a left at a green light on 96th and then another at Second Avenue. We just made that one.

"Doubling back, hub," I said. "Y 'know, we've been lucky with these lights. Chubs."

"Tell me about it."

The red light caught both of us on 91st and Second.

"Hey," said Chubby, "isn't this the block Cousin David lived on?"

"Close enough, he was on 90th between Third and Second."

"Man," he said wistfully, "Those were good years."

I thought about it. I was a teenage kid from Brooklyn running wild in the streets of Manhattan with my family. No responsibilities; no disappointments.

"Yeah," I said, "the best."

Velleto's cab made a left on 90th.

"I think I know where he's going now," I said.

I was right. The cab let Oswald out on the southwest corner of 90th, right in front of a non-descript five-story brick building with blacked-out windows. The door was oak with one of those speakeasy peepholes that slide back and forth. He knocked three times, the slit slid open and he stated his name. The thick door opened and he quickly scurried inside. Now to the hurrying passer-by, the place had all the charm of a scab factory. Only the two foot long, half a foot high, aged bronze plaque over the lone door gave away the establishment's identity: DARBY HOSPITAL. Maybe this was a work night for Velleto, I thought. Maybe.

Chubby and I decided to hang around a couple of hours to make sure. We found a parking spot a block away on the northeast side of 89th and right across the avenue from a deli. I stopped in and, with the kindness of my heart, treated my uncle to a host of snacks and goodies.

At about eleven, after we had shot the shit - and realized we had to shit - we were ready to call it a night when we saw Oswald stepped out of sainted Darby. Wearing just a sweater, his hands jammed into his pockets, he looked plenty anxious as he trod downtown.

"Where's he going dressed like that?" asked Chubby,

"Wherever it is," I answered, "it ain't far."

It wasn't. Velleto, half-shivering, jogged to the deli.

"Oh, Doctor Vee's hungry," said Chubby.

Doctor Vee? Vee. Don't tell me, I thought as I put my hands over my eyes. Nah, this schmuck couldn't be related to Jimmy Vee. Or could he? This I had to check.

It turned out later, he wasn't. I found out the next day, during a short trip to the library, the Vee in Jimmy Vee stood for Vicious. (As in Sid.) His last name was really Gagilano. But I got so wrapped up there, I almost missed a key clue. Thank god my uncle was with me.

"Ahhh, the tucker's just having a junk food attack," he said. Look at the shit he's buying."

I rubbed my temples and looked. Maybe I could get a cheap chuckle out of this, I thought. No way. Not after what I saw.

Velleto was buying bags and bags of Cheez Doodles. Must have had seven of them on the counter. I had a feeble notion. Maybe, I thought, he's buying them for an office party. At a plastic surgery shop for the rich? I don't think so. Then I saw him open a bag up at the counter, finish it and then open another. The way he tore into those Doodles was like a hungry wolf ripping into a chicken. No, they were all for the cheese homeboy. I knew it.

"Let's go home. Chubs."

"You sure, Freddie? You got what you need?"

"Oh yeah," I said as he fired up the car.

When we pulled out into traffic, I was one serene individual. With Cheez Doodles as bait. I'd caught the rat. I had put the Wizard at 320 East 124th Street, at last.

TWENTY-EIGHT

"...**LET ME GET** this straight, Freddie. You want me to arrest Velleto because he eats Cheez Doodles?!"

I was sitting with O'Reilly at the back of Pepito's in the Throne of Honor. It was lunchtime and he wasn't quite in agreement with my arraignment suggestion. I tried to explain further.

"Listen to me, will ya? What did we find at 320?"

"You mean besides bodies and crack vials?"

"Yes."

He shrugged.

"Alright, we found a couple of empty Cheez Doodles bags."

"A couple? C'mon, O'Reilly, there were more bags in there then you'd find in any neighborhood bodega."

"Granted, but that does not give me the right to arrest the man. You usually need a little more than that."

"Not up here, " I snorted.

"I don't play that game," he snorted as he adjusted his sport jacket.

"With wealthy white doctors?" I sneered.

"With anybody."

"His wife mentioned at dinner the other night that Velleto eats junk food whenever he's stressed. He tells me he's under

153

extreme pressure. His brother-in-law is found dead in a building with Cheez Doodles bags all around him. That's got to be probable cause."

"You watch too much television, scribbler. It's not enough."

I threw up my hands.

"Okay, Columbo, what do you have?"

O'Reilly moved in closer.

"I followed up on that license plate you gave me. Belongs to a private car company in Flushing, Queens which specializes in funny cars. "

"Funny cars?"

"Yeah, you know what I mean. You want to hire a hearse for a gag date or a school bus, these guys will get it for you."

"So you have to make an appointment with these guys?"

"Exactly."

"What's the company's name?"

"Mystery Car. And dig their ad line: 'Why you want our cars is a mystery."

"Kooky."

"I called the dispatcher over there to get a line on the driver. Did you ever see him?"

"No."

"I made up a tale. Told him that the driver might have been a witness to a hit-and-run. Some witness remembered seeing a checkered cab with a 6869 license plate in the area. The dispatcher told me that was impossible."

"Why?"

"None of the drivers had signed 6869 out that evening."

"How come?"

"It been in the shop for a month."

"Does Mystery Cab do their own repairs?"

"Not on their premises," said O'Reilly.

"They farm them out to a sister garage. The Y.B.R garage."

"Where?"

"A hundred and twenty-fifth and Second Avenue."

Right around the corner from Cary's killing. I asked him if he checked it out.

"Uh-huh. This morning. Seemed legit. Found out some of

our guys go there."

"That's another good reason not to talk on the phone."

"Thought about that too," said O'Reilly. "But I didn't see a checkered cab in there."

"Then get a warrant."

"Freddie, I'm not going to get a warrant just to look for a checkered cab," he said impatiently. "You need more than that."

"Man, am I sick of that tune."

He shifted gears.

"Did you ever hear of a guy named Harve Breindel?"

"No," I said. "Who's he?"

"He owns Mystery and YBR. Wealthy. Runs the Breindel Foundation. Born into it. Father owned lots of different businesses. They call it diversifying now, don't they? Forty-ish. No record. Fairly straight guy in the community. Hosts fundraisers for poor kids. Lives in Douglaston. And when I got a computer printout on the Angelo Pharma-what-ical Company, his name was listed on the Board of Directors. Turns out he's a Harvard grad. Just like your boy."

Finally, a connection. A chum from college. And he wasn't a Latino. Man, I felt ashamed.

"Anything else?"

"Yeah," he said. "The twins called in a few favors and checked on that number Velleto called from Yolanda's. The call went to a disco in Chelsea called The Perpetual Erection. Ever heard of it?"

"Heard of it? Hell, I spend my whole life trying to find it."

"No jokes, Freddie. Do you know it?"

"Yeah. Supposed to be the hottest place in town."

"Velleto called an office number there. Now the club's run by a guy named Edgar Lorenz. Shady character. Unfortunately for him, not as shady as he wishes."

"Mob wannabe?"

O'Reilly nodded.

"Let just say he's an unmade man. I had to bust his head about three years ago when he tried to open up a couple of social clubs around here."

"In El Barrio?"

"Yeah, they were for rich white boys who wanted to slum and get it on with some minority meat."

"'Get it on.' Well, I'm impressed."

O'Reilly tugged on his lapels.

"Hey, man. I'm chill. I'm fresh. I'm dope. I'm butter. I'm jiggy with it."

"No doubt about it."

"Lorenz got the hint and headed downtown. Now, he may fool them assholes but not me. I know he doesn't have the capital to open a spot. He's fronting, Freddie."

Fronting? Man, O'Reilly was really into this. He was on a regular fuzzroll.

"Do tell, cop-man."

"So I checked the owner of record, the parent company who's paying the bills…"

"… and you got…"

"… the Breindel Foundation."

"Oh, shit."

He threw up his hands.

"But so far, Freddie, it's all circumstantial."

"But we are getting closer."

"That we are. In fact, the twins are going to the Perpetual Erection tonight to do some recon on Lorenz."

"The twins. Undercover. That I'd like to see."

"Me too, " he said. "What are you going to do tonight?"

"Follow Velleto… say that reminds me, could you check on a place called the Darby Hospital on York and 90th? That's where Velleto works."

"Okay…hey, where's our lunch?"

"Pepito was kind enough to hold it while we talked."

I signaled him to bring over the plates.

"That was nice of him," said O'Reilly.

"Sure was."

"You know, there are a lot of rumors about this place being a mob front."

"Really," I said, "Well that's news to me."

Pepito dropped off two hot plates of arroz con pollo. The steam from them suckers made my eyebrows molt. O'Reilly and I scarfed up a forkful, placed it in our mouth and let loose with a couple of satisfied sighs.

"Oh, one more thing," I said with a garbled mouthful, "What does the YBR stand for?"

He reached in his blazer for his notes.

"The Yellow Brick Road," he said.

TWENTY-NINE

IT WAS LATER that night - our second evening of shadowing Velleto - that we finally struck a bullseye. At about 9:00, Chubby and I were trying to figure out exactly who came up with the idea of the sheepskin condom and what ghoulish way this was to take advantage of old wives tales when he saw Velleto leave his apartment. This time he was all duded up, wearing a sharp dark brown suit with a black banded collar shirt and matching shoes. Draped over his left arm was a black leather trench and in his right was the Gucci briefcase.

"I think the Doc's making a house call tonight," said my uncle.

I wondered what house it was. House of style? House of commons? House of pancakes? House of cards? Whorehouse? House of pain? House of wax? House music all nite long?

"Peep this shit, nephew."

It was ye olde checkered cab pulling into the curb. It was a moment which needed a cliche so I came up with one.

"Bingo," I said with my baritone Barry White growl.

Velleto got into the back seat and the cab took off. So did we.

"Be careful. Chubs, I don't want this guy to make us,"

"No shit, Sherlock," he said as he eased off the accelerator.

"Just hang back on this guy."

158

It was pretty much a straight run with hardly any turns. We found ourselves red-lighted on Sixth Avenue and 14th about two cars behind them.

"Well, we know one thing, Freddie. He ain't going to the hospital tonight,"

"No he's not," I said.

The overhead traffic light turned green and we were in motion once more. As the cars ambled down the avenue, I gazed through the windshield at the buildings lining the oncoming blocks. I could see on the northeast corner of 21st street, on the roof of the building, was a large cast-iron construction derrick with a five yard-wide hook swaying in the wind from its arm. I pointed it out to Chubby.

"He's heading there," I told him.

"What's that? A construction site?"

"Used to be. Now it's a club. The Perpetual Erection."

He laughed so hard I thought he was going to crash the car.

"Oh, those blancos. They are so funny."

Just as I suspected, the checkered cab pulled up right at the club. Oswald vaulted out, the taxi sped off only to be caught at the light.

There was no time to waste. I unbuckled my seatbelt - a must in the Monte Carlo - and turned to my uncle.

"Follow the cab," I told him, "I'm staying with Oswald."

I told him I'd call him later at the bar. He told me to be careful and took off after the taxi.

The sidewalk was packed with the usual club mixture of outrageously garbed (we-are-talkin'-your-chain-links-leggings-and-mascara-here-people) revelers and your mentally bankrupt bridge-and-tunnel denizens trying to get in. Velleto, however, was obviously expected. The second he got out of the cab, four steroid-loving doormen cleared a path for him and he disappeared inside.

The immediate question was how was I going to get in? I scanned my outfit: black jeans, shoes, socks, turtleneck sweater, pea coat and gun. I kinda sorta had the artiste/dockworker thing going on. I didn't think it would work here. Then I had a brain flash.

I went up to one of the doormen. He was your typical mastodon with bulky biceps and a neck the size of a city mailbox. Vain, too. As cold as it was, all Kong had on were jeans, sneaks and a T-shirt with PERPETUAL ERECTION across the front. (I had news for him, I thought, if he kept drinking those steroid milkshakes that T-shirt would be a check he'd never cash.) Perpetually smoothing back his gelled, shoulder-length mane, he also had on a thick gold chain with a medallion that read BENSONHURST RULES. Perfect.

"Wait in line, fuckhead," he growled at me.

I kept staring straight at him until he lumbered closer.

"I said, wait in line, nigger or what ever the fuck you are," he told me.

I gave him my best Book-lynn accent. "Do you know who you're talkin' to, asshole?"

He sneered. I guess he thought it was gonna be ass-kicking time shortly.

"No, boy, who?" he mocked.

"Jimmy Vee sent me, you fuckface cocksucker. That's who."

The hulk flinched. That was the last name he expected to hear from this ornery sambo/spic. He repeated Jimmy Vee's name but it wasn't the same. He'd lost a lot of his bluster.

"You know whom I'm talkin' about, you swollen faggot," I said. "Now I don't want to have to disturb the man and tell him that some beefy punk motherfucker is disrupting our business."

Like Carol Merrill used to open the curtains on Let's Make A Deal, I opened my coat and let him see the Sig Sauer P220. He blanched.

"But I will if I have to," I continued. "Now he won't like it and I won't like it and when we're through with you, you won't like it. Unnerstand, you rat bastard?"

Even in the freezing cold, the beads of sweat were forming on Gigantor's face. He was experiencing some thing new; he was having to think.

"Maybe I should call somebody to check on this," he whined.

"You call the wrong person, goombah, I will personally fuck your mother's dead body."

His right eye began to twitch.

"My m-m-mother's n-n-not d-d-dead," he stammered.

"Not yet," I said before patting my gunside. "That all depends on your next move, shit-for-brains."

He ran his hands through his hair then turned to look at his fellow beasts. They were busy ogling the scantily-garbed chicks in the crowd.

"I'm losing patience, buttfuck, and you've run outta time," I said before heading for the door.

I passed him by but then came face-to-chest with his compatriots. Guess they tired of the pavement freak show.

"You wanna get outta my way?" I asked the three muscle-bound stooges.

"Is this guy okay. Patsy?" one of them asked.

I turned back to look at him. He was petrified.

"Yeah...Patsy," I taunted, "am I...okay?"

He bobbed his head up and down. Textbook jitters.

"Don't obstruct the gentleman's path," he beseeched, "let him in. He's a friend of ours."

THIRTY

WHEN YOU STEPPED inside the Perpetual Erection and made your way through the long,: dark, narrow entrance hallway past the bored coatcheck girl to the actual - and packed - dance floor, the effect was like a bucket of Cherry Garcia tossed in your face. First, the music boomed so loud you could actually feel it in your chest, I pitied anyone who came in with a pacemaker. Second, the place itself was as big as an aircraft hangar. The decor was Spartan with a series of steel girders crisscrossing along the bare brick walls. Concrete slabs were tactically deployed throughout the disco for use as go-go stages. The bar at the far end consisted of three cement slats stacked up table-style with the liquor bottles stashed in a hole in the wall. (Obviously, the PE's designer's muse was early Bedrock.)

This was a true terpsichorean throng. Except for the occasional beer bottle held aloft on the dance floor, there was not a soul around the bar. Whatever the feeling on temperance sure didn't extend to cigarettes. The thick smoke rising to the ceiling was so omnipresent I thought I was in a Jack The Ripper movie set in Victorian London.

Behind the bar was a nylon ladder. The ladder went up to a cage. In the cage was a deejay spinning his records on two turntables. Aside from some basic electrical equipment and a few vinyl platters, there was nothing else in there. The ladder seemed to be the only way in and out of the cage. I felt sorry for the dee jay that had to go to the john. Deaf and on dialysis is no way to end up your golden years.

To the left of the bar, in the corner, was a closed door. The only door in the place. I decided to investigate. (That's part of my job, right?) I'd made it three-quarters of the way there when I felt two hands on each of my arms. The bouncers? My head did the lambada swivel. To my shock, I was being accosted by two drag queens with heavy black eye makeup, rosy cheeks, ruby-red lipstick, red corsets, black fishnet pantyhose and fire-red fuck me pumps.

"Thanks, but I've seen Rocky Horror already, fellas," I said.

"Going..."

"..somewhere.."

"...Freddie?"

Double take. Could it be?

"The Trimble Twins?" I asked.

"That is..."

"..right, it's.."

"...us. We're…"

"..here.."

"...undercover. "

"Well, that answers my next inquiry," I said.

I filled them in on following Velleto. They said they spotted him when he came in and that he had headed to the open door in the corner, and had not come out.

"Well, c'mon then," I said, "let's check it out."

"But we're..."

"..not.."

"...armed."

"You guys didn't even stick a derringer in your cleavage?"

They shook their cute little heads,

"It wouldn't…"

"..be.."

"...regulation. "

"Well, I'm packed," I said before opening my coat. "Now I

don't care if you Ru-cops cover me with your fuckin' heels but we are going in there. Right?"

"Right," they chimed in unison.

"Good," I said. "C'mon, you bitches. Let's go to work."

The sign above the door was a small one. It said: OFFICE/BATHROOM. (Talk about conservation of space!) I recognized the lettering. It was the same as the sign over Darby Hospital. Coincidence? I didn't think so.

I went in first, with Cagney and Lacey close behind on my flanks. It was a tiny alcove with a steel door on the left next to a solitary, splotched commode.

"How's that for colonic stress," I whispered to the twins.

"How..."

"..unsanitary.."

"...too."

Tad watched the outer door while Tod and I put our ears to the steel one. There were only two men talking. Their voices were so muffled we could only make out snatches of conversation.

"....be patient, Oz,...."

"....they 're on to me...."

"....can't postpone delivery...."

"....call Breindel...."

"....have to confirm with your superior...."

"....is our superior...."

"....the night after next...."

"....gives the go-ahead...."

"....usual spot...."

"....not giving the orders...."

"....have to trust Edgar...."

Finger snap. Tod and I turned to Tad. He was pointing to the outer doorknob. Slowly turning. I waved them back towards the commode. Sat down on the toilet seat and heard the most horrible squishing sound. Almost puked on the spot. Pulled Tod sideways down in my lap. Tad caught the hint and sprinted towards my other side. Put his hands all over my face to conceal my identity. Perfect. I could see them, they couldn't see me.

Some grunge Joe College kid walked in to the room. About twenty. Hair shaved at the sides, bleached blonde up top. Wearing fucked-up, torn and tattered 501's, Airwalks and a Bilko T-shirt. Went to the steel door and banged three times, paused, then five times. Paid us no mind.

The door opened. Heavy-set white guy, dark-brown hair, unibrow comes out. Wearing a white shirt open to the navel - showing eight gold chain and his tits - pleated and cuffed dark-blue slacks. Gives us the fish-eye, sucks his teeth, then turns to Joe College to speak.

"Whaddya want?"

Joe looked at the twins nervously. Tod rubbed my head harder. I let out a fake moan. Disgusted, Fatso waved us off.

"Just a bunch of preverts, now, what's up?'

"Mr. Loring..."

"Edgar, kid. My father's Mr. Loring."

The kid took a second to figure it out. Edgar rolled his eyes.

"Edgar, the kids need more Sunset."

"Sure they do, those greedy little bastards, how much more?"

"About 200."

Lorenz paused a moment to calculate in his mind. "I'll expect twenty thou at the end of the night."

"I've got to go," said a voice behind Lorenz.

Oh fuck, I thought, Velleto. I grabbed the Trimble twins closer than life.

Lorenz turned inside to say something but Velleto shot past.

"C'mon, Wiz," pleaded Lorenz.

"No, I must go," said Velleto.

Thank God his back was to us.

"I have to report in," he said.

"Then I'll see ya when I see ya," winked Lorenz.

Velleto harrumphed then made like a banana and split. Lorenz turned his focus back on the kid.

"200, huh," he said, "then I expect 20 grand at the end of the night."

"You know I wouldn't screw you over, Edgar."

"Better not or I'll have Patsy, Larry, Manny and Baby

personally stomp your nuts till they bleed,"

Baby? I thought. Go figure.

Then Lorenz produced a plastic bag. The bag was full of multicolored pills. He tossed it to the kid. Looked like a flying rainbow.

The kid caught it, jetted and slammed the outer door behind him. Lorenz turned to us.

"Hey, you sweet-meats want some Sunset?" He pointed towards the door. "There's more where that came from."

"No thank you," said Tod.

"We've already got our groove on," said Tad.

"Whatever," he said with curled lips, "just don't come on my floor, you fucking pansies."

Then he closed the door.

We waited until we heard the sound of a lock turning before we got up. Then we counted to ten and started to tiptoe out of the alcove.

The music was deafening. Wall to wall teens. I felt old. There was good news. Velleto wasn't anywhere in sight. The twins and I commandeered a corner to talk. I noticed the college kid schmoozing on the dance floor, slipping something in the dancers' hands and getting what seemed to be a twenty dollar bill in return. I pointed it out to the twins. They were perturbed at my actions.

"Could you..."

"..be more.."

"...careful?"

"Sure I could," I said, "but this restless style of mine seems to work best for me. Now, relax. Nobody saw me. Now here's what I want you to do. I want you to buy some of the shit the kid's selling."

"But..."

"..we.."

"...can't"

"Why not? Didn't we go through this? You guys are undercover. You can do anything. Just look at your outfits."

"But we..."

"..don't have.."

"…any money."

"What?" I asked. "Why not?"

"We used…"

"..all of our.."

"…money to…"

"..get in.."

"…this place."

"Where were you keeping this money?"

I felt like a scolding grandmother.

"In…"

"..our.."

"…cleavage."

"Both cups?"

"Yes, this…"

"..is a.."

"…very…"

"..expensive.."

"…place."

"Boys, couldn't you have tucked some mad money in the tops of your pantyhose?"

"And…"

"..ruin our.."

"line?"

"Vanity. Sheer vanity"

I pulled 60 bucks out of my pockets.

"Here," I said, "pay me back later. Just buy the stuff, get it tested then give me a call."

"Okay," they said.

"Remember, whatever they're planning takes place the night after next. That doesn't give us much time so let's stay in touch."

The twins looked puzzled.

"Aren't we…"

"..supposed to tell.."

"…you that?"

"Yeah, but I knew the way you guys sat on top of me and stroked me that you wanted me to take charge. You know, to be the top in this relationship."

The twins were non-plussed.

"We'll... "

"..call you.."

"...later."

"Okay," I said, "just make sure it's business related, you big galoots,"

I pulled a Patsy and didn't stay for their reactions. Just walked outta da joint. Speaking of Patsy, I saw him on the sidewalk. Gave him the old extended index finger and thumb as I strutted on by. The way he clutched his chest, you'd thought I shot him. Ah well, there's always tomorrow.

THIRTY-ONE

DID'YA EVER HAVE one of those nights where you didn't feel like going home? When it didn't matter or not whether you had somebody waiting there for you or not; you just didn't want to be there. And if you didn't have anybody waiting for you at home then you definitely didn't want to be there.

Well, that's how I felt. I knew I had to call Chubby at the Barcelona later but that's all I had on the schedule, I wasn't going to try to tail Velleto. I had no idea where he was and I was on foot. It was late, close to midnight, and I had nobody to call to ask if they wanted to come out and play.

So I started walking. No particular direction in mind. (At least, consciously.) The night was brisk, the foot traffic light and the time was all mine. I put my collar up, my hands in my pockets and started to stroll.

It took me a few blocks before I realized I was heading downtown but I thought that was a cool thing. The further away from my apartment, from my jail cell, the better. Jail cell? Was that how I really felt? Was that what this case was all about? A parole. A reprieve. And who put me behind bars? My parents? Clarice? Cary? Me?

Me. It was all my doing, wasn't it? I'd shut myself off from the world leaving myself emotionally marooned in a bandbox of an apartment in El Barrio. I had had dreams once. I'd had ambitions, too. I had emotions as well as insecurities but I had let the insecurities win out and turn me into a bitter bitch of a man.

Somehow, I had to right the wrong; get back on track; blaze the trail; navigate the ship; drive the car; grab hold of the reins; ride the pony; tame the savage beast. I had to become a person again. Be human. Be whole.

A tooting car horn woke me out of my self-help reverie. By not watching where I was going. I'd stepped off the sidewalk, into the street and right in front of a speeding Jeep Grand Cherokee. The horn blared; I barely jumped out the way. The driver called me an stupid asshole; I thanked him for his concern and went on my miserable way.

Where was I anyway? I looked around. Bumper-to-bumper traffic, ill-mannered drivers, steel-shuttered businesses and fast-food joints with signs in Mandarin. I didn't walk over a bridge so I wasn't in Flushing. I was on Canal Street not far from the Holland Tunnel.

Didn't know if I had the guts to do what I wanted to do. Surprised myself by doing it anyway. Walked over to Yolanda's and went in.

Blondie was there, standing by the floor with some wraparound shades on. Those things never hide what really happened. Looked like she'd been smacked around pretty hard. Like to say I was sorry it happened but I can't lie. I wasn't. My theory is you want to play with mob fire, don't be surprised if you get burned, beaned or knocked off.

Needless to say, she recognized me. Flinched just like Patsy. I got the same perverse kick out of it.

"Mr. Vee's not in tonight," she quivered.

Mister? I guess she got demoted, I thought.

"I'm not here to see Jimmy," I said before glancing down at the floor, (God, I felt so shy.) "I'm here to see Juanita."

Her eyebrows shot up.

"Juanita Benjamin? The waitress?"

So her last name was Benjamin..

"Yes," I said. "The one that's employed here. The waitress."

I couldn't help but glare at Blondie. She seemed to bring out the Norman Bates in me.

"I meant no disrespect by my statement...sir," she stammered. "It's just that I'm surprised."

Hard stare.

"And I mean no disrespect by this statement, " I said, "but can we cut the chatter and just get Miss Benjamin over here."

"Certainly!"

Blondie called over a waiter with a fish-face and told him to get Juanita. He informed Blondie that Juanita had finished her shift and was cleaning up in the back and getting ready to leave.

"Get her anyway," she commanded.

He did.

It took a couple of minutes before Juanita sauntered onto the scene but it was well worth it. She walked like a matador entering the ring, full of confidence and bravado. Miss Thing was wearing a faded blue denim jacket with matching pants and red cowboy boots with a matching sweatshirt. So round, so firm, so fully proportioned. Ooh-wee, I swear, dungarees never looked so good. On top of her head, framing her beautiful brown face, was a New York Mets cap. Perfect, I thought, let's play ball.

Juanita walked past Blondie without even an acknowledgement and stood in front of me. She was an inch away and, with the boots, three inches higher. I felt like a mountaineer waiting to climb Everest.

"You rang?" she purred.

"I rang, knocked and sent up a flare," I responded.

"You must be in trouble," she smirked.

I answered with more emotion then I wanted to.

"More than you know," I said.

She caught it and grabbed my hand.

"Let's go," she said.

Her touch was kinetic. When I gazed into her face, it was like there was no one else in the room, in the city, in the universe. I'd grown to fear the power a woman could hold over me. I'd been made a fool, a cuckold, alone. But not with

Juanita. I don't know if it was the Amazon thing; all I know is I wanted to surrender. To her.

As if she read my thoughts, she held it a bit tighter. Her kindly eyes sparkled in the dim light. Take me to your leader, I thought. She gave a yank and led the way. Meekly, happily, I followed her outdoors.

We stood outside Yolanda's for a few minutes. Juanita seemed deep in thought. There was a steady breeze now blowing off the Hudson River. Simultaneously, she and I started to shiver.

"I don't know where we've going, doll," I said, "but I only hope we get there quick."

"That's what I'm debating," she said, "I'm not sure where we're going to go."

She looked away.

"I mean, I just met you. I don't know you in any meaningful way. Yet I'm willing to dis my boss, hold your hand and stand here freezing while debating in my head about a future with you."

"Welcome to the ills of attraction."

"Oh, don't patronize me, Freddie," she snapped. "This is more than a simple attraction and you know it. I work in the public sector. I see attractive men every single night. Gorgeous men. This is something else."

"What do you need to know?" I sighed.

"Everything. "

"I don't know everything and this is my life we're talking about so why don't we just pare it down to a few hundred essential questions."

"Fine, smart-butt. Are you disease-free?"

"Except for an unnatural captivation with this city, I most certainly am. How's about you?'

"Yes," she said. "What do you do?"

"For a living? I'm a private investigator."

"Isn't that dangerous work?"

"So's being the only Black waitress in an overpriced bistro."

"Speaking of that, how do you know Jimmy Vee?"

"We've bumped into each other through the years?"

"Do you know he beat the hell out of Melissa because of the way she treated you?"

"Is that her name? No, I didn't."

"Well, how do you feel about it?"

"I'm all broken up about it."

"That's a smart-ass answer."

"I can be a smart-ass guy."

"I noticed. How do you feel about violence towards women?"

"The same way I feel about violence towards men," I said, "I'm anti."

"Would you ever hit a woman?"

"Not unless she slugged me first."

"Don't you know you're never supposed to hit a woman no matter what?"

"Whoever came up with that notion never got decked by a woman from my neighborhood," I said.

I knew I was coming across too harshly so I decided to soften the tack.

"Listen, sweetheart. I don't like wife-abusers, women-beaters, gay bashers, rapists and child molesters. As far as I'm concerned, they should be sautéed in a frying pan on national television. Better yet, make it a pay-per-view event then take the proceeds and the time to educate people not to fuck with other people. My credo is a simple one: don't lay hands on me and I won't lay hands on you. Call it self-preservation, call it childish, call it stupid. The bottom line is I've managed to survive for over thirty-odd years in this city by that code and for a minority man that's pretty fucking good,"

There were tears running down Juanita's face. It was my turn to squeeze her hand.

"What happened, honey," I inquired, "did your last boyfriend kick. .were you in an abusive relationship?"

She nodded. I asked her what did she do to get out of it.

"I waited until he was asleep then I took a baseball bat to both his arms and legs."

Ironsided the sucker.

"He all right?"

"I don't know," she said. "I didn't stick around to find out."
Just up and left him. Ballsy.

"Where'd this happen?"

"Portland."

"Maine or Oregon?"

"Oregon."

"Took all your stuff and moved here."

"Kinda sorta."

"You're a brave woman," I said, "I like that."

I wiped away a tear on her cheek. Rubbed it on my lapel. It got me a smile.

"I also like when you smile," I said.

"I like to find stuff to smile about," she answered.

"Look. I'm going to lay it on the line," I told her. "I haven't been too successful with women. I've been hurt. I've been betrayed. And I haven't been with one for a loooong time. That accounts for my residual hostility. Which you no doubt have noticed. But I like you. Don't ask me why? It's been such a short time that it shouldn't make sense. But I genuinely do. And it's mucho importante to me that you like me too. I want to know more about you and I'm willing to take the time to learn. But tonight...tonight I want to be with you. To spend some time with you. It doesn't have to be sexual, although that would be nice, but it has to be intimate. I don't want to bullshit you, Juanita, I simply want to talk, laugh, huddle, cuddle and, if we're both lucky, kiss. If you can handle that....fine. If you can't. I'd rather you told me now so I can draw up my suicide pact."

I held her face in my hands.

"Whaddya think?"

"Now, Freddie," she said deliciously, "would you respect me if, the very first night we spent together, we slept together?"

I eased real close to her wonderful mouth.

"Respect you? Hell, I'd be admiring you for your great taste."

"Speaking of taste," she whispered while putting her arms around me, "why don't we get that kiss out of the way right now?"

I snaked my arms around her back.

"I knew I liked your style," I retorted.

I could feel Juanita's massive breasts heaving against my chest. I suddenly felt short...of breath.

Logistically, I hadn't had to kiss upwards since the 10th grade with Annie Lopez. (Back then, even in my bubble-toed platform shoes, I had to tippy-toe to get to those chops.) So I did what I did then: closed my eyes, bent my head back at a 45 degree angle - just call me Scarlet - and opened my big mouth to a 25 percent capacity.

When I felt Juanita's warm, wet tongue slowly exploring my mouth, my knees buckled, my eyes rolled back, my pores opened, my skin heated, my hearing faded down to the sound of a heartbeat and Little Freddie started to roar. (It's a good thing I was wearing a long coat or I would have been arrested for wielding a concealed weapon.) Goddamn, I thought. I'm having a fuckin' orgasm from a kiss.

It was the sort of kiss you lean your neck into; full of passion and want. When our lips parted and we opened our eyes, so sure was I that our ardor was some type of combustible force, I swear I expected to see a new cosmos encircling us. Instead, I got Juanita with a quizzical expression on her wonderful face.

"Freddie," she said, "What the hell is this gunk on your back?"

Then she showed me her hands. They had a greenish-brown substance smeared on them. In horror, I tossed off my coat to the pavement. There, towards the lower third, was some alien substance in the shape of a toilet seat on it. Both of us got real ill real fast.

"I think," said Juanita, "we best be going before we throw up like rabid dogs in the middle of the street."

"Plus, it never looks too good to spew in front of a restaurant," I said.

She started jogging. I followed. Turned out she lived only three blocks away - on Varick - in one of the few tenements in Tribeca. (I guess that's why she wore such a light jacket to work.) Gingerly, using fingertips only, she took her keys out of her jacket pocket and unlocked the front door.

"You sure got a funny method to get a girl to take you to her apartment, Freddie," she stated while unlocking the hallway door.

I had to agree so I pulled a Howdy-Doody and idiotically grinned.

We walked up the next four flights in silence. It wasn't a favorable sign. Another rule of mine in these times of crisis is when in doubt do Jerry Lewis. When we stopped in front of an apartment door I, the ace detective, presumed to be hers since she put a key in the lock, I let loose with my best impression.

"Hey laaadddy," I screeched.

"You poor, deluded child," deadpanned Juanita as she popped the lock. "Anyways," she added as she opened the door and flipped on the overhead light, "I was a Dino woman myself."

Some people in New York have small apartments, some have bandboxes they call studios. They would've seemed like estates next to Juanita's. Her pad - and that was about the size of it - was literally one room. Going clockwise around the room from the entrance, there was room for a gingham sofa-bed, a CD radio player atop a five tier bookcase which housed tapes, compact discs, magazines and hardcovers, a closet, a television on a four-drawer dresser, a closet with an empty hanger on it, another closet and then a small half-table with two chairs with a mini-icebox underneath it.

The good news should have been that there was a lot of closet space. Three of them, to be exact. The bad? Well, only one of them was a real closet. The one to the left of the TV was converted into a bathroom with a tiny double-fauceted sink which looked like it came right out of Barbie's playhouse, a stand-up shower a yard wide in circumference and an oddly-angled commode that unless you placed your legs under the sink while sitting on it, you couldn't close the door to do your bizness in private. (As it was, as an intestinal boomer, I could easily imagine, unless the TV volume was jacked to the max, some very embarrassing bathroom excursions.)

The one located to the far right of the boob tube, past the genuine closet and to the immediate left of the half-table, had been reborn as a makeshift kitchen. Bisected by a steel shelf, a miniature four burner electric stove took up the bottom half and assorted spices and canned goods reigned on top.

"Isn't that a fire hazard?" I asked.

"That's why I work in a restaurant," she said, "I certainly don't want to cook in here."

She took my coat and headed to the bathroom.

"Excuse me while I wash my hands and.... this."

Somehow, she managed to squish her fine healthy frame into the toilet and closed the door. As I heard the water running, I ventured - what venture? Two steps tops! - over to the telephone.

"Mind if I make a call?" I shouted to the door.

"As long as it isn't to your wife," was the muffled reply.

I punched in the number of the Barcelona. My uncle picked up on the first ring.

"Speak to me," he said.

"I'm speaking. I'm speaking."

There was relief in his voice. (Well, what in my family passes for relief.)

"So asshole, you finally decided to call. Where the fuck are you?"

"At a ladyfriend's house."

"That's okay, Freddie, " shouted Juanita from behind the door, "you can tell whoever my name."

"Listening in, you pulchritudinous snooper," I shouted back.

"Who is that?" screamed my uncle. "What's going on?"

"That is the wonderful maiden. Miss Juanita Benjamin, in whose apartment I am calling you from."

"Flattery will get you somewhere, Freddie," she said.

"You mean, you have a chance at a piece of pussy, nephew? Oh my lord, how I prayed for this day."

"Very funny," I snorted. "Where did your friend go?"

"Oh, he wasn't feeling well, so he stopped at the clinic."

Darby Hospital again.

"Really, " I said. "Is he going to stay overnight?"

"No, just a couple of hours. Remember, he has to take his car to the shop in the morning."

Back at YBR. I was going to nail that fucker.

"Gracias, Tio,"

"Will I see you tonight?"

"Not if I can.. .help it."

"That's my boy," laughed Chubby. "Call me whenever you get in. Your apartment, that is."

He hung up just as Juanita came out of the bathroom and tossed my coat back to me. It was wet but clean.

"Who was that?"

"My uncle..."

Satisfied that I no longer was a walking billboard for Son of the Green Slime, I tossed my coat back. She hung it up for me while I ran into the bathroom to wash my hands.

"...I love him very much," I said.

Juanita was sitting on the sofa when I got out. She pounded the cushion next to her. Like a gazelle with MS, I leapfrogged into her arms. She laughed, we kissed, we caressed, clothes got ripped off, limbs got spread, protection got put on and then the earth stopped moving again.

Later that night I awoke being cradled by still-slumbering Juanita. The lights were out, the bed was open and we were lying naked on top of what-were-crisp-now-sweaty cotton sheets. My head was nestled right between her breasts. (If her big, brown nipples had been spikes then a blind man would now be telling you this story.) Like a slow windshield wiper, I licked them both, back and forth, forth and back, savoring the sweet, salty taste of each one with every swipe of my tongue. Her dark areola were as broad as her nipples were large. (They reminded me of IHOP's nickel-sized flapjacks.) I opened my mouth as wide as their width and then, one at a time, carefully, leisurely sucked.

I could feel Juanita's nipples harden under my lip-o-suction technique. Each passing of my tongue brought a sharper intake of my breath. When I thought she had almost fully roused, I shifted my emphasis downward, spotting her tummy with wet kisses and love bites, placing my tongue in her belly button and jabbing it as Little Freddie had done her Candyland a few hours earlier.

(I'd told her that Candyland sounded like an amusement park. She responded by opening her legs as wide as outspread as Cinerama and suggesting I try a ride. I did and didn't want to get off.)

She began to awaken. I gave her belly a kiss and her button a back tongue fare-thee-well and headed south to Candyland. It had been so long I had forgotten how much I loved a woman's pubic hair. See, I'm not a believer in defoliation. I'm a naturalist. I don't care if a woman has a Don King hairdo down there just as long as it's clean. As Shakespeare said in one of his censored sonnets: If the hirsute cavern is real and tight, then it's a meal all right.

I simply enjoy the feel of it, the curly texture, the way it cushions your nose - ah, the smell of it! - and tickles your cheeks. I also adore the way it sops up a woman's juices, her sweat, her passion. And to prove that God was a creator with a master plan, I love the way than I can use it to wipe off any excess saliva or perspiration on my lips. (Talk about your wetnaps!)

While nibbling on Juanita's inner thighs, I used my nose as a divining rod to determine precisely where the slits and the folds were. Then, savoring each flavorful drop, I started my Candyland oral quest in search of the magic button of undistilled ecstasy.

My tongue dipped and dabbed until it found its destination. I knew I reached it when I suddenly felt Juanita's hands grip both sides of my head.

"Right there." she hoarsely murmured while using my noggin as an NBA double-palm job. "A smart-ass and a cunning linguist, too. I love it."

After proving my ambidexterity by caressing Juanita's breasts while providing mouth-to-nappy-dugout resuscitation, I slipped my hands down her torso and slithered them - thank my maker for those sweaty sheets - under her thick, muscular butt cheeks.

As I pulled them up towards my face, she wriggled down the bed, kicked her legs up and onto my shoulders and began to grind her pelvis in my face. Sabor! I love a woman who not only know what she wants, I thought, but how she wants it.

My face was drenched. I felt Juanita's juices dripping off my chin onto my neck. After cupping her cheeks and slightly spreading them, my right hand glided up and under Candyland. Just like a good funkateer should, I extended my index finger and pinky and slowly, gently, inserted them into her pussy and anus.

Juanita gasped - the fit was so tight - and started to buck as I rocked my fingers back and forth. Her moans got louder with each lick and wrist flick. Her hands covered my ears as she began to compress my head like a supermarket melon. I couldn't hear a thing. I remember thinking that if this is how Beethoven went deaf then he must have been a fortunate man.

Then somewhere in the aural distance, I could make out the fruit of my oral favors. Juanita shouted out my name as if it were the most important name in the world and ram-jammed her chochita to the back of my throat. Her kitten and bunghole began to contract and spasm uncontrollably. As I eased them out, she was still screaming my name. I felt honored and, for a night, special.

Still breathing like an asthmatic in a dust storm, she reached down and yanked me up from my chin. Then she kissed me even better than she had the whole night before. When we stopped playing test the tonsils, she licked off all of the juice on my face. (As the joke goes: I must've looked like a glazed donut.)

"Wow, Freddie," she said breathlessly, "what a way to wake up a woman up." She kissed my forehead. "You were terrific. Thank you. "

"It was my pleasure," I muttered through novocained jaws.

"My gosh, what inspired you?," asked Juanita. "The last thing I remember was we were knocked out asleep. Then I wake up and your head is between my legs doing such wonderful things," she chuckled. "I mean, what happened? And what do I do to make certain it happens again?"

"You really want to know?"

"Yes, of course."

"I just figured we'd fucked before. Now it was time to make

love. "

Juanita's eyes softened. She reached out to hug me. I hugged back.

"Freddie, that is so sweet...tell me baby, what can I do for you?"

I exhaled.

"This is gonna sound strange coming from a guy but ..ah.. can you just keep holding me?"

"Of course, my baby, of course," Juanita said.

Then she let out a little satisfied laugh and held on even tighter. It was the tenderest vise I'd ever been in and I didn't ever want to be let go.

THIRTY-TWO

WHEN I STAGGERED into the Barcelona Bar early the next afternoon I'd looked as if I'd gone 12 rounds with Tyson. (That's Mike, not the model.) My back was bent, my legs were rubbery and my eyes were the law firm of swollen and bloodshot. I'd had so many orgasms the night before that by morning, like a kid's basketball pump, all Little Freddie was shooting was air.

Thankfully, Miss Juanita had finally had mercy on my diminished capacities and my sensually emaciated body and fell asleep at around ten in the morning. I forced myself up, wedged my body into the shower and let the lukewarm water run awhile in an attempt to partially resuscitate my beaten flesh.

It worked. I managed to fall into my duds and write the still-sleeping, still-smiling Juanita a mush note full of love and appreciation before I bid her adieu with a kiss on the forehead. Then I lurched to the nearest subway station and took the train home.

My uncle was behind the bar with Papo expecting me. He had that goofy prideful look on his face that older male family members get when they know a younger male family member has gotten laid. (Or as Chubby's generation would call it: getting lucky.)

"Look at my nephew, Papo," he said, "my boy got some act-shun last night. Look he can barely walk. A wo-man put a tough whipping on my man's man last night!"

The way he talked you'd have thought I'd discovered a cure for cancer instead of just getting fucked. Then I thought about it. Up until last night, the former was a lot more likely than the latter.

"Let's get right to it. Chubby," I said.

He did.

Seems like the cabbie drove straight to Darby, got out and went inside. I asked what he looked like.

"White guy, about six feet, two-eighty..."

"A big boy," I interjected.

"Real big," said Chubby, "and not much fat either. He's balding in the back, thick mustache and goatee. Dressed okay for a cabbie."

"Meaning?"

"Meaning he had on a blue three-piece pinstripe suit and wingtips. Looked more like a stockbroker than a hack."

Stockbroker type. Businessman. Breindel. Eight to five it was Mister Investment himself. But why?

"How long did he stay in the hospital?"

"About two hours. Then he headed uptown to the YBR. Drove the car inside and that's the last I saw of him."

"How long did you wait?"

"Ninety minutes," he said, "then I had to come here to take care of my business."

"Understood and not a criticism," I assured.

I told him what'd happened at the PE.

"Sounds like there's dissension in the ranks," Chubby said.

The bar door flew open. It was O'Reilly.

"Somebody say something about a pension," he said.

"Dissension, not pension, flatfoot," laughed Chubby.

"What gives anyway? I haven't seen this much of you since me and my boys used to chase you away from that girl you dug. What was her name?"

"Magda Maria Mercedes Martinez," grinned O'Reilly,

"And whatever happened to her?" asked my uncle.

"I married her."

"Once again the strength of our race's blood gets watered down, nephew."

Retreating to higher ground, I changed the subject. I repeated to O'Reilly what I'd told my uncle and what he'd told me. Then I asked him what he'd found out about Breindel.

"Well, first off. Chubby here just gave a fairly good description of Breindel hisself. Second, according to a couple of my sources downtown, Breindel's in a cashflow girdle and the money's getting tighter and tighter."

"Then it would make sense for him to get into the drug game," I said. "Low overhead and big monetary returns."

"Now you told me that Lorenz was pushing some pills at the club called Sunshine?"

"Sunset," I corrected, "and he was charging twenty bucks a pop. Now he had a dealer guarantee him a twenty grand return. And it wasn't the first time that night that kid had gotten shit from Lorenz. Suppose he had a few more guys pulling double shifts selling Sunset. Let's say, conservatively, five guys are doing this for a week. Then Lorenz and Breindel are clearing..."

"One million, four hundred thousand," said Papo.

Papo? We all stared at him.

"I always thought this guy was a mute," said O'Reilly.

"Nah," offered Chubby, "just your ordinary introverted financial genius. Why do you think I have him behind the bar?"

"Good point," I said.

I looked at Papo.

"You don't happen to do tax work too, do you?"

He nodded sagely.

"Good, we'll talk later."

"You'll talk later," corrected my uncle.

"Anyway, you see what I'm saying," I said. "Add that with whatever money they were making from selling crack at 320 East 120th and you've got a two-prong assault at solving your financial problems. "

"Hitler got burnt fighting a war on two fronts," said Chubby.

"And so will Breindel," I told him before turning to O'Reilly. "You find out about Velleto's cashflow?"

He let out a sigh.

"Oh yeah, Velleto's in much better shape. Angelo Pharma-who-cal has a majority interest in a bunch of hospitals located in such major cities as Boston, Providence, Los Angeles, Palm Beach, Chicago and San Francisco."

"Where the high-rollers are," said Chubby.

"Uh-huh," said O'Reilly. "The one in Los Angeles the company owns outright. It's named after the one they founded here in town."

"The Darby Hospital?" I asked.

"You got it. It's named after his mom's maiden name."

"Hospitals," said Chubby. "Don't they have a high overhead?"

"Normally," said O'Reilly. "But Velleto's sly. He has tax-shelters galore. The most convenient, the most profitable one is something called the Carrington Foundation."

The Carrington Foundation. Mayra's baby. Oh shit.

"But that's not all," said O'Reilly. "In the last year. The Carrington Foundation has been buying up inner-city real estate in major cities for the purpose of renovating tenements to house low- income unwed mamas and their bastard offspring."

"Don't tell me," I said. "The Carrington Foundation is the owner of 320 East 124th."

"Give the gentleman a cigar," he said, "and do you know who's been overseeing these property purchases?"

Please, Lord, not Mayra Molina. Not her. I asked O'Reilly who it was.

"A special advisor appointed by Dr. Oswald Velleto himself; Mr. Harve Breindel."

Nice and neat.

"Whatever is going on is going on in Darby Hospital," I said. "I can feel it."

"Certainly sounds like a lot of activity goes on over there," said O'Reilly.

"Too much," asserted Chubby. "And it's gonna go down

tomorrow evening. "

"Yeah," nodded O'Reilly. "Freddie, we've got to talk about how we're going to handle this."

We, huh? I must've come a long way, baby, I thought. I tugged at my clothing, Man, I felt rank, I hadda change.

"Guys, can we talk about this in a few? I just wanna run upstairs to my apartment and put on a clean set of clothes."

"Thank god," said my uncle. O'Reilly sniffed the air.

"I did smell something foul when I came in, scribbler but I was thinking something in the deceased rodent family."

"You were just smelling your upper lip, copper. Now everybody stay put. I'll be right back."

"We have to," said Chubby, "that odor is paralyzing."

"Bottle that shit and I guarantee we'd have kicked Saddam's ass," said Papo.

"Papo!" I screamed. "Twice in one afternoon. This is a day to remember."

It turned out that I was right. But, unfortunately, for nefarious reasons.

THIRTY-THREE

I RAN UPSTAIRS, stripped off my funky fashions and jumped in the shower for the second time that day. (Not a record but dangerously close.) As I lathered up, I thought all sorts of naughty things about Juanita but I must have been missing a penile synapse or something cause Little Freddie just wasn't responding. (It was like stroking overcooked linguini.)

I realized I didn't have the ability to reanimate the dead so I stepped out to towel off. Well, you know what always happens then. That's right, the phone rang. I wrapped my terrycloth around my held-in waist Tarzan-style and ran into the room to answer it. Surprise, surprise. It was Mayra Molina Velleto. And she sounded scared.

"Omigod, Freddie, thank God you're home," she babbled, "thank God!"

"Take it easy, hermana, what's the panic?"

"Remember at dinner, I told you something was wrong with Oswald, remember?"

"Of course I do. You said he was in over his head."

"Well, now he's drowning. He came home early this morning ranting and raving about being forced to do things he didn't want to do. . . . .How he feared for our safety. . . .. .That Junior's death was a message to us not to back out... How he'd given you a retainer to protect me. ...Is that true?"

Uh-oh. It was truth or consequences time. No contest. I'll take consequences for ten thou, Alex.

"Nah, he must have been hysterical," I said.

"But he sounded so sincere, Freddie."

"Sounded to me like he was sincerely rambling."

"Maybe but he got so scared I got frightened. I begged him to share with me what was going on but he wouldn't. He kept repeating that if anything happened to him tonight I should run straight to you. Then he ran out of the house without telling me where he was going. I don't understand what happening. We don't have an enemy in the world."

Tonight? What the fuck was going on tonight?

"Mayra, are you sure he was talking about this evening?"

"Oh yes. He was babbling about hoping to get through another night. He said how he wanted to live to see another dawn with me but he had to do something this evening... a meeting, he said... that he might never return from. And then he showed me a gun."

"A gun? What kind of a gun?"

"A nine-millimeter. Actually, he showed me two of them. He gave one to me. He said he'd gotten them for our protection and I had to be prepared to fight like him. He said he'd use it in a second if he had to. He said I had to be the same. I had to be ready to kill for survival. Chulito, I'm so afraid! I've never seen him like this. He terrified me! He terrified me!"

Mayra started to sob uncontrollably. I didn't know what to do. My head was swimming with so much information and I've never been adept at comforting women. Especially over a telephone. Still, I tried to get her to remain focused. I asked her was there anything else Oswald said that she thought might be helpful. If he'd mentioned any of his planned whereabouts for the evening.

"No, no, Chulito, nothing. Ohmigod, do you think Oswald's mixed up in Junior 's death? Oh god," she bawled, "I'll never forgive myself."

"Calma, calma. " I said in my best Lite-FM voice, "let's not speculate, hon. We don't know that's true."

Man, I was lying through my in-need-of-bridgework teeth. In my rush-to-judgement, I was convinced Oz was involved but I didn't want to alarm Mayra. She was close to the edge as it was. All she kept repeating was 'omigod, omigod.' Since He wasn't answering, I decided to keep the queries coming.

"Mayra, honey, think about it. Is there anywhere he'd go? Does he have any good friends in town?"

"Well," she sniffled, "his only amigo in town is an old college roommate Harve Breindel."

Yowsah, yowsah. Hell, I almost dropped my towel. (What a treat that would've been for my across-the-avenue neighbors.)

"How well do you know this Breindel?"

"We've socialized, that's about it. Oswald considers him a best buddy. You know that male bonding thing you guys like to do. Football games. Baseball games. Bowling. They get together to do those things."

"They're close?"

"Close enough that Oz has him on the board of directors for everything we do. And, I've got to say, he's been a help. Especially in real estate. He has us all over the place,"

"Breindel handles that end?"

"Him and Oswald. I prefer to deal with the people, the girls, the kids." Mayra's tone shifted. "Why are you asking all this stuff about Harve?"

"Just curious, doll. Covering all the bases."

"I guess so. That reminds me I should give him a call."

"Breindel? How come?"

"To tell him my husband's not well enough to see him tonight."

Yes, and it counts! I tried to sound calm as I asked Mayra what Breindel and Velleto were meeting about. I think I half-succeeded.

"They were supposed to meet to discuss the budget for the Carrington Foundation's upcoming fiscal year."

"Really," I croaked, "where at?"

"At the Darby Hospital about nine," she said.

"Okay, honey. I'm gonna tell you a few things and I want you to stay quiet and don't flip out. I don't want you calling anybody. I don't want you picking up the phone unless it's me or someone I've said is alright. I'm also going to get police protection for you. Now, if a cop knocks on your door, even if he or she's in uniform, ask him to produce ID and a note from me authorizing that officer to be there. Do you remember my handwriting?"

"It's sort of like a serial killer's."

"Well, it hasn't gotten any better but, in this case, that's good. My evil scrawl simply cannot be duplicated by any other human so you'll be certain I sent them. I'll call later to make sure. Otherwise stay away from the door."

"What if Oswald calls?"

"Well, that's your judgement call. You can talk to him, try to get him to come in to the police for protection. If that happens, I'll be there if you want me to be."

"Protection? Is it that bad, Chulito?"

"Could be. If he does call while the policia are there, notify them. Maybe they can put on a trace. Whatever you do, don't tell him the cops are there. We don't want to scare him off or make him do something rash."

"Where will you be?"

"As close as a phone call away. I'm gonna hit the streets and get some information. Hopefully we'll bring your husband back home to you."

And not in a bodybag, I thought.

"Chulito, thank you. Thank you for everything."

"Don't thank me yet. Let's see what happens. Meanwhile, stay put and no phone calls."

"Okay. I'll speak to you later?"

"Count on it," I said as she hung up.

So, I'd misunderstood what I'd overheard at the PE. The meet wasn't set for tomorrow's twilight time: it was tonight. I was certain about one thing. Visiting hours at Darby Hospital began at nine and I wasn't going to miss them.

THIRTY-FOUR

I'D CHANGED BACK into my usual funereal outfit - boy, does black clothing keep down those laundry bills - and rushed down to the Barcelona where Chubby, Papo and O'Reilly were impatiently waiting,

"Goddam, Freddie," exclaimed my uncle, "I know dead people who dress quicker than you."

"There was a necessary pause in the action," I answered,

"What?"

"Mayra Velleto called me."

That got their attention. I ran down everything she told me. Then I told them my plan.

"You want Tod to tail Breindel?" asked O'Reilly.

"And Tad to follow Lorenz," I affirmed.

"Why?"

"Because I'm convinced they're meeting with Velleto tonight at Darby."

"You believe his wife's story then?"

I got slightly insulted.

"Of course, I do."

"He's just checking, nephew," said Chubby. "Chill out."

"That's what I always tell him," said O'Reilly. "Chill."

"Okay, okay. The twins allow us some flexibility in case one or none of them shows up for the meeting tonight."

I pointed to O'Reilly.

"Either way you and I will be staking out the hospital this evening. If the Trimbles spot Velleto, Breindel and Loring someplace else - which I doubt - they will then contact us by telephone, radio, fax or smoke signal and stay put until we get there."

"'They' and 'we,'" said O'Reilly. "Sure sounds like you're running this investigation now."

"I'm not running it," I said, "just offering an assist you simply cannot refuse. Any objections?"

He threw up his hands. "Nah, you got as much right to nail them as I do."

"More," I said, "and I'm exercising my right under close police parental supervision."

"Granted."

"Now," I said, "if I am correct about Darby being the hot spot, then the twins will meet us there and we can organize an armed assault on the premises."

"Hold it, nephew, this isn't a United States Embassy or a pro-life rally we're talking about," said Chubby. "This is a hospital. What about probable cause?"

"I got that covered, too. If all the players show up there on time as I suspect they will, then at 9:10, an anonymous call will be placed to police headquarters that there is some suspicious activity going on at the Darby Hospital. The Trimbles and O'Reilly and I will just happen to be getting together for dinner close by at the time so they will be the first to respond to the call."

"What about you being there?" asked Chubby.

"He decided to assist as a good citizen," answered O'Reilly.

"Precisely," I said, "That gives us a ten minute head start to get inside and see exactly what's going down."

"Even more with the response time," said O'Reilly.

"So you want me to make the call?" asked Chubby.

"Fuck no," I said. "With your tendency to ham up, the cops will think you're the son of the unibomber or something kind of surgical stalker. I want Papo to make this call. No one in the outside world has ever heard him speak so there's no possible way anyone will recognize his voice."

I turned to Papo and asked him if he would he do it. He nodded yes. Guess he was saving his voice for his evening performance. I thanked him profusely then faced my uncle.

"Chubs, what you can do is drive Papo to a pay phone in the neighborhood so that if there's a trace it matches the area. After that, get the fuck out of there and I'll call you later at the bar."

"Sounds good," said O'Reilly, "anything else?"

I remembered Mayra and her situation. I asked O'Reilly if there were any cops he trusted who could watch her until we were through. He said he thought he could finesse it through official channels and get a couple of friends to do it on the clock. I gave him a note to give to them to verify I'd sent them. He peered at the letter intently. I casually inquired if anything was wrong.

"It's your handwriting," he said.

"What about it?"

"It's God-awful," he laughed.

"I supposed I hit the nail on the head when I started calling you 'scribbler.' Or maybe you hit the nail on your hand."

"You're a regular fuckin' psychic. In fact, after you're done talking to the Trimbles, why don't you drop a line to Dionne Warwick?"

"I already have," he said while getting up, "in my mind, where it counts."

"Cheaper, too," opined Chubby.

O'Reilly, the cop Kreskin, said his good-byes and booked. But not before reminding me to meet him outside at eight. I concurred.

"You're going through with this," asked Chubby, "huh?"

"Got to."

Using both hands, he yanked out a big sealed box from under the bar then used a carpet knife to open it.

"Then you're gonna wear this," he said.

A bulletproof vest. My uncle was giving me a freakin' bulletproof vest. God love him.

"Thanks," I said. "I'm really overwhelmed by your kindness.

It's such a thoughtful gift."

"Gift, my ass! I added the cost onto your bar bill."

"Oh," I said sourly. "Well, it is the thought that counts."

"Yeah." He put his hand on my shoulder. "And I want to see you around to pay it. "

"Well," I said soberly, "I half-agree with you."

THIRTY-FIVE

IT WAS EIGHT on the dot when O'Reilly picked me up in front of my building. He was driving his deliberately undistinctive-every-New-Yorker-knows-this-is-a-cop's-car blue four-door Dodge sedan. This was only topped by his battle garb. Under a beat-up black bomber jacket, he had on a blue-black heavy cotton jumpsuit with a zipper down to about his breast bone to show his badge on a steel- linked necklace. Oh yeah, his black combat boots looked in worse shape than his jacket. I gave him a concerned look as I shimmied into the passenger's seat and off we went. It took a few blocks before he seized the bait.

"What 's the matter?" he asked. "What's with the face?"

"It's that outfit of yours."

"What's wrong with it?"

"It looks like you should be humming the theme from SWAT."

"Good. It's meant to look that way so I don't get accidentally shot by a fellow officer. You should've have worn something that identifies you."

"Like an 'I'm with Stupid' T-shirt?"

"Very funny, scribbler," he sneered. "Lucky for you I used my newly-found psychic powers and tossed a couple of NYPD baseball caps in the back seat."

"You mean I finally made to the majors. Skip? To the Big Show?"

"Why no, kid, we needed a ballboy," he chuckled. "The hat comes with the job."

"Ballman," I corrected, "And I do plenty fine carrying my own big, massive black bat, thank you very much,"

"Maybe, but I hear you cork."

"It's better than using pine tar for a lubricant," I said, "and, anyways, you can't be too careful these days."

"Speaking of careful, here we are."

The time was half-past eight. O'Reilly parked the car on the northwest corner of 89th. Gave us a clear view to the hospital. I broke out a pack of gum and had a good chew while O'Reilly filled me in on everything.

The twins were tailing Breindel and Lorenz. They were calling into O'Reilly's cellular phone every hour on the hour. I asked if there was any test results on Sunset. There were. The result: a never-before-seen synthetic heroin/amphetamine hybrid. Highly addictive. Highly.

"Looks like the Angelo Pharma-suit-ical Company has an unqualified, illegal smash hit on its hands, " said O'Reilly.

"Talk about your rave reviews."

I pointed outside the windshield. Mr. Edgar Lorenz had been to first to arrive.

"Still think I'm wrong, O'Reilly?"

O'Reilly craned his head looking for Tad.

"I never said you was wrong, Freddie. I merely laid out other possibilities. Hey, there's Tad, across the street in the Jeep."

O'Reilly honked his horn twice in short bursts. Trimble acknowledged back by honking back three times before he left his car and headed over to us carrying a backpack full of surveillance goodies in hand. He was wearing the same outfit as O'Reilly except he had on a black leather baseball jacket.

"The clothes are bad enough but what's this with the toots?" I asked. "Cop Morse code?"

"Just signals," said O'Reilly, "in a city this big no one ever notices honking horns."

"Well, if you want to be so subterranean," I said, "next time use car alarms. Nobody ever pays attention to them."

"Hello...guys," said Tad as he slid into the back seat.

"How's it...going?" I asked.

"Fine...fine. Any sign of...my brother?"

"Not...yet," I said.

"...but we'll let you know," chimed in O'Reilly.

"Not...funny," said Tad.

While waiting for Tod - wasn't that a Beckett play? - Tad hesitantly filled us in on Lorenz's day. He went from the club to dinner alone at Tad's Steakhouse - no relation - on Forty-Deuce to here. No other stops. I don't know why but that struck me as strange.

"You'd think a guy trying to pull off a huge drug deal would stop a number of places," I said. "Try to shake a tail or something."

The other guys agreed. Just when we began postulating, Mr. Harve Breindel showed up to be our next contestant on The Jig Is Up. He looked just like Chubby's description. Maybe heavier.

"Portly fellow," I said.

"Stout," said O'Reilly.

"Husky," mused Tod.

"Try fat pig," said a voice from behind us.

We all jumped and pulled our pieces. It was Tad and, yes, dressed just like Tod.

"I feel like I'm Tony Orlando and you guys are Dawn," I said.

"Well, knock three times and tie a yellow burnoose on the old fat pig because all that guy did was stop and eat, stop and eat and stop and eat," spewed Tad bitterly.

"Tad," said O'Reilly, "I'm shocked, I've never seen you so angry."

"I've never seen you put so many words together," I added.

"It only happens when..."

"..he.. "

"...gets pissed off."

"Now, that's the enigmatic Trimble tandem I've grown so

much to admire," I said.

"How many places," asked O'Reilly, "did Breindel go to eat?"

"Five."

"Fast food joints?"

"Yes."

"You know, Freddie, you're right. This doesn't sound like normal behavior before a big deal."

"I told you. How many guys would risk indigestion and diarrhea before something like this.?"

"I…"

"..don't.."

"…like it."

I glanced at my watch, 8:52.

"Time to get ready," I said. "Everybody know the plan?"

"You two are..."

"..going in.."

"...the front."

"Right," said O'Reilly, "and you guys are going to hit the back."

"There's an old loading dock back there," I said, "from the building's old factory days. O'Reilly and I spotted it on the drive here. There's gotta be an entrance into the building, find it, use it and we'll meet you in there somewhere along the way."

"We're counting on the element of surprise," said O'Reilly, "everything this gang has done has been semi-private in public places. They're betting the farm on their flair for concealment and that they're smarter than the average Joe. Let's show 'em they're wrong."

"And let's show 'em quick," I interrupted, "because our guest of honor has arrived."

All heads swiveled towards the hospital entrance. Rapping thrice on the door was the disheveled, distressed, distraught, debased Dr. Oswald Velleto. And his depraved dreams of drug dealing dominance were about to be discovered, dashed, disrupted, dissed and detained by four determined, diligent deputies of due punishment in a dumpy Dodge. (That's including one alliteratively challenged shamus, of course.)

THIRTY-SIX

THE SLAT IN the hospital door slowly slid open.

"Let me in for Chrissakes," shouted Velleto, "it's fucking cold out here."

Those must have been the secret words because, with its rusty iron hinges creaking all the way, the mysterious portal to the Plastic Kingdom flung open to welcome the good doctor home. And with the speed of a descending mousetrap, the door just as quickly slammed shut behind him.

The time was now one minute to nine o'clock. A mere sixty seconds to zero hour.

"Places, everybody," I said, "annnnnd. . . action! "

The Trimble twins put on their NYPD caps, pulled their badge necklaces from under their T-shirts and jumped out the car with guns in hand. As they turned the corner to get to the back, I saw Tad slip on the backpack. Excellent, I thought, we were going to need that stuff later.

I glanced at O'Reilly. He handed me my brand-spanking new NYPD cap. I adjusted the plastic in the back - I'm a second holer - and put it on.

"Looks good," he said. "I don't want to make a habit of this headwear," I said.

"May save your life."

"In some places, may cost me it, also."

He put a steel chain around my neck. It had a badge on it. I lifted it up to the light.

"It's my kid's merit badge," he said with a wink. "In the dark, nobody will be any wiser."

"I'm touched."

"Don't get used to it, though. I want it back when this is all over. Now, let's roll."

We got out and slowly made our way to the entrance.

"You're gonna knock on the door," I asked, "right?"

"I thought you wanted to do it?"

"Listen, when that sentry sees this brown face, we don't stand a chance of getting in."

"You sure you're not playing the race card here, scribbler?"

"Y'know, that term has angered me since the day I first heard it. Does white America think that niggers and spics sit around all day plotting when they're gonna use the race card? What about you all using the trump card on us poor folks? In all my years of living in this city and dealing with all types of people, I have never heard that line of bullshit used by anybody but pasty-faced motherfuckers. I got a question for you: how can we keep playing the race card when y'all got control of the deck?"

"Jesus, Freddie, I was just kidding around. It was a joke not the intro for a polemic."

"There are some things I don't joke about: The race card; Mothers; The fact that you still haven't returned my pen. This is the stuff that keeps me up at night."

"Okay, okay," O'Reilly said as we reached the door, "don't have a cow. Here's your pen."

He reached into his inside pocket and gave it to me. I checked it for bite marks or scratches. Everything seemed in order so I put it in my jacket.

"Jesus, Freddie, I'm sorry if I offended you. Now are you ready to take these fuckers down?"

"Soon as you turn your cap around. No need announcing who we are right now."

O'Reilly gripped the bill and twisted it backwards.

"O'Reilly, hip-hop detective," he muttered.

"Hey, there's an idea for a hit soundtrack."

"Not to mention, four videos." "O'Reilly, you hipster!"

"Hey, I've got two teen-agers. I can funk."

"Two Irish Ricans? Sounds like a cookie."

"Yeah, and I want to see them sweet kids again so guns out."

We unholstered and cocked our weapons. O'Reilly had a nine; me with my two-twenty. Together, I thought, we had two-twenty-nine. God. I felt giddy. It's so strange the silly thoughts that fix in the nervous mind before a major confrontation.

Instinctively, while O'Reilly stood in the center of the door, I shifted, out of sight, to the far left. Just like with Cary, I thought. But this time, I vowed, would be different.

O'Reilly and I made eye contact. The time was now. He knocked on the door three time. His gun was below the peephole's eyeline as the slat's slit slid open. "Who's there?" asked a gruff voice from behind the door.

"Velleto asked me to meet him here," said O'Reilly.

"Who?"

"Cut the shit, asshole," yelled O'Reilly. "Now that son-of-a-bitch and I've got business. Open this door now before I blow this entire motherfucker up!"

"Hey, take it easy," said the voice. "Why don't you come inside while I get him? Just stand back so I can get the door open."

O'Reilly and I had figured these guys weren't going to do any shooting in public. Bad for business. They wanted to do their dirty work behind closed doors. We were right.

The door started to open. The guard was a tall pumped-up blond thug of considerable mass in a gray silk shirt and slacks. (Doesn't anybody hire below-average size muscle anymore?) He was pushing the door with his left hand. His right held a 357.

He flung the door open and was raising his right to point the mag at O'Reilly when I leapt forward and put the cold muzzle of my Sig Sauer on Silky's left temple.

"Police," I said, "drop it or lose it."

He dropped it. O'Reilly, his hat now straight, picked up the mag and stuck it in his holster. It fit too. Then he stuck his gun in the thug's puss. He backed the ape into an empty hallway. We stepped inside and closed the door behind us. The coast wasn't only clear; it was deserted.

"Including Velleto," asked O'Reilly, "how many more?"

"Five," the thug answered, "including Velleto."

Five, I thought. Seemed like a skeleton crew for such an important operation. Maybe there were reinforcements on the way.

"Where are they?"

"The basement."

"How do we get there?"

"It's the green door straight in the back of the hallway."

"Any booby traps, alarms?"

"No sir."

"Ooh, such respect," I said. "Who's upstairs?"

"The post-op patients, night nurses and the lab attendants."

There was a lab upstairs? Things were getting clearer.

"Just you down here?" I asked. "This is probably the first this word has ever been said in regard to you but that sure seems light."

"Fuck you, nigger," he said.

Then Silky spat at me. I swung the butt of my gun at the bridge of his nose. He missed; I didn't. Split his schnozz open from top to tip. Blood spurting all over his bug-spun shirt, Mr. Thug-man buckled and took a knee.

"Police brutality," he said.

The notion brought a smile to O'Reilly's lips. I, instead, dug the two-twenty into his temple.

"You can't file a brutality report from the grave, you peroxide albino whore's cunt," I said. "By the way, what nationality are you?"

"I'm German-Irish."

"Correction," I said, "You kraut mick peroxide albino whore's cunt,"

"C'mon," said O'Reilly, "cool it and cuff him"

We hog-tied the thug, cuffing him behind the back, hands to ankles. O'Reilly reached into his jacket and pulled out a small roll of electrical tape and put it on Thug-man's mouth.

"You sure," I asked, "he won't have any problems breathing?"

"Not since you were kind enough to open his nasal passages."

We started to head towards the back when O'Reilly suddenly turned around, ran towards Thug-man and kicked him hard in the ribs. I could hear the ape's muffled yelps as clear as a sneeze in the New York Public Library.

"Whatcha do that for?" I demanded as we passed the admitting room.

"That was for the half that wasn't Irish," he retorted.

"Wonder if he'll check off bi-racial on his next tax return," I said.

"Not where he's going."

We walked through the waiting room. There were so many portraits of famous folk on the otherwise bare walls I thought we had stepped into some theme-park restaurant. (Planet Plastic. perhaps.) I wondered were they all outpatients or just used as scalpel-attainable examples of beauty.

"Say, Freddie, isn't that a picture of Mr. Ed?"

"Sure is."

"Now, who the hell would want to look like Mr. Ed?"

"Deliberately?"

"Yeah."

"Outside of Catherine the Great, I can't think of anybody."

"That's sick," he said as we stood in front of the green basement door.

"Maybe, it's a form of subliminal organized crime. Hear me out. Velleto and his cronies fix horse races by taking mediocre racehorses and cosmetically alter their appearance so they look like Mr. Ed thereby fostering a warm and fuzzy feeling of familiarity in prospective bettors who wager and lose their shirts on these non-placing nags."

"That's even sicker then drug pushing," said O'Reilly as he placed his hand on the knob. "Let's nab these bestial bastards."

THIRTY-SEVEN

DELICATELY, WE OPENED the green basement door. The lighting was near-nonexistent but it was enough to make out the outline of stairs in front of us. I took a test step. They were like Long John Silver's right leg: made of wood and kinda creaky. This fact duly noted, we lightly and slowly descended.

The stairs were at a steep angle. They seemed to go on for miles. In the distance, I could hear a major argument going on. The people shouting were so angry the words were garbled. (Sounded like a Brando hog calling contest.) Thankfully, it was profanely loud enough to cover our footsteps on the down low.

The discussion stopped exactly when our feet hit the concrete floor. Cautiously, silently, I reached out in front of me. Felt like a brick wall. Seems, the staircase was so long we'd walked all the way to where the building's York Avenue exterior was.

Noise! Behind us! I pivoted around as did O'Reilly. Nothing in sight. Just mumbled profanity. We'd just been revisited by the clamor of agitation. Like two stubby-legged men in a potato-sack race, we staggered ahead at a snail's pace. In the distance was a solitary sliver of light. With each ungainly lurch, it seemed to expand. The decibel level was also rising. We were definitely getting closer to something. But what?

The nearer we got, the cooler, clammier the basement air.

Clearly, the cellar was larger and emptier than any of us could 've hoped to imagine. For quite a while, O'Reilly and I had been trudging on without bumping into a single object. It was like being in a deserted airplane hangar. Only this bad boy was underground.

Head towards the noise, I thought, so I stumbled about like a bat in a brand new belfry. By the number of times he bumped into me, I could tell O'Reilly was having the same problem. At moments, he was so close to me, you'd swear we were Siamese sons of different mamas.

By my judgement, we'd walked way past the above loading dock when I finally made out exactly where the light source was emanating from. It was coming from a rusty iron door which was opened just a hair. Gotta be a sub-basement, I thought. It made sense. Easier to stash things, harder to detect. O'Reilly and I were a yard away from each other and verifying my theory when, out of the darkness, a pair of guns were shoved in our faces.

Game over, I thought. Then I realized I never even got to play. This motherfucker was over from the opening coin flip. That fatalistic line of logic continued in my mind until I heard the soft speaking voices at the other end of the barrel.

"Freddie, O'… "

"..Reilly, is.."

"...that you?"

Praise those double-Y chromosomes. It was the terminating Trimbles themselves. Tad whispered in my ear that, in the few minutes they'd been there, they'd heard five separate voices. Unfortunately, most of that was unintelligible. From the fragments they were able to make out, it appeared a drug exchange was the hot topic of discussion. But they couldn't get any specifics. So, being the anal retentive duo they are, the winsome twins whipped out the tape machine, slithered a mike past a door hinge and recorded the inaudible mess anyway.

After thanking Tad, I pitched to the side like an old man listening through a funnel to see if I could make head or tail of the conversation below. All I got was Velleto describing the cost of a run to, or through downtown. Maybe, I thought, that's where the stuff comes in from. There's the docks, the seaport, the river. All perfect spots for a delivery or a pickup.

I was going to pass my precious pearls of profundity along to my partners but I didn't have time. Regretfully, as soon as I turned to my head to whisper my great discovery, the iron door flew open and there we all stood, in the blinding light, face-to-face, with five armed men.

THIRTY-EIGHT

OKAY, LET THE Maestro set the showdown scene, Hmmmmm. There was Tod on my left, me, O'Reilly, and Tad on his right. Facing us from left to right was an armed stranger who resembled a bulldog, Lorenz, Oz, Breindel and yet another unknown blond gunman. Warehoused behind them was a kaleidoscopic treasure trove of pills and empty crack vials. There we are pointing gats at each other like an outtake from a John Woo flick. Normally, at this juncture, I would've been thinking of something snappy to say like 'this must be ze place.' Not this time. I was too busy making a book on which group looked the most surprised: the Velleto Five or the Perez Quartet. Actually, I knew the answer. It was Oswald and Company.

"Freddie," inquired a stunned, dropped-jaw-and-all Oswald, "what the fuck are you doing here?"

The first thing that came to mind was a typically smart-assed statement that I thought would break the tension. I was wrong.

"You should know, Oz," I said, "You sent for me."

I guess to a fat schnook like Breindel the whole set-up seemed pretty hinky. I mean, here's his compatriot-in-crime Velleto on a first-name basis with one of four armed guys wearing NYPD baseball caps and badges around their necks who've just crashed their secret meeting place and - as we later discovered - distribution center. Velleto, Breindel probably thought, had been acting strange the last couple of weeks. In fact, Harve must've said to himself, he's been edgy since the killing of that cop and the discovery of his brother-in-law's body. The jumpy bastard, the fat man aptly reasoned, has been fighting with Lorenz at the Perpetual Erection and he spends all night arguing with me. Stalling me. Breindel, in all likelihood, added up all this circumstantial information and came up with one conclusion: this rat cocksucker sold me out.

So, as calmly as one reaches for the spices in a kitchen cabinet, Breindel raised his gun - a pearl-handled 357 - to the back of Oz's left ear and splattered his brains all over Edgar Lorenz.

Blinded by brain matter, Lorenz screamed like a baby who's wet his diaper. I cut that shit short with a squeeze of the trigger.

Pop. Pop. In true minimalist fashion, the Trimbles entombed both of the unknown soldiers.

That left O'Reilly and Breindel. They were doing the two-gun two-step, waving their weapons in each other's mug and trying to out-Eastwood the other.

"You're not taking me, copper," said Breindel.

"That went out with Cagney, asshole," retorted O'Reilly.

"Oh yeah, fuck you, shit-for-brains."

"No, fatso, fuck you."

"Fuck your mother, punk."

"Fuck your mother, father and your unfaithful bitch of a wife, tubby."

I glanced at the Trimbles. We seemed to agree that this exchange of ideas had to end. So we all raised our guns and pointed them at Breindel.

"Boys," I said. "Now I don't care if you're quoting Shakespeare, Mamet or Rudy Ray Moore but this shit ends now."

Breindel eye-jiggled us. I saw he was calculating the odds. He had to know they were lower than a Black defendant in Simi Valley. I hoped he'd put the gun down and give up. Then I peeped it. He had that I-don't-give-a-fuck look. (I'd seen it too often on New York subways to miss it.) The others caught it too. The second his wrist tightened, we let the barrage fly. He got off one shot - missed O'Reilly by an inch - before we perforated him.

As what was left of Breindel fell to the floor, we heard something scurrying behind us. We wheeled round to see a Rockette line of about half a hundred armed cops aiming nines at us.

"NYPD!" shouted a tall uniformed man in the middle of the police wolfpack. "Identify yourselves!"

"Detective Tod Trimble, NYPD, Twenty-Fifth Precinct!"

"Detective Tad Trimble, NYPD, Twenty-Fifth Precinct!"

"Detective Joseph O'Reilly, NYPD, Twenty-Fifth Precinct!"

I glanced at my badge and spoke out.

"Private Detective Freddie Perez, Eagle Scout, Troop 140, Sunnyside, Queens."

THIRTY-NINE

IT WAS ANOTHER festive late night in the two-five's famous interrogation room, (It was known on the street as the Motel Criminal cause suspects come in and they don't come out.) Furnished in early Dragnet, it consisted of a large, ancient 6' by 9' rectangular oak table and some matching moldy mud-brown chairs. So many perps had sat in these seats, the varnish had been wiped off by their buttsweat.

Like bad students serving their detention in a study hall closet, we were squished in - shoulder-to-shoulder - at the long end of the table at the far side of the room. (We were so close we could've done precision harmony.) There was Tad Trimble who sat cemented next to O'Reilly who was glued to Tod who was pasted to me.

Facing our do-gooder's daisy chain some three yards away were two somber men who probably woke up wearing three-piece suits and sour dispositions: the Captain of the two-five, Lou Ebekel and his compatriot in repugnance, Manhattan Assistant District Attorney William Fames. (It seems the Mayor and the Police Commissioner were at a fund-raising banquet and couldn't be disturbed. That is, not until the photo op.) As a living oxymoron - a noted Black Republican - Fames scared me the most. I guess that's why he was yelling the loudest.

"You expect us to believe that four guys, who look like they were dressed for a Soldier Of Fortune convention, just happened to to be getting together for dinner when they hear a radio request and get involved in a mass shootout? You expect the Captain and I to believe that?"

"It does sound like the scenario for the average gangsta rap video," I granted. "But es verdad, jefe. "

"Shut up, Perez," thundered Fames, "and don't think the color of your skin is going to help you here!"

"It hasn't so far," I said, "why should the inside of a police station be any different?"

"I meant," clarified Fames, "don't expect any sympathy or favors from me."

"I don't, Mr. Ass-istant District Attorney and I'm sure neither did any of the one hundred and fifty men of color you've bragged in the tabloids about convicting in this calendar year alone."

"One hundred and fifty-two," he corrected, "and may I remind you, Perez, the year isn't over yet."

"Mister Perez to you," I chided, "and may I remind you, Judge Joe Brown, not one of those poor one hundred and fifty-two souls, broke up a major drug ring!"

"Alleged drug ring," Ebekel wearily stated.

"Bullshit, Captain," O'Reilly said. "There were enough pharma-who-ticals in that basement..."

"About two million's worth," I interjected.

"..to start your own chain of drug stores across the country."

"Which was…"

"..probably what.."

"...they were doing..."

"..Captain."

"Maybe so," said Ebekel, "but five guys are dead and that has to be looked into. Now you say Breindel capped Velleto - ballistics can verify that - Perez shot Lorenz..."

"Only in self-defense, " I added.

"Of course," Fames said caustically, "why else would you shoot him? It's not like he was a dead guy or something?"

"Well, well," I said. "Word does trickles down to the DA's office. Slowly, perhaps, but it gets there."

"It does when someone shoots up a corpse, Perez."

"I certainly hope they call me when you qualify as one, Fames."

"Why? You want to practice on my cadaver, gumshoe?"

"I wouldn't waste a paper clip on your dead body," I answered. "I just want an excuse to throw a party."

"Knock it off, Perez!" Ebekel paused and then continued. "I'm sure it was a righteous shoot. For all of youse. We've got the audio tape the Trimbles made for support evidence to your stories. Mr. Fames and I just want to make sure it all jibes together. Okay?

"Sure, Captain," I said.

"Good," said Ebekel.

"Now, Detectives Trimble, did either of you recognize the men you shot?"

"No..."

"..sir."

Ebekel tossed a photograph the length of the table to our end.

It was a picture of the bulldog Tod drilled.

"His name is...was Lonny Braxton. Known as a professional ne'er-do-well, he owned a string of go-go bars, porno bookshops and select sleaze-oriented properties."

"One former property," said Fames, "was a notorious 320 East 124th Street locale."

"It seemed he purchased it from the city a few years back," said Ebekel. "He had it for a couple of months..."

"Long enough to drive out the building's tenants," interjected Fames.

"..and then sold the building to Harve Breindel," I said.

"Right," said Ebekel.

"Who then gave the building over to the Carrington Foundation," said O'Reilly.

"Which was..."

"..run by Doctor.."

"...Velleto."

"Sounds like a connection to me," I said.

Ebekel slid another photo down the table. (This was

beginning to feel like Mission:Impossible Meets Cheers.) It skidded to the edge on our side. I'll have a snapshot and a frothy brew to go, I thought.

"This was, thanks to Tad, Chef Babcock, Braxton's attorney," said the Captain. "He was known as his aide-de-camp..."

"Capo de tutti felony?" I asked.

"Sort of," grimaced Ebekel.

"Wherever Braxton went businesswise, so too was Babcock."

"We suspected Braxton was possibly fronting for Babcock in a number of unsavory business transactions and vice versa," said Fames.

"A crooked lawyer," said O'Reilly, "imagine that."

"He was under investigation for numerous offenses," said Fames. "We were trying to revoke his state license."

"Instead he got disbarred the hard way," I said. "Gee, Fames, I sure hope Tad doesn't start a trend."

"His death isn't what bothers us," said Ebekel, "It's the circumstances."

"We've gone over what happened," said O'Reilly, "a thousand times. "

"It's not your actions we're really worried about," said Ebekel, "it's theirs."

"What are..."

"..you talking.."

"...about?"

Fames started counting on his fingers. "Braxton. Babcock. Breindel. These are three dangerous guys who were known for their caution.. "

"..as well as their toughness," said Ebekel. "Yet, they go to a drug meet without any muscle?"

"And we're not counting that doofus O'Reilly and Perez hog-tied upstairs," said Fames, "as muscle by any stretch of the imagination. "

"It doesn't make sense," said Ebekel. "And then we searched the premises for cash, money, any currency involved in the deal. None. "

"Maybe they used credit cards. Captain," I said.

"A drug deal on credit? I don't think so."

"All of which boded well for you guys," said Fames. "If there had been any cash lying around, we would have started to think we were dealing with some rogue cops looking to rip off some dealers."

"While answering a call? On York Avenue? I don't think so," growled O'Reilly.

"None of the men has any records of transaction, a notebook, a sheet of paper, a computer disc on them," said Fames. "We find that unusual for a major drug deal."

"Did they at least have a deck of cards on them so we could charge them with gambling?"

"That's enough, Perez," admonished Fames.

"How about dominos?" asked O'Reilly. "After all, we know hundreds of armed near-felons who play a game of dominos surrounded by empty crack vials and a shitload of pills, don't we?"

"I'm merely pointing out how unusual the circumstances are," Fames calmly said.

"And I'm pointing out the exit door in this hellhole," I said. "You've got five men - all dead which saves the city the cost of a trial - caught with millions of illegal drugs around them. One of them might 've even killed a New York City police officer in the line of duty. That's enough headlines for a week to hide the brutality cases in the Bronx, the woman who was blown away by her ex despite an order of protection in Brooklyn, the serial rapes in Queens, the child abuse/neglect cases downtown and the fact that nobody in their right mind gives a shit about what happens in Staten Island."

I stood up. So did O'Reilly and the Trimbles.

"So, Fames, either charge me and the boys in blue here with a crime and get another set of headlines or shut the fuck up and tell me when I can pick up my medal and reward."

Fames sputtered, turned as red as black can get but said nothing. Ebekel took his choked silence as a cue.

"Freddie, you can go, with our thanks and well-wishes," he said. "I'd like my fellow three officers to stay a bit longer but only to finish and hand in their written statements. After all, and I'm sure I speak for Assistant District Attorney Fames here, we want make sure our department heroes go home and get their rest."

He extended his hand. I guess that was my hint that I was supposed to shake it when I went by. Instead, I gave him the long distance wave-off and half-turned to O'Reilly.

"When the file on Braxton and Babcock and that tape comes in," I whispered, "send me a copy."

He nodded and gave me a high-five. (For the Trimbles, I had to high-ten.) I headed to the door but stopped when I got to Ebekel.

"Who's gonna notify Mrs. Velleto she's a widow?"

He seemed surprised by the question. Guess he hadn't considered it.

"I..I don't know," Ebekel said. "Do you have any suggestions?"

"Yeah," I said as I left the room. "Send Mr. Ass-istant here. He's used to burying people and then talking about it. He got that natural mortician touch."

I'm sure Fames cursed me eight ways till Sunday but I didn't stick around to find out. I just wanted to get home and hear Juanita's voice.

FORTY

THAT EVENING I didn't have the best night's sleep. Oh sure, Chubby and Papo were happy to see me. And when I told them what happened, they were absolutely ecstatic with drinks for everybody on the house. (One round of the cheap stuff, of course.) The liquor was plentiful and there were, for a change, some single eligible ladies - now this is important - around my own age group. But after an hour of imbibing, I passed on the bar pussy and went upstairs to call Juanita.

It was well past two in the morning but, bolstered by boozed-up bravado, I rang her up anyway. She picked up on the third ring, sounded drowsy but that didn't inhibit me a bit from chattering on about my exploits that evening.

When I finished she was silent for a while. Then she told me she never realized how close I came to death for a living. I responded truthfully: neither did I.

We kinda left it there. She asked if I wanted to come over. I did but I didn't tell her that. Instead, I explained to her that physically I wasn't able to even hazard an attempt. But, I added, I wanted to see her soon. Real soon.

She told me that was a good thing and she would leave my appearance at her doorstep at my discretion. Then she told me she loved me and hung up the telephone before I could reply.

As gently as I had touched her the night before, I placed the receiver in its cradle, opened up my sofa-bed and laid down in it fully clothed.

Then I shut my eyes so tight I could see splashes of color and tried real hard to forget that, with the simple squeeze of a forefinger, I had taken a man's life so easily.

FORTY-ONE

I DIDN'T BOTHER to attend the press conference at One Police Plaza downtown. Too much bullshit hoopla for me. (Plus I wasn't made to feel my presence was sorely requested.) I did see highlights of it on the evening news as Fames and his bosses announced the bust-up of an important drug ring after months of undercover investigation and the seizing of - in estimated street value - over eight million dollars in illegal narcotics.

Lies, lies, lies.

O'Reilly and the Trimbles looked about as happy as a dead fly in a swatter to be sitting onstage behind Fames as he rambled on and on about his potential political prospects, the importance of parents in the ghetto to control their children and the need for the country's drug czar to be unshackled by Congress. Interesting topics over a late latte one Sunday night at the coffee bar perhaps but, unfortunately, none of them had to do with this case. I didn't attend Velleto's funeral either. I simply couldn't bring myself to face Mayra. Even though I had done what she asked me to do and probably unearthed the killer of her brother, the circumstances were too painful, too raw, for me to talk to her. Hell, I hadn't even called her to collect the rest of my money so you know I was feeling awkward.

So I was spending my days mostly lazing around the pad,

talking to Juanita every now and then on the phone - why was I so afraid to see her? - and trying to figure out my next step when my uncle came upstairs briefly to bitch about the cold weather and drop off the day's mail.

It wasn't much - some magazines, a manila envelope and a letter - but it was the most non-bill material I had gotten in weeks. Besides, to up the emotional ante, the envelope was from O'Reilly and the letter was from Mayra.

I had to make a tough decision on which one I was going to open first. I decided to repress my natural cowardice and unsealed Mayra 's missive instead.

It read:

Dear Freddie,

I know you have been hesitant to speak to me and, to be honest, I can understand why. It's not an easy thing to tell an old friend that her husband is not only a drug dealer who has used the non-profit foundation she has worked her whole life to set up for his own devious, nefarious purposes but he is also responsible for the death of her brother. I know that when I got the call from Mr. Fames, I was unbearably angry at you as if this whole nightmare was your fault and your fault alone.

Then I remember the thousands of families who are living nightmares that Oswald and his friends created and capitalized on. How many lives have they destroyed? How many people have they killed?

These are the questions that keep me up nights. These are the answers I hope to find. So I write you this letter to tell you I'm leaving New York in three days to go back to Los Angeles. There are too many bad memories here for me to feel comfortable and I have much work ahead of me. But I couldn't leave without telling you all is forgiven. Believe it or not, you have been a help to me. I want you to know that and, while you're at it, drop by. If not to wish me well, then, at least, to pick up your cat. (She truly hates me!) I hope I'll see then.

Con mucho afecto,

Mayra. P.S., Here's a little something for your troubles.

My jaw dropped. There, taped to the bottom of the letter, was a check made out to yours truly for twenty thousand dollars! I suppose she did forgive me, after all.

I was thinking about the joys of economic solvency when I tore open the manila envelope. In it were files on Velleto, Breindel, Lorenz, Braxton and Babcock. It began, quite frankly, as cursory reading - I was still sky-high about the twenty grand - but then started to get interesting quick.

Fames did have a point. These gentlemen were the cautious type. In fact, Braxton and Babcock were rarely seen together outside of court engagements and never with the other three fellows.

Braxton, Babcock and Breindel - sounds like the law firm from Hell - were also bodyguard junkies. These were men that didn't even like to go to the store without a platoon guarding them. But that night they'd travelled freely and alone.

Speaking of guards, the one that O'Reilly and I encountered - one Cecil Vincent Harrison - turned out solely to be the Darby's house muscle. Oh, he knew what was going on there, Harrison confessed from his hospital bed, - without his attorney present, stoopid! - but the crux of his job was to deny entry to 'suspicious' (that's a laugh) non-hospital people. And he swore that evening was the first he'd ever seen of Braxton and Babcock and only the third or fourth time Breindel and Lorenz had shown up. And, he stressed, the first time he'd seen those two together. In Harrison's eyes, he was a 'victim of a set of unfortunate circumstances. ' Seems he was the only regular worker not given the night off. He was - all together now - 'in the wrong place at the wrong time.'

Not given the night off. That's right, I thought. The Trimbles didn't run into anybody by the loading dock. O'Reilly and I only bumped into Harrison. Pretty slim protection for a major deal going down. How were the pills or the vials going to be loaded and unloaded? Were the five dead men going to do it? Without any muscle to lift or safeguard the stuff?

Unusual, to be sure. Of course none of this information was going to help Harrison's case. As the sole survivor of a vicious police shootout where he tried to prevent officers from doing their duty - Fames's words - Harrison was getting the book thrown at him by the DA's office. He was being charged with everything from conspiracy to distribute narcotics to complicity in the death of a New York City Police Officer to plotting to overthrow the government of the United States. Fames wasn't just throwing the book at him; he was hurling the whole goddam Encyclopedia Britannica. I guess that's why Harrison later plea-bargained a thirty-year bid. He was afraid, after Fames was through with him, he'd get the chair and then a lethal injection.

I put down the files and called O'Reilly at the station. After we exchanged salutations, I told him about my misgivings about the lax security. He admitted the thought came to him also and he'd pressed his commanders to stakeout Darby Hospital for a week. They reluctantly agreed and set up a 24-hour surveillance but all the effort was for naught. Outside of the normal hospital staff, nobody unusual showed up.

"Maybe we just got lucky that night," he said.

"Maybe," I said.

I thanked him for his time and promised to call him if anything new came to mind. He told me he'd appreciate that and bid me a fond adieu.

O'Reilly had placed a copy of the Trimbles' tape in the envelope. I took it out and popped it into my boom-box. Supposedly, the tape noise had been cleaned up but, except for a few brief passages, it still sounded like a garbled, muddied mess to me. (Sort of like alternative rock without the angst.)

As I felt a headache coming on, I was about to give up on this aural jumble when I heard Velleto's voice come in clear as a bell.

"..the boss about this run through when I head downtown."

I bolted upright. I rewound the tape to listen to that section again.

"..the boss about this run-through when I head downtown."

In the hospital's basement, I'd heard it all wrong. It wasn't the cost of a run to or through downtown. It was a run-through, a rehearsal. No wonder there wasn't any muscle around, they weren't needed yet. That's why the five guys were so surprised and that's why Breindel felt set up. It was all a rehearsal. One, most likely, at the boss's request.

This all made sense now. Everything. I glanced at my watch. 1:00 PM. Cool, I thought. I had a couple of hours to replay the tape a couple of times, get dressed, run to the bank, deposit a check and then pay a little visit to the mastermind behind it all.

FORTY-TWO

IT WAS PAST five when I knocked on the door. Even in the hallway, I could hear the salsa music blasting away on the other side of the thick oak as clear as a bell. The disc playing sounded like Gilberto Santa Rosa. Good stuff. I felt a residual chill from the cold air outside, pulled at my pea coat and pounded at my semi-numbed crossed arms with my fists. Then I rapped again - this time a little harder - and placed my ear against the wood. (Call me eavesdropping Freddie.) I heard the blaring trumpets and the driving rhythms slowly fade to silence. There was a hushed pause which was rapidly broken by the click-clack of approaching footsteps. The golden doorknob twisted open to the right as the portal peeked open a pinch and I could see a wary brown eye peering at me through the inch-wide space.

"Freddie?" said a voice behind the door. "What are you doing here?"

I let loose with my warmest smile.

"Well, Mayra, you did invite me. Sort of."

"Oh, you got my letter."

"And your generous check."

I took a deep bow.

"I thank you," I said.

"Oh, it was nothing, really," she said. "You deserved it."

"I thank you again."

I looked around the hallway.

"Uh, can I come in or are you more comfortable chatting through a door? I mean I feel like I'm on The Dating Game or something."

"Oh, I'm sorry."

Mayra flung open the door and backed up two steps. She was wearing a gorgeous sleeveless black dress with a plunging backline, frontline and matching pumps. I strode into her apartment. The kitchen light was on and that's all that was needed. With the shades from the window up, the place was as well lit as a Christmas tree. (Natural light: there's a Con Ed nightmare.) As I locked the door behind me, I couldn't help but notice she twitched a bit when she heard the tumblers slide into place.

"Something wrong?" I asked.

"I've just been in a fog lately," she said, "...well, you understand, Chulito."

"Sure I do," I comforted. "You're been through a lot. Say that's quite the killer outfit you've got on there"

Her eyebrows shot up for a moment. But only for a moment. "This very old thing? It's Norma Kamali's," she said.

"Well, what ever you do, don't give it back," I grinned. "I doubt if she could do it justice."

"No, silly," she laughed while pinching the bodice with her thumbs and forefingers, "Norma Kamali designed this outfit."

"Oh, I thought you borrowed it," I said as I opened my coat. "You must forgive me, Mayra, my fashion sense is straight out of the Spiegel Catalog."

"I suppose we all have to start somewhere," she laughed. "By the way, how did you get upstairs without me buzzing you in?"

In actuality, I'd picked the lock and, if she hadn't been home, I'd have done the same thing to her apartment door. But I couldn't tell her that now, could I? So, I fibbed and said somebody must've left the downstairs door opened.

"That's unusual," she said.

"And dangerous. That's an easy way for a thief, robber or worse to get into an apartment. It's an invitation to disaster."

"That's a bit melodramatic, Freddie," she said, "don't you think?"

"Maybe, but not as dramatic as that dress," I said as I took a seat on her couch. "That's some cleavage, sister."

Mayra got a little self-conscious and try to tug the material around those big boys up. No such luck. If gravity couldn't bring those golden globes down yet, it wasn't gonna let them up either.

"I just wanted to look good," said Mayra wistfully, "this dress was Oswald's favorite."

"He had good taste, honey," I said, "in most things."

"Yes he did."

Mayra stared at me. It wasn't a puzzled gaze or even a perturbed one. Nah. This was her enigmatic, helpless, heavy-lidded, pouty-lipped little-girl look. This was the one that would 've had most men gasping in joy. They've mistaken it for a sign of interest in the come-hither realm. Not me. I'd fallen for that goo-goo eyed shit in grade school but this was an older and barely wiser Freddie now. I knew this was her power-play. Hell, I didn't even get a pee-pee rise. I was so proud of myself.

"Something on your mind, sweetheart?" I asked.

Her lips tightened and her brown eyes went from heavy-lidded to narrow and suspicious. Little Chulito had refused her charms and she wasn't sure why.

"Aren't you hot in that coat?" she asked.

"Nah," I said, "just hot looking."

"Suit yourself, I'll go get Macha for you," she said as she trotted up the staircase. "I locked her up in Junior's room."

I would have ransacked the place while she was heel-stomping above me except what was there to ransack? The kitchen for a recipe? I wasn't gonna do that. I was thinking of getting the Food Channel on cable anyway.

I could've tried to come back later in the evening, perhaps even get her out of the house under some type of ruse and then tossed the upper level but then what? Who's to guarantee I'd find something incriminating? If anything, my visit this afternoon probably raised Mayra's antenna. Whatever evidence was around would be hidden or destroyed by the time I got back. No, I thought, in this instance I was going have to rely on one of my God-given gifts.

I was going to have to be annoying. Extremely annoying.

With a loud 'meow,' Macha came hurtling down the winding steps. She was running so fast, she almost screwed herself into the floor. As it was, she had to take a extra lap or two around the stairs to regain control over her furry body. The third time around, she managed to right her ship and sailed into my arms. I was stroking her head and getting some mighty contented purring when Mayra finally came down the stairs.

"I told you that cat loves you," said Mayra.

"I'm sure she loves you too," I said.

Mayra shook her head and pointed out some scratches on her left hand. They were fairly intense and so was the huge ring on her fourth finger. When she saw I was peeking at it, she unconsciously pulled away.

"That's quite a rock you've got there," I said.

"Yes," mumbled Mayra, "it was a birthday gift from my late husband."

She started to twist the ring inward towards her palm.

"I like to wear it now and then," she said with a clenched left fist.

"Poor Oswald," I intoned.

"Yes. ..poor Oswald."

"You know, we wouldn't have gotten him without your help."

She nodded her head, walked around the counter and into the kitchen. She pulled out a can of ginger ale from the icebox and pointed it at me.

"Want one?"

"No thanks," I said. "I'm trying to cut down to three quarts a day."

She shrugged her bare shoulders and popped the can open as she leaned forward against the counter between us. As she took a swig, I knew the message she was giving me with her body language: here's my castle wall, Freddie, come try to knock it down.

With a philosophy of one brick at a time, I decided to take a whack at it.

"Really, Mayra, I couldn't have done a thing without the wealth of information you gave me."

Another sip.

"Wealth?"

"Sure, honey," I chuckled. "You were the one to hip me about Oswald acting strange over dinner at Yolanda's, remember?"

"Sure I do. but...."

"And," I interrupted, "you're the one who told me about his junk food habit which indirectly led me to discover his predilection for Cheez Doodles which tied in with the bags and bags of Cheez Doodles we found next to your brother's body at 320 East 124th Street, a building your Carrington Foundation owns."

"I..I didn't know about that..."

"About what?" I grinned.

"About all of that."

Time for my killer smile.

"How could you, hon? We're talkin' classified info here. This is stuff only the cops and I know. Right?"

Another swig, another nod.

"And the fact that I found out about that building from a cat stashed for a couple of weeks under a pizza box - whose license around her collar, by the way, is a phony - in your dead missing brother's room here in your apartment is simply a fortuitous coincidence, don'cha think?"

A rather frosty nod this time.

"Just like you telling me about that meeting he was holding at Darby Hospital which turned into, according to Assistant District Attorney Fames - and I'm quoting - 'a necessary bloodbath to spearhead the war on drugs,' was yet another fortuitous coincidence, wasn't it?"

She drained the can, crumpled it and tossed it into a wastebasket.

"Now," I asked, "shouldn't we be recycling those?"

"I do not think I like your conclusions, Freddie."

"They're not conclusions, Mayra. They're insinuations."

"Well," she yelled, "I don't like them either. Now get the fuck out of here."

I didn't move a muscle.

"Such language. You know what's funny, sweetheart. Here I was thinking that Oswald and these guys were doing this mega-deal and then I find out today it was a rehearsal for the real mega-deal that we took down. Disheartening."

"What the fuck are you talking about?"

"I'm telling you, your husband and the four stooges were sacrificed so that the real payoff could go off without a hitch."

"Real payoff?"

"Yeah," I said. "It's all on this tape recording we made just before we took the boys down. Oswald was quite loquacious about the big boss. Quite."

"Really," she said calmly.

I leaned forward. There wasn't a bead, a drop of sweat on her fine little head. Had to give it to her. Mayra was gonna play it cool to the end.

"I hope you get him," she smirked.

"My, aren't we gender-specific?"

"Meaning?"

"Meaning..."

I was about to say something important - what I don't know since I was stalling my ass off - when Macha suddenly made any conversation moot. She sprung out of my lap, onto the counter and took a clawed swipe at Mayra. Mayra swept the cat off her paws with a swoop of her left hand.

Mayra swung with such fury, she momentarily stumbled backwards. As she tried to regain her balance, her open left palm flailed into one of the bare windows' path of direct sunlight. Off her ring finger flashed a glint of green in my eyes. It was a sight I'd seen but once before and that was at the butcher's block known as 320 East 124th Street.

To her credit, Mayra recognized my look of recognition before I even realized it myself. With a swift twist of the torso, she dove forward behind the counter. Before my hand was halfway to the inside of my coat - and my two-twenty - she'd popped up like an armed Jack-in-the-box holding a sawed-off double-barreled shotgun at me.

"Not bad," I said, "but can you make a soufflé?"

"SHUT UP!" she screamed.

"I should 've known," I said. "You were born in May - a Taurus - and your birthstone's an..."

"An emerald," she said, "I ought to just off you right now."

"But you can't."

"Why not?"

"You've got to divulge all of the diabolical details of your master plan"

"You're shitting me?"

"Hey, it's a tradition," I said. "Now you don't want to break a tradition?"

She shook her head,

"You are crazy, Freddie,"

"I'm insane. C'mon, darlin', humor me," I pleaded. "For old times' sake."

She bent her head a bit to improve her aim. I just smiled.

"Ah, why not? You're going to die anyway. Fire away. No pun intended," she chuckled.

"None taken," I said. "So was I right about everything?"

"Pretty much."

"You were the mastermind?"

"Uh-huh. There's good money in those pills."

"From the beginning?"

"Yes. Oswald liked the idea but lacked the vision. We agreed he'd be the frontman and I'd be the power behind the throne."

"Just like the Wizard of Oz."

"Close enough."

"Where did the real deal go down?"

She glanced up at the ceiling.

"Right here. The stuff was in Oswald's room."

"Right after the cops notified you about Oswald's demise?"

Carefully, I clapped my hands together. I wanted to get the stiffness out.

"Mayra, you cold-blooded little animal, I am impressed."

"Watch the name-calling, Freddie, and the hand-movements."

"Who did you do the deal with?"

"Some overseas businessmen."

"Get a lot?"

"About ten million in cash and bonds." She licked her lips. "And, thanks to you, I don't have any partners to split it with."

"Aaahh, poor baby. So you used me all along?"

"Every step of the way. You know I always could."

"Did you seek me out?"

"No. Bumping into your mother was a pure accident but once she told me what you were up to...well, let's just say I felt as if it was as though Fate herself was giving my plan a blessing."

It was a good thing I was scared, I thought, because my self-esteem was sure taking a beating. I was nearly out of questions and time when I spied something on top of the refrigerator that gave me a little hope.

I had to keep stalling so I inquired about Junior's death. It was the only incident that appeared to truly upset Mayra. Tears swelled in her eyes as she spoke.

"That ...that was an accident," she claimed. "He was messing around with Sunset, drinking, smoking perico, snorting it. Oswald said his heart just gave out. It was my suggestion to keep him on ice until we could figure out what to do with him. Then I ran into your mom and the missing persons idea just seemed to fit into my 'master' plan so we went with the flow."

I looked past Mayra. C'mon, C'mon.

"But there wasn't any room for Oz, huh, cutie?"

"He was weak," she said, "losing it."

I kept darting my eyes back and forth from the refrigerator to Mayra. C'mon, I thought.

"So you lost him?" I asked.

"Yes."

Uh-oh. She started to take aim.

"I'm getting bored with this twenty questions shit.."

My vision was getting blurry from all my eye-jiggling.

"Just three more, Mayra, for old times' sake."

"Only three," she growled.

"How are you going to explain my death?"

"I'm not," she laughed. "I'm going to blow you away and let them figure it out. I've got a private jet waiting for me and a Swiss bank account. Fuck 'em. I dare them to find me. They can't even find Hoffa."

"How do you know I didn't bring the cops here?"

She laughed uproariously.

"If you had, they would 've been in here now. And don't give me that Get Smart shit that there 's a SWAT team downstairs waiting for me. Trust me, I'll take my chances. Last question."

Finally. Eye contact. C'mon, baby. Do it. I looked back at Mayra. Gave her the hard stare.

"Why did you kill Cary?"

"The cop? He was in the way. Just like you..."

"NOW MACHA!" I screamed.

I threw myself to the floor just as Macha hurled herself off of the refrigerator top and onto Mayra's head. Startled, Mayra managed to squeeze off a round as she fell back. It splintered the tenth step on the staircase.

I leapt off the floor and, as I pulled out my gun, vaulted onto the counter top. There, on the ground, was a screaming, bloodied Mayra swinging the shotgun butt towards her face in a desperate attempt to stop Macha from clawing her eyes out. It was only at the sight of me that Macha stopped and slinked away.

"Freeze, Mayra," I said. "Now, using just your right hand, toss the shotgun away from you."

Mayra speedily obeyed both of my commands and chucked the weapon a couple of yards away from her. She started wiping the blood from her brow with her back of her hands.

"Please, Freddie, hear me out," she begged. "I listened to you."

Before you tried to kill me, I thought. Still, I wanted to hear what she had to say.

"There's ten million dollars upstairs in a trunk filled with untraceable bills and bonds," she calmly said. "Let me go and I'll give you half."

I said nothing. Her voice leapt an octave.

"Come on, Freddie, it's five million tax-free. I'd give you

more but I need to pay the pilots and the custom people. Come on, Chulito."

I stayed silent. Now, Mayra sounded desperate.

"Pleeease, Chulito. We can work this out. You can have half the money and I promise to deposit a million dollars in the off-shore bank account of your choice on a quarterly basis. That's another four million dollars to you, tax-free, every year. I'll even tell you where I'm going so you can find me at any time. I've got nothing to hide from you. We've known each other for too long. What do you think?"

I remained mute and stared right through her.

"Freddie, Chulito, I don't know what to say. I'm offering you a chance to be my partner and share in 50% of my earnings. I'm pleading with you to let me go, as I let you go at 124th, to live my life."

She flashed me one of her most dazzling smiles.

"I'm beseeching you, Chulito, for old time's sake."

I thought about what she said then let out a chuckle. Her eyes widened just a tad.

"There's just two problems, Mayra," I said. "I work alone and I'm not nostalgic. Oh, one more, you murdered my best friend."

With that, I aimed and pulled the trigger.

FORTY-THREE

THE FIRST SNOWFLAKES of the season were falling in New York City, children were playing in the streets, Christmas decorations were being put up, carols were being sung and there I was half-asleep on the sofa watching Jerry Springer on a sunny afternoon. But this time I wasn't feeling guilty about my listless nature. I figured I'd earned it with all the machinations I had to pull after Mayra's death.

First, I'd rummaged through her upstairs rooms in hopes of finding this mysterious luggage containing a tax-free fortune. I kinda doubted its existence but I found this old, dented trunk wedged under the desk in Oswald's office. I jimmied it open only to find ten million dollars in bucks and bonds staring me in the face. In addition, there were three reporter's notebooks written in some kind of numerical code.

I had to act fast. In one of Mayra's closets, I discovered an empty black valise. I filled it up with about three million dollars. Then I took both it and the trunk downstairs.

I moved Mayra's shotgun closer to her and placed the valise in her left hand. I left the apartment briefly and ran to the corner pay phone. Then, I called the Barcelona Bar and told my uncle to get his ass to Franklin Street pronto and, as sneakily as possible, pick up a old trunk from the second garbage can in front of the building next door, 140 Franklin. He told me he was on his way and hung up.

I raced back upstairs, grabbed the trunk - boy does the lure of easy money make you strong!!! - and dragged it into the street. Luckily, no one was around. I placed it in front of the second trashcan in front of 140 Franklin. Then I unzipped my pants and urinated on it. (I figured the smell of pee would act like a deterrent.) Then I went back into Mayra's apartment, picked up the phone, dialed O'Reilly, told him most of the story and asked him to get up here with Fames. He said sure, reminded me not to touch anything - too late! - and clicked me off.

Twenty-five minutes later, I was stroking Macha and enjoying a ginger ale when I heard the sirens. O'Reilly with Fames and his flunkies came barreling in ninety seconds later. I explained what happened - how I defended myself in self-defense - and pointed out the valise and all the money in it.

Fames' eyes bugged out at the sight of all that green then he grew suspicious. He insisted the apartment be searched. After it was and no additional cash turned up, he maintained I must have hidden it somewhere and demanded I'd be strip-searched. After O'Reilly loudly suggested the only asshole in the place that truly needed airing out was Fames, his order was rescinded.

Nevertheless, Fames kept me there for over three hours hoping to find a flaw in my tale. He couldn't and I walked out a tired but oddly exuberant man.

O'Reilly noticed it to on the drive back to El Barrio. He said I appeared abnormally happy for a guy that just killed a grade-school classmate. I told him he had it wrong. The act of killing bothered me but I was happy I had fulfilled a vow to myself and found Cary's murderer. The answer appeased him and he wished me a good night when he dropped me at the Barcelona.

When I walked in, Papo jerked a thumb to the crates by the wail. A pushed button, a knock, an opened door and I was in Chubby's office. He was sitting on his desk with his legs stretched out along Mayra's trunk. The room smelled like freshly-sprayed Lysol.

"Do you want to tell me now," he asked, "what the fuck I had to garbage pick for this pissed-on trunk for??"

I took the case and flipped the lock.

"This," I said as I showed him.

He took one look and fainted dead away.

The next day, I watched on the bar's television Fames' press conference about Mayra's death and the seizing of a million and a half dollars they recovered.

"This is blood money that will go directly to fight the drug war," he said.

My uncle turned to me.

"One-point-five?" he asked.

"I guess the price of justice in New York is more expensive than I thought," I shrugged.

We laughed a lot that day. Especially, Chubby after I gave him a finder's fee gift of one million dollars. (I slipped in an extra 150 K for Papo.) I had only one stipulation: don't flaunt it. He told me he wouldn't then turned around and bought himself a black Humvee. Well, at least it wasn't sky-blue. And he is - slowly - fixing up the bar.

My parents are doing the same thing to their house. I went out to visit them in Canarsie and explained I'd come into some money but no questions could be asked. Then I gave each of them a million dollars. They were very happy and not the least bit curious. They're off on a Hawaiian cruise now. My mother sends me postcards telling me about how my father brags to everybody about his son the private eye. To be honest, I felt kinda proud. As for Juanita, well, I told her I love her and gave her a gift to prove it: Macha. They get along swell with Macha sleeping between us whenever I stay over. I haven't told her about the money yet but I promised myself to spend at least half a mil on her next year.

As for me, well I just keep kicking back in the neighborhood I've grown to love, enjoying my 52-inch television with surroundsound, my new high-end stereo system, my four-head VCR, DVD player, my satellite dish and my hundreds of tapes and discs. I even got me a lap-top. I spend at least four hours a day on it trying to break Mayra's coded notebooks. I just know there's money in them thar pages.

Other than that, I don't do much. But I've never felt better about myself in my whole life. Whether it's catching a movie at the Cosmo or eating at Pepito's or having a beer at the Barcelona or placing my head between my lover's legs, I've never felt more alive.

Shit, I might even stay up for Oprah.

THE END